C

L

CJ Wood.

For Mum and Dad

One

Detective Inspector Andrea Statham hurried as fast as she could across the car park at police headquarters. She failed miserably to avoid the puddles forming on the black tarmac. Struggling to position her umbrella into the swirling wind to prevent it from blowing inside out or, worse, from being blown away. The rain was unrelenting, hitting her at all angles. She touched her card against the security access pad and the automatic door slid open, providing her with instant refuge from the weather. She stepped inside, shaking the rain from her brolly.

"I think I'll go and have another coffee rather than go out in that. You look like a drowned rat, Ma'am," A uniform officer commented. Andrea hadn't noticed the cop hanging back from the door inside the building. He was usually outside having a cigarette when she arrived. She was curious to find out what his job was. It certainly wasn't a demanding one. He never looked under pressure.

"I don't blame you. It's wild enough out there to make you give up smoking. And then the job gets an extra eleven minutes work out of you." She walked towards the elevators in the atrium, not waiting for his reply. Her feet felt soaking wet, and her black trouser suit was saturated. She stepped inside, catching a glimpse of herself in the mirror. Drowned rat! Cheeky git, mused Andrea. The lift was empty; she tidied her windswept hair, putting it up into a ponytail, using the mirror whilst the lift ascended. Andrea walked into the open plan major incident room through the banks of desks where her team of detectives were working at their computers. She replied to a few greetings of "Morning Ma'am," as she passed by. The office was on the fourth floor of the building, with panoramic views over the wet rooftops towards the city centre. She reached her office and placed her handbag on the meeting table before leaning against the wall radiator. She closed her eyes and enjoyed the warmth on her legs as it dried her trousers. Andrea's team were based at headquarters temporarily whilst the incident room at the Serious Crime Division building was refurbished. The headquarters was a new build; the exterior looked modern and slick, finished with corporate blue shaded glass. As with most police buildings, there wasn't sufficient car parking. But she could live with that. It was a great place to work.

"Morning, Ma'am," DS Pete Higgs greeted cheerfully; Andrea reluctantly accepted that her peaceful quiet moment was over.

"Why are you dry, Pete? I got drenched coming in. I'm soaking wet!" She sounded mockingly aggrieved.

"If you weren't on the last minute, you'd have got a parking space closer to the door."

"I suppose so. Good morning to you too, Pete. New suit?" Pete was wearing a dark grey pinstripe suit that Andrea hadn't seen before. She thought he looked pretty dapper.

"No, I've had it for a while; I just couldn't get the trousers on until I lost a few more pounds." Pete still had a beer belly but looked a little slimmer. The heat from the radiator was starting to burn Andrea's legs. She stepped away and closed the office door.

"I can see you've lost some weight."

"Why, thank you. I was shamed into it; I was playing five-a-side football, a lads and dads match. I sprinted for the ball and struggled to get my breath back. My lad looked worried and asked me if I was alright. He must have thought I was going to have a bloody heart attack!"

Andrea smiled, amused by the source of his newfound motivation to shed some pounds. They took a seat at the round meeting table. Andrea could see through the open horizontal blinds, which went floor to ceiling over the glass window partition. Her team looked busy at their computers; they were supporting Divisional CID, investigating child abuse gangs. The investigation was stretching the divisional team's resources to the limit. Andrea had offered the support of her team, following a lull in the number of murders in Greater Manchester.

"I might be able to let you go on your attachment to the Drug Unit if you still want to abandon us?" Andrea teased.

"Excellent, it will obviously be a drag to leave you and the team, but I could do with a new challenge. It's something I've always fancied," Pete said. Andrea felt a tinge of disappointment that he still wanted to go.

"DS Lee McCann is leaving covert operations, and he's coming to work with our team as an acting detective sergeant. He will be your temporary replacement. DI Dave Ferguson is more than happy to have you on his team, and your knowledge of Jason Hamilton's crime gang will be invaluable to him."

"Thanks, Ma'am, I owe you one. How long is the attachment for?"

"Add it to the list of favours you owe me, Pete. Let's say an initial six months and review it then; you may even be begging me to come back by that stage." They were interrupted by a knock at the door.

Pete leant over from his chair and reached out to open the door.

"Good timing Lee, I was just talking to Pete about you joining us." The last time she saw Lee, he had a few days growth of stubble and longer hair. He was now clean-shaven, and his brown hair was cut short and tidy. He was six foot tall with a muscular, athletic physique.

"Do you two shop together? Or, are grey pinstripe suits on special offer?" She teased, regarding their similar tastes in suits.

"I didn't want to upstage the main guy. It's a backhanded compliment to his fine taste," Lee said, with a cringing smile, shaking Pete's hand.

"Take a seat, Lee." Andrea caught a whiff of his fresh, aromatic aftershave as he sat down. "Welcome to the team. It's great to have you with us."

"Glad to be here, thank you."

"Well done with the Jason Hamilton result mate, I'll make you a brew in recognition of that performance," Pete said.

"Cheers, Pete, great team effort as usual, good to see him behind bars, a bit of a psycho that one." Pete stood up to leave the office and make the coffees.

"Will Pete be my mentor?" Lee asked.

"I'm afraid not, albeit he would be a good one. He's been waiting patiently for an attachment to the Drugs Unit for a while now, so I'm reluctantly letting him go. You will slot into his role, and be working alongside me, so I'll keep an eye on you."

"Sounds good, I've got all my experience as a divisional detective to bring to the table, so I feel like I'm good to go."

"I'll focus on developing your management skills to get you through your promotion board. I'll diary us a meeting later in the week to see what areas we need to look at." Pete carefully edged his way back into the office, balancing three mugs of coffee.

"I believe you're moving on, Pete; it's a shame I was looking forward to working with you," Lee said.

"Likewise, mate, but I had to snatch her hand off; she's been dangling this carrot for ages." Pete winked and smiled at Andrea.

"I'll show you the ropes and brief you on the investigations before I leave. You'll love it here. They're a great team. The boss isn't too bad either."

"Steady on, Pete. You've got your move rubber-stamped; it's in the bag. You can cut the crap now," Andrea said shaking her head.

"Come on, Lee, I'll introduce you to the team and show you around," Pete said. Andrea stood up from the meeting table and returned to the computer at her desk. Through the glass partition, she could see Pete introducing Lee to each member of staff in turn. Andrea was looking forward to working alongside him; he had made an excellent first impression and came with a reputation as a grafter and thief-taker.

She would have preferred not to lose Pete and was surprised that he still wanted the attachment. They worked well together, and Pete had seemed happy with his lot until recently when he had seemed a bit out of sorts. He had hinted at relationship problems at home, but he was the strong silent type, so Andrea hadn't delved any further.

Jason Hamilton had not had the pleasure of enduring the Manchester rain that morning. The weather didn't feature on his agenda these days. He had adapted well to life inside. The stale air, artificial light, and gloomy grey and magnolia décor of his new surroundings in HMP Strangeways was now the norm. The wings in the Victorian prison extended from a central atrium, like the spokes of a wheel. Following his initial assessment on the induction wing, Jason had been moved to B Wing. Much to his relief, it had a laid back feel about the place. There was a good mutual understanding between the prison officers and inmates. If the inmates toed the line and didn't cause the officers any grief, the regime was relaxed, at least compared with the other wings. The wing consisted of rows of cells accessed by landings on either side of the building. Not only did the landings have iron rail fencing, but also safety nets hanging across the void to prevent items from being dropped on those below or inmates attempting to self-harm.

The cell doors on the landing were unlocked and open for association time; prisoners were out of their cells, socialising. There was a constant hum of noise from chatter, shouting, televisions and radios.

Jason was sat on the edge of his bed in his cell, catching his breath, following a rigorous workout. The cell walls were magnolia, the dark blue door to the landing was at one end, and a small iron-barred window at the other gave only a limited view to the outside world. Inside was a bed, stainless steel toilet, sink basin, writing table and television on a corner shelf next to the door. He looked towards the door, sensing someone was approaching; he saw it was Dean Hall, one of the prison officers. Dean almost filled the doorway. He was six feet tall with the stocky build of a bodybuilder, enhanced by steroids. His sunbed tan contrasted against his white short-sleeved uniform shirt. He had a confident manner for a twenty-six year old, having only been in the prison service for five years, and he was now one of the senior officers in terms of years in the job.

"Good workout?" Dean asked.

"You know the score; it's not easy getting motivated, but once it's done, you feel great."

"I was training last night, chest and arms; I'm feeling it today."

"Did my lad sort you out with some steroids?" Dean looked uneasy and checked over his shoulder. "Yes, cheers, proper stuff too, I can tell the difference already. They're a good bunch of lads at the gym."

Jason eyed the officer before Dean broke the silence, "Is the single-cell going okay? Some of the lads say they miss having someone to talk to when they're padded up alone."

"After two weeks of being banged up with the Don on the induction wing, it's heaven. Jeez, that guy doesn't take a breath. Great for helping you to nod off, though, boring bastard."

"I've brought your mobile phone in," Dean whispered, once again checking over his shoulder.

"About fucking time, Dean, I was beginning to think you'd bottled it." Jason didn't want to sound too appreciative. He needed to keep Dean eager to please. He now had him where he wanted him, in his pocket. Dean had accepted the invite and ensconced himself with Jason's boys at the gym.

"It's in the linen room, we can exchange your bedding later, and you can pick it up. Are you ready for your visit?"

"Yes, let's go." Jason followed Dean along the landing and down the black iron steps to the visiting area. "I'll get the money transferred into your account tonight. Is there a charger with the phone?"

"No, it's safer to bring that in separately."

"That's okay; I can charge it through my electric shaver charger; for now, we don't want you getting rumbled, do we?" Jason was amused by Dean's obvious discomfort when he talked about his corrupt favours on the landing. Grooming Dean had been easy. In Jason's eyes, he was a naive lad, more of a soft puppy dog than a tough guy, which is how Dean saw himself. Their shared interest in weight training had opened the door for Jason. They entered the visiting centre. Around ten other prisoners were already seated at tables, wearing bright orange bibs, talking to their visitors.

Jason made his way to the table in the corner where Frank Burton was sitting. Frank had dressed casually in a departure from his trademark black suit. Grey chinos, a white shirt and a blue woollen sweater. His grey hair and rotund build completed the look of a respectable middle-aged, average guy rather than a bent solicitor. Jason, in contrast, looked much healthier; six-foot tall, jet black hair, with an athletic build, wearing a black sweatshirt and grey jogging trousers. He was ten years younger than Frank, at forty. His tanned complexion was fading due to his time spent indoors. Jason pulled back the metal frame chair, scraping the legs on the polished grey lino floor.

"Good to see you. You're looking well, Jason."

"You too, Frank, but I'm guessing life is treating you better," Jason replied. Privately though, he thought that Frank was a health disaster, drinking and smoking in excess to the detriment of his health.

"Did Dean give you the phone?"

"Yes, he brought it in. I'm collecting it on the way back to the wing. Pay him a good wedge tonight; let's work on his greed for the cash. And make sure they film the handover, in case he gets a bit windy."

Frank slid a paper bundle across the table, "I need you to read through this property update. If you're happy with it, I will proceed with the purchase." Jason skim-read the first page, and turning to the second page, he took the mobile phone sim card from the bundle and secreted it in the wristband of his sweatshirt.

"Very impressive. Have you been practising that?" Frank asked. Jason didn't deem a reply worthy. He waited a few moments to ensure there was no reaction from the prison officers and slid the papers back.

"Once Dean has the money, there's no going back for him. He's in my pocket anyway. He was getting a load of grief from a gobshite on the wing, so I had a word with the prick and made him apologise to Dean. I got one of my boys to throw some boiling water, mixed with sugar, over his head just for good measure. He's still receiving treatment on the healthcare wing," Jason said, smirking at the inmate's misfortune.

"Have you given any more thought to an early release?" Frank asked, changing the subject.

"I seem to be managing things well from in here, and it will be much easier with the mobile. The screws think I'm no trouble, model prisoner, just keeping my head down, doing my time. We need a contingency, though, a fake illness to get me to the hospital, maybe. It shouldn't be hard for you to get me out of here." Jason held his gaze on Frank as if weighing up his ability to perform the task. Jason thrived on putting Frank under pressure. He knew that Frank was very devious and capable. He always delivered.

Frank changed the subject, "I've not heard a peep from Ryan or Kirsty. Wayne has spoken to them, and he's content that they pose us no threat."

"That's not important for now. If Ryan is stupid enough to elope with my girlfriend, after everything I've done for him, that's his problem," Jason said.

"You did try to have him killed," Frank reasoned.

"Obviously the right decision with hindsight. I need to get the job done properly next time. But I've got bigger fish to fry for now. Talking of which, have you made any progress in tracking down Lee McCann. I can't let an undercover cop get away with befriending me and then getting me sent down."

"Are you sure that's a good move, Jason? Going after a cop is serious shit. It will bring too much unwanted attention to us."

"Never been more certain, Frank. He's the reason I'm banged up. He befriended me, gained my trust, and fucking set me up. I can't let him get away with that, can I?"

"I've not spoken to my bent cop for a while; I'll get him to do some digging."

"Make it your priority, Frank. You need to get a move on." Jason stood up, pushing the chair back. "I'll be in touch Frank, good to see you." He walked to the gate, ready to be escorted back to the wing. Dean had been chatting to another officer. He walked over to Jason, "How did your visit go?"

"Nothing special, just business, signing papers." Don't you be getting too familiar with me boy, you're an errand boy, not a fucking bestie, Jason thought.

"We can collect your clean bedding on the way back," Dean suggested. Jason didn't answer. He was ruminating on his conversation with Frank. The need for revenge on his nemesis, Lee McCann, was eating away at him. He knew he couldn't rest until he had taken his revenge. He had his reputation to uphold. He followed Dean up the metal staircase and onto the landing. Dean stopped at the linen room and unlocked the door, he went inside whilst Jason leant on the balcony rail, looking down through the safety nets to the landing below. Jason was deep in thought, planning Lee McCann's demise. He was going to make the him suffer. Dean brought him back to the present, "There you go, a full set of clean bedding." Jason took the bedding bundle from him and returned to his cell. He set about changing his bedding. Retrieving the mobile phone, he gave it a quick once-over before concealing it into the foam cushion sole of his training shoe.

It had been a busy day for Andrea, with numerous management meetings, phone calls, and inevitably catching up on the endless stream of emails. She wondered where some people found the time to write them. She struggled to find time to read them. She left headquarters via the main entrance and headed for Central Park Metro Link Station, eyeing the leaden sky, but relieved that the rain had stopped.

The station came into view with its central metal spike, supporting a slanted, curved copper and glass canopy. She reached the top of the stairs and walked onto the concrete platform, sparse with commuters. The yellow tram glided into the station, the brakes hissing and spitting. She had arrived just in time. The doors slid open, and she took her seat facing forward, sitting in the other direction gave her travel sickness. Out of habit, she didn't catch the eye of any other travellers; instead, she read for a short while until her tram came to a smooth stop at Exchange Square, Manchester. Stepping onto the platform, she noticed a homeless guy sitting cross-legged next to the ticket machine. He had long brown braided hair and a beard, wearing a padded black puffer jacket. Andrea placed a couple of coins into his paper cup and smiled as he thanked her. The growing number of homeless people on the streets of Manchester concerned her. She had represented the police at multi-agency meetings concerning the wellbeing of 'rough sleepers' as they were now called, in preference to 'the homeless'. She found some of their life stories that had led to their current plight heart-breaking. Andrea made her way along Deansgate, which was busy with shoppers and commuters. She reached the Mexican restaurant and pushed the door open. The gorgeous smell of spices hit her senses straight away and made her realise how hungry she was. It was one of her favourite places to eat. The walls were finished with rustic dark wood, which contrasted with the colourful Latin American pieces of artwork. The paintings gave the place a joyful ambience. She looked around and saw her friend Sarah Lovick sitting at a nearby table, engrossed in the menu. Sarah looked up and waved at her. Andrea made her way over and took a seat opposite Sarah. The table and chairs were basic minimalist furniture, no-frills, but the food here was great.

"Hi Andrea, you okay?"

"Yes, I'm ready for some lunch; I'm starving. Have you started on the vino already? I need to catch up with you," Andrea said, looking at Sarah's glass of wine.

"It's only my second one. I got here early and couldn't be bothered shopping, not that I need an excuse."

"I'm ready for a glass or two. You look great. Have you had your hair done?" Andrea asked.

"Yes, it's a bit lighter than usual and a bit shorter, easier to manage." Andrea usually saw Sarah with her hair tied up, wearing blue scrubs and wellies at the mortuary in Oldham. They shared professional mutual respect. Andrea preferred to work with Sarah in preference to the other Home Office Pathologists. They had developed a close friendship over the last few years and enjoyed meeting up. There was a lull in the conversation whilst they perused the menu.

"Brazilian lime chicken for me," Andrea said, closing her menu and handing it to the waiter.

"I'll have the beef and chorizo casserole, please, and could we have another bottle of prosecco?" The waiter scribbled down the order and headed for the kitchen. "He's a bit of a dish." Sarah said with a smile, "but too young for me!" How's your online dating going?"

"It's funny, you should ask. We have a new DS on our team, and he's gorgeous."

"Bring him to the next post-mortem, and I'll give him the once over." Sarah laughed.

"He seems a decent guy too, obviously works out and looks after himself. Not a good idea, though, mixing work and pleasure is it? He's a suitable replacement for Pete Higgs."

"I thought you and Pete would see your retirement out together?"

"So did I; we work well together. Although Pete's not been himself lately, he seems a bit distant and preoccupied. Maybe he just needs a change of scenery?" More prosecco arrived on the table, and with a clink of glasses, Andrea could feel the tensions of the day slip away.

Two

Ryan and Kirsty were sitting at a table outside their favourite cafe in the old town, Marbella. It was a beautiful building, the rustic stone façade surrounding the dark wooden entrance contrasted against white-washed walls. Climbing plants spread upwards, intertwining on the black iron railings of the first floor balconies, towards the terracotta tiled roof. It blended perfectly with the other buildings around the cobbled stone plaza. The slower pace of life here was idyllic compared to the main resort, where Ryan worked at one of the bars and Kirsty in the salon of one of the higher-end hotels. They were picking at the complimentary olives and sun-dried tomatoes whilst drinking lime and sodas.

"I think I'm fitter than I've been for years," Ryan announced proudly.

"It's all that running, yoga, and the Mediterranean diet; you're a new millennium man Ryan." Kirsty mocked. She gave him a once over, covertly from behind her shades. His short hair was a lighter blonde now, bleached by the sunshine. At 5'9" he looked proportionate with his wiry, athletic physique. But she didn't care much for his Hawaiian shirt and pink shorts.

"What time's your flight tomorrow?" Ryan asked.

"It's about two o'clock, I think. I need to double-check when we get back to the villa."

"I'll drive you to Malaga; it will only take forty minutes to the airport. Are you looking forward to it?"

Kirsty nodded, "Yes, I've missed the staff at the salons. It will be nice to see my mum and dad too. I just hope all the drama and chaos has died down. I might even visit Jason to try and calm the waters. I've never been inside a prison before."

"If you do visit him, try and find out where I stand with him. I'd be surprised if he lets it go. He wants his pound of flesh from me. Even though it was Carl who was grassing to the cops, all along."

"I'll do my best. You know what Jason's like." Ryan didn't fancy going with her. He had adapted to his new life in Spain with more enthusiasm than Kirsty. There was also the little matter of Jason wanting to have him killed. It wasn't safe for him to go back.

The move to Spain was what they both had needed. The change of scenery had been a shot in the arm for both of them. It was not only a beautiful holiday destination with great weather but another world away from their life within Jason Hamilton's crime gang. Ryan knew that Kirsty was happy with her decision to leave Jason. She had no regrets. Ryan was also aware that there was no long term future for his relationship with Kirsty either, but they would remain friends. They both felt the same, so there were no hard feelings. After the initial knee jerk whirlwind romance of getting back together, the spark vanished pretty quickly. But they were both in a good place.

"I'd better get going. The bar will be getting busy," Ryan said reluctantly.

"I'll walk down with you. I'm meeting a pal at the marina." Ryan placed some Euros on the table, and they set off through the narrow streets shaded by the tall villas on either side. Ryan walked on, to the seafront plaza, for his afternoon shift at Mas Tequila. The Plaza was busy with holidaymakers boozing and dining. Kirsty walked alone in the opposite direction to the seafront marina, she wasn't meeting anyone, but she had a sensitive phone call to make.

"Hello, Kirsty, how are you?" Frank Burton made the question sound overly sincere like he looked forward to her calls.

"I'm very well, thank you, Frank. I'm soaking up the sun on the seafront as we speak. I just wanted to let you know; I'm flying to Manchester tomorrow for a visit. I need to get around my salons and check all is well."

"Thanks for letting me know, Kirsty, is there anything I can do for you; lift from the airport?"

"No thanks, I just wanted to touch base to make sure I've nothing to fear. How is Jason, by the way?"

"He's just focused on doing his time. I thought ten years was a bit harsh. But with good behaviour, he shouldn't even serve half of that. You will have no problems at all. It's all water under the bridge." Frank made the previous months of bedlam sound like a minor inconvenience.

"Just for the record, Frank, me and Ryan are not together. You need to drill that into Jason's head. We are just supporting each other; after everything we've been through, that's all it is. Jason has no reason to go after him. We all need to get on with our own lives and move on."

"Of course, Kirsty, I couldn't have put it better myself." Kirsty cringed at his condescending tone. "Is Ryan visiting too?" Frank asked gingerly.

"No, just me. I'll be available on this number if you need to contact me, cheers Frank."

"Just one more thing, Kirsty, the police are still sniffing around. If they approach you, don't speak to them before calling me. They can be quite devious and tie you up in knots."

"I've nothing to hide, Frank, and I'm not stupid. I won't be telling them anything."

Kirsty felt better for the conversation with Frank as she walked along the seafront. The cool breeze blowing in from the sea helped her to feel calm and relaxed. She loved it here, but her life, family, friends and business were back in Manchester. She soaked up the moment, knowing that she wouldn't be back for a while.

The news of Kirsty's visit was of no concern to Frank, but he did like to be kept informed, so he appreciated the call. He wanted to believe that he kept all the plates spinning during these difficult times. He stood up from his desk, grabbed his black raincoat from the stand, slipped it on, and walked out of the building, stepping onto the wet pavement. He stood close to the red brick wall for shelter and lit a cigarette, shielding the lighter flame with his cupped hands. He took a long drag and continued to walk towards the Northern Quarter. He turned into a cobbled back street, walked past the tattoo artists shop and into his favourite greasy spoon café. He savoured the smell of the bacon cooking on the grill. A presenter on a local radio channel was chattering away, like irritating white noise in the background. The ambience of the place wasn't dissimilar to a truckers café. The wooden chairs and tables, beige emulsion walls, menu boards, and a simple counter at the far end provided a no-frills appearance. It was a popular place with locals. Frank walked over to the window seat in the corner where Wayne Davies was sitting reading the paper's sports pages.

"Morning Wayne, have you ordered?" Frank loved a fry up and couldn't hide his enthusiasm.

"No, I just got a brew whilst I was waiting for you." He waved at the young waitress, who dutifully walked over. Frank slung his coat over the back of the dining chair and sat down. Having ordered their breakfasts, Frank looked around to make sure no one would overhear their conversation.

"Jason has been on my back to find out some background information on Lee, the undercover cop," Frank whispered.

"Jesus wept. What's up with him? He's in self-destruct mode. Why do we need to stir a hornets' nest?" Wayne dropped three sugar cubes into his cup and stirred his coffee.

"I know, it's been eating away at him, and he wants his revenge. He's banged up for most of the day, sat seething with hatred. He's nothing else to do. He's taken it very personally. I don't think it helped that he took such a shine to Lee. It was like they had a bromance going on. You know Jason better than me. It's all about his reputation; he's obsessed with being feared. He thinks if he doesn't retaliate, word will get out that he is losing his bottle."

"No way, I'm not in on this one, Frank. We don't need to go to war with the cops. We will lose too much money. They'll be all over us and the business like a rash. You need to bring his focus back to the business."

"I don't think we have a choice, Wayne; are you going to say no to him?" Wayne didn't answer and took a drink of his coffee.

"Look, Frank, you're the educated one amongst us; you need to guide him away from this. He listens to you. Christ, he's banged up in Strangeways because of an unnecessary fuck-up. We don't want another one."

"I'll do some research on the cop, and we can take it from there," Frank concluded. He could see that Wayne was pissed off. He knew he had been working hard on the drug supply business whilst Jason had been inside. Frank also knew it would be to his benefit, building a solid rapport with Wayne. In Jason's absence, he was Frank's new business partner.

Wayne was looking out into the street as if he had washed his hands of the matter. Frank slid a piece of paper across the table to him. "That's Jason's new number. Don't call it. He will call you."

"You need to talk him out of this, Frank, or he can sort it out himself when he's released. It's not worth the risk or the unwelcome attention we'll attract. Between you and me, Frank, I'm getting pissed off with him, big time."

"Well, I've not finished yet. There's another issue, Jason might be wanting you to spring him out of Strangeways."

Wayne shook his head slowly, "Fucking priceless, is there anything else he wants? What's the point of escaping? He'll be out in four years or so anyway."

Frank sat back in his chair. He wondered how many more of Jason's demands Wayne would take before he went off like a powder keg. He took his cigarette pack out of his pocket and placed it on the table. "I'll just have a cigarette whilst you ponder that one." Frank left the café for a smoke. He stood still, enjoying the nicotine hit and a moments respite

23

from trying to bond with Wayne and get him onside with Jason's plans. His attention was taken through the window by the waitress placing their breakfasts on the table. He returned inside to eat.

"You can tell Jason I'm not getting involved in going after a cop. There's no need for it. What will it achieve? It's between the two of them, nobody else. He can either hire someone to do it, Wayne paused, "Or on second thoughts, he's probably better sorting it himself when he gets out. We know where that got him last time. I would rather walk away from the firm than get involved in that." Wayne continued eating. Frank could see that Wayne was seriously pissed off. He was like a dog with a bone. He wouldn't let his dissent to the subject drop.

"You know Jason. It's all about ego with him. It always has been. I'll get on with my research and see where it takes us. We might not even find out who Lee is… problem solved at the outset," Frank reasoned.

The waiter brought two more drinks over. Frank changed the subject to lighten the mood. Kirsty is back in town, from Spain, visiting her salons. Ryan isn't in tow with her."

"If he's any sense, he should practice becoming the hide-and-seek world champion. I take it Jason is still after him too?" Wayne said, shaking his head.

"I think Ryan's on his back burner for now," Frank said, briefly in an attempt to cool things down.

"That's another fuck up too. I could do with Ryan here, and he'd be fine if I kept him on a tight leash. I've got some trusted lads working for me, but it's not the same. Test the water with Jason, will you?" Frank guessed that Wayne wasn't happy with his lot these days. Albeit he enjoyed the money and trappings, just as Frank did, their business was lucrative, but that came with high risk. Frank had accepted a long time ago that he was up to his neck in criminal underworld dealings now. Walking away wasn't a viable option. He just needed to keep lids on things, especially Jason's ego.

"Right, I'm out of here Frank, thanks for breakfast. Nice to see you, pal. Make Jason see sense before he takes us all down," Wayne said as he tucked his chair under the table.

"I take it I'm paying," Frank muttered. He left a twenty on the saucer. The waitress set about clearing the table and thanked him as he put his coat on. The last thing Wayne said resonated with Frank as he smoked a cigarette outside. Frank knew he couldn't cope with a prison sentence. The thought of doing time scared the life out of him.

Wayne was growing on him; since Jason's incarceration, there seemed to be less drama, and the business was running smoothly. Frank flicked his cigarette to the floor and stepped on it, stubbing it into the pavement. He had a call to make, which he had been putting off for a few days now. He took out his mobile and selected the name from the contacts.

"What do you want? I thought we were quits now," DS Pete Higgs said.

"I'm in the same boat as you Pete, it's quits when Jason says so. It's better for all of us if we play together nicely."

"Jason's inside because of his own mistake. We all delivered on our side of the deal. I'm walking away now."

"Pete, we both know you can't do that. You're up to your neck in it. You can't take the cash payments and then walk away when it suits you. It doesn't work like that. Jason might argue that you ripped him off. Where was his warning that the undercover cops were infiltrating him? You're supposed to be our man on the inside," Frank paused and let the silence hang for a moment. "I'll meet you at the usual place at seven o'clock." Frank ended the call before Pete had the chance to reply. He felt some empathy for Pete, but just like himself, Pete had allowed his greed to get the better of him. There was no easy way out. He was now one of Jason Hamilton's assets.

Pete returned to the major incident room, placing his mobile phone into the inside pocket of his suit jacket. He could see DS Lee McCann and DI Andrea Statham talking in her office. He strolled over and knocked lightly on the door as he entered. They both looked up at him from the meeting table.

"Ah, you're back, Pete, good timing. Let's all sit down and make sure we've covered all of the bases for your handover... You okay, Pete? You look like you've got the worries of the world on your shoulders," Andrea asked.

"Yeah, I'm fine. My daughter's school just called; she's not feeling too well, and they'd like me to pick her up."

"You'd better get off then, and we can catch up tomorrow," Andrea suggested.

"I'm okay for another half hour. They're going to give her some lunch and see how she feels." Pete pulled back a chair and joined them at the table.

"Rather than get embroiled in the child abuse investigation, I've asked Lee to familiarise himself with the Paul Smethurst and Carl Smith murder investigations. A set of fresh eyes might spot an opportunity." She looked over to Lee, "It will also be good for refreshing your memory and re-acquainting you with the HOLMES database software."

"No pressure then," Lee said.

"I've given Lee a briefing of the investigations and copies of the closing reports. I won't be far away if I'm needed anyway," Pete said.

After their meeting, Pete made his way to the car park, and sliding into his car, placed his hands on the top of the steering wheel, leaning forward, head on hands. I need to fight fire with fire here, he decided. It's all they understand. I need Burton onside though, what a mess. What was I thinking about getting involved with these fuckers, Pete lamented. The smell of the new car interior was a reminder of his predicament. It had been paid for with cash from one of Burton's brown envelopes. Pete's head was all over the place with anger and regret, but there was nowhere to hide. He had to face this head-on. He started the car and drove into Manchester. He parked in the multi-storey car park and walked down the concrete staircase that stank of piss and god knows what else. He paced across town, ready for a row, and reached the anonymous-looking red brick Victorian building near the Cathedral. The black wooden door looked anonymous and uninviting. He selected the intercom button on the wall next to the door.

"Hello, can I help you?" said the voice of a young male.

"Yes, I'm here to see Frank. Tell him it's Mr Higgs. It's urgent and won't wait."

"Just a moment, Sir." Pete took out his phone and checked his text messages. His wife was on his case again, pecking his head about the money he'd blown at the weekend. "For god's sake, give me a break," Pete said aloud.

"Mr Burton will see you now; come up to the second floor, please." Pete heard a buzzer and the click of the door lock opening. He pushed the door open and entered a sparse but clean and tidy functional staircase.

On reaching the second floor, there was only one door; he pushed it open and walked into a small reception office. A young lad in a cheap, black suit that looked too big for him was sitting behind a desk tapping away on a laptop.

"Shouldn't you be in school?" Pete asked, immediately regretting his cheap, snide remark. It wasn't the lad's fault Pete's life was a clusterfuck.

"Go straight through, Sir," he said, pointing to the only other door in the room. Pete knocked politely on the door and regretted this courtesy right away; old habits die hard.

"Come in," Frank's voice bellowed from behind the door. Pete stepped cautiously into the office.

"This had better be good, Pete. You should not be visiting here under any circumstances. More so for your benefit, not mine." Frank glared at Pete, who remained standing.

"I want out. I've done my bit for you now. Jason fucked up. He put himself inside..."

Frank interrupted, "Lower your voice, and listen to me. The reason you still have a roof over your head is down to us sorting out your mortgage arrears. Then there are the credit cards, and did you drive here in your new car? Don't be so bloody naive. You still owe us, big time. Whether you like it or not, you're just a bent cop in Jason's pocket. Now get the fuck out of my office."

"If that's the way you want to play it, Frank, bring it on. But don't forget, you've got as much to lose as I have." Pete was unable to muster anything further. He was taken aback by the unexpected aggression from Frank.

"Pete. You need to wake up. One call to your senior officer, and you're fucked. I've even got her number in my contacts. You have nothing at all to threaten me with, so wind your neck in and get the hell out of here."

Pete turned about and hurried out of the office. The young lad in reception kept his head down. Shit, what was I thinking? I shouldn't have come here. Pete hadn't bargained on Frank standing up to him and taking such an aggressive stance. To date, he had always been a mild-mannered inoffensive middle-aged guy. Pete felt anxious; he had hoped to reconcile his exit from the arrangement with Frank but had now been left in no doubt that he was with them for the long term.

As Pete walked down the stairs, Frank reached into his drawer and took out a bottle of scotch. He hesitated, then poured a large shot and necked it in one. He stood up and walked over to the window, lighting a cigarette. He was just in time to see Pete leaving the building in haste as he disappeared out of view.

Three

Association time was coming to an end, and the cacophony from the landing was gradually quietening down, pre-lockdown. It was the time of day that Jason looked forward to; peace and quiet gradually replacing the madness of daytime incarceration. During that time, he kept himself busy by reading most of the time or working out. A prison officer silently looked into his cell, then locked the door. Being one of the quieter officers who didn't have much banter with the inmates. Jason was wary of him and instructed Dean to keep him at arm's length. Jason continued to read for another hour or so, to give the prison officers time to leave the landing before retrieving his mobile phone.

"How you doing?" Wayne answered.

"Can't complain," Jason replied cagily.

"Business is good, running smoothly, No issues," Wayne reported.

Jason sensed Wayne was being a bit stand-offish and felt a rise in tension between them. "Frank tells me you're not keen on taking revenge on the cop," Jason said, getting to the point.

"I'm having nothing to do with it, Jason. It's a bad move. Are you sure now is the time? Surely we don't need any more attention from the cops?"

"I can't let this one go, mucker. The cop took the piss out of me, flirted with Kirsty, drank my beer in my house, and stitched me up. He's the reason I'm sat in this cell right now. I'll look like a right twat if I let him get away with it."

"I hear what you're saying, mate, but let's not be hasty, eh? There's plenty of time to take your revenge when you get out. Our main focus now should be business, surely? You're inside, Carl's dead, and Ryan's done a runner because you want to kill him. That leaves me to run the show. I've got enough on my plate. Why don't you leave it for now, let him think he's got away with it? He'll probably get complacent with his security and make it easier for you when the time comes."

Jason was getting tired of listening to Wayne's bleating. He was irritated that Wayne had been challenging his instructions more since he'd been inside. "So, can you get me out of here? Or is that an inconvenience too?" Jason asked in a menacing tone, a spontaneous reaction to the negativity he heard from Wayne.

"You know I'd help… just think it through. You'd be on your toes, looking over your shoulder forever. The cops wouldn't rest until they busted you. On the other hand, if you keep your head down, you'll probably be out in three or four years."

"Leave it with me. I'll consider my options," Jason terminated the call and lay on the bed, looking towards the ceiling in the darkness. He was seething at Wayne's reluctance to see things his way. Being inside made him feel less effective.

The reason he wanted to get the cop killed whilst he was inside was to send a message to rival gangs that he was still a force to be reckoned with, even from behind the bars of Strangeways. Having the cop killed whilst he was still inside would eliminate any physical evidence linking back to him. I bet Lee the cop thinks he's the dog's bollocks, home and dry. Well, he's not. He's got it coming to him, Jason brooded.

On impulse, Jason dialled a second number. Kirsty answered in a surprised tone, "Hi Jason, Frank said you might call, but I didn't think you would. How are you doing?"

"I'm settled into a routine now. I can't complain. It's a breeze in here. You okay?"

"I've been better, and I needed the break in Spain to get my head sorted. I really didn't need all that shit going on. I warned you that this would happen."

"You still with Ryan?"

"No, I was never with Ryan. Nothing happened. You know what he's like, he was looking out for me, that's all. You need to give him a break; he's still a loyal mate to you. Let it go and make up with him. I just wanted some time to myself, and he needed to get away because his head had gone, which is no surprise after you tried to have him killed. There was an empty silence. Anyway, it's up to you. I'm back in Manchester. I'll visit you if you want me to?"

"We'll see."

"Let me know if you need anything sorting out for you. There's no reason to fall out. We can still be friends."

"Let's just see how things go. Keep your head down. If the cops start harassing you, call Frank. He'll get them to back off. I've got to go. I'll think about the visit."

"Okay, speak soon."

Jason concealed the mobile phone; although it was unlikely, he knew that a screw could look through the spyhole at any time. Talking to Kirsty had chilled him out, but he wasn't hasty in jumping to conclusions about their relationship. For now, Jason would take things one day at a time. As for Ryan, he would let him sweat for a while longer yet.

Closing his eyes, he began planning his revenge, re-thinking his options, before the deadly silence of the prison wing lulled him into a fitful sleep.

Pete's last day on the major incident team had ended with Andrea indulging him at their favourite Rusholme kebab shop. They were sitting on bar stools at a bench, looking out of the window onto Wilmslow Road, watching the passers-by. Andrea was lamenting the loss of a key team member. "There's still time to change your mind, Pete," Andrea teased, giving him a nudge.

"I didn't intend moving, as you know, but it's probably my last opportunity to work on the squad, and I've always fancied it." Pete took a bite out of his kebab. Andrea took the hint that he probably didn't want to discuss it any further. He seemed awkward about it.

"Well, I'll have you back if it doesn't work out for you, you know that?" Andrea changed the subject, "This chilli sauce is red hot, how's yours?" Pete didn't have time to answer. His mobile was ringing. He looked at the caller display, and his face dropped.

"I need to take this, Andrea. I'll be back in a minute." He stepped down from the stool and walked out of the shop, turning right into a side street. Andrea watched him through the window. His speech looked animated as if he was having a row with someone. He didn't look happy. Andrea carried on eating, watching from the corner of her eye. She didn't want Pete to catch her spying on him. Maybe he was having relationship problems; things didn't look good in Pete's world. Pete walked back into the shop and took his seat. Andrea could see he was stressed.

"Is everything okay, Pete, you've not been yourself lately?"

"Thanks for asking, but just the usual stuff at home, nothing major, you know the score, we're going through a bit of a rough patch, nothing serious." Andrea sensed that Pete was making light of whatever issue was pissing him off.

"Who was that on the phone?"

"It was the builder, and he's trying to sting me for more cash." The answer didn't convince Andrea, but she wasn't about to challenge him. It did make her more curious, though. But for now, time to steer away from that subject.

"Kirsty Hamilton is back in Manchester. I think I'll visit her; she's the weak link. You never know what she might let slip."

"I'm sure she knows more than she lets on, but she will also be frightened to death of Jason Hamilton. Going to Spain with Ryan Young won't have done her any favours. But nothing ventured, nothing gained, I suppose, if you catch her at the right time, you never know."

"It would be nice to get some evidence to stick on Hamilton for the Smethurst or Smith murders. It looks like he's covered his tracks. Not only that, people are terrified about giving evidence against him. All we need is one witness, and then others will come forward. Especially whilst he's locked up."

"I doubt anyone will come forward. People know what he's like; even though he's inside, he would still get to them through his cronies… Well, that was delicious." Pete stood up from the stool, "Give me your plate." Pete took the paper plates and plastic cutlery and dropped them into the bin.

Back at the office, the team had assembled to wish Pete all the best on his attachment to the drugs squad. Andrea said a few words in a farewell speech and presented him with a bottle of his favourite Scotch whiskey. Following cake, coffee and banter, Pete returned to his desk and started to go through his emails. He was struggling to concentrate and was still seething about how Frank Burton had spoken to him, over the phone, outside the kebab shop.

Burton had tasked him to get background information on DS Lee McCann, his address, what gym he went to, where he drank and so forth. Pete had tried to talk Frank out of it but to no avail. Pete's head felt mashed. He was between a rock and a hard place. Setting up a colleague for a beating by some gangsters went against every principle he held. But it was getting to the stage of self-preservation. He had to face facts. If he didn't produce the goods for Burton, he too could be attacked by Jason Hamilton's men. Even worse, he had made himself vulnerable to the blackmail of Burton, grassing him up to police command. He felt shit, and truth be told, he wasn't sure of which way to turn. He decided it was time to confront Frank Burton again. He needed to make him have it. Why should he take shit from a snake like Burton?

Four

Andrea parked her car at the roadside and walked along the tree-lined pavement in Urmston, passing the neat and tidy gardens of the red brick semi-detached houses. It was a suburb that estate agents would call desirable or sought after. Beyond the houses, she saw a row of three shops, a florist, a newsagent, and a hair salon, set back from the pavement. Hair by Kirsty was closest; it looked stylish and upmarket. Andrea stepped inside and smelled the familiar strong aroma of hair products. Young women occupied all four black leather stylist's chairs. Not a salon for blue rinses, she mused. Andrea was impressed with the setup; the furniture was black, set against white designer floral wallpaper. One of the four stylists broke away from her client and approached Andrea at the reception station. "Would you like an appointment?" The stylist asked politely, A young woman, with immaculate hair and makeup.

"Andrea held out her police warrant card, "I need to speak to Kirsty Hamilton, is she here?"

"You've just missed her. She's been here for most of the morning. What is it concerning? I'm the manager." The woman who looked no older than mid-twenties appeared a little flustered by the unannounced visit of a police officer. Andrea was sure that her presence hadn't gone unnoticed by the four customers in the salon chairs. The chatter had stopped, all ears straining to hear above the noise of the hairdryers to capture any worthy gossip.

"It's a personal matter. Do you have a number I can contact Kirsty on?" Andrea already had a mobile number for Kirsty, but it was always worth asking the question, on the off-chance, she had a second phone. The manager took her mobile phone from the pocket of her stylish black apron and scrolled through her contacts, reading the number to Andrea aloud. "Thank you, is she busy today?"

"I'm not sure; she may have been going to her salon in Bolton."

"How long has she been back from Spain?"

"I'm not sure, maybe three or four days," the manager said hesitantly.

"Do you know Kirsty socially?"

"I'm sorry, I need to get back to my client. The dye needs washing out." The manager looked flustered and apologetic.

"Well, do you?"

"No, I've not worked here long," She replied, already walking back towards her client.

"Thanks for your help. Nice to meet you." Walking back to her car, Andrea smiled as she wondered what chatter had ensued after her departure. Oh, to be a fly on the wall, she wished.

Andrea sat in her car and took a drink of the now lukewarm cappuccino. She still enjoyed it all the same.

Kirsty eventually answered the phone, just as Andrea was about to give up. "Hello."

"Hi Kirsty, It's DI Andrea Statham. I need to ask you some questions about your boyfriend. Are you free to meet up?"

"Look, I've nothing more to say that will help you. I've already explained this to the detective before I went to Spain. I was as shocked as the next person. I'm trying to move on and get my life back on track."

"It will only take ten minutes, just loose ends that need tying up. It's not going to go away until we've spoken," Andrea interrupted.

"I'm at the Trafford Centre, and I'll be here for another hour or so. Do you want to meet here?" Andrea agreed to meet for a coffee. She was only ten minutes away.

She parked her car in the shadow of the iconic blue dome that was now a familiar sight on the skyline of Manchester. It was the first time she had visited for business purposes. Her regular visits here would involve shopping and dining with her friend Sarah in the Orient.

Andrea walked along the polished marble floors of the shopping mall, past the shops and imported Californian palm trees that stretched up towards the glass roof.

She saw Kirsty sitting at a table, "Hi Kirsty," Andrea took her coat off, placed it over the back of the chair and sat down, "You've got a nice tan. How was Spain?"

"It was just what I needed. I could be tempted to live out there quite easily," Kirsty smiled politely.

"I've heard you flew out with Ryan Young. Are you two an item now?" Andrea wanted to get straight down to business.

"No, I've known Ryan for years since our school days. We're just pals. Christ, don't you fan the flames of that rumour as well," Kirsty retorted.

"I bet Jason doesn't see it like that. Will he not hit the roof when he finds out?"

"Have you got some questions for me, or are you just here to gossip?"

Andrea was taken aback by Kirsty's confidence. "How did you feel when Jason tried to have him murdered?" Andrea continued to probe.

"Are you ready to order, ladies?" A young waiter had approached them. He was a tall, skinny lad wearing a traditional waiters uniform that looked like it needed ironing. Andrea initially cursed his timing. She was building momentum to her questioning, but on reflection, she was thankful for the pause. It allowed Kirsty some time to consider the gravity of her questions. They ordered their coffees.

After ordering the drinks, Andrea broke the silence, "I bet it hit you hard, your boyfriend paying to have Ryan killed. You need to be pretty evil to do something like that. Or is it his ruthlessness that attracted you to Jason? They do say that girls are attracted to bad boys, don't they?" Andrea was doing her best to press Kirsty's buttons, hoping for an emotional response.

"I was shocked. I thought they were good pals. Everything changed when Lee, the undercover cop, came on the scene. He was a bad influence on Jason. Maybe he influenced Jason to do it. I wish we'd never met Lee."

Andrea restrained herself from laughing. "The thing is Kirsty, I know he's involved in two murders, Richard Smethurst and Carl Smith. He's a nasty piece of work this fella you're protecting. Why would you offer him such loyalty?" Andrea was surprised at Kirsty's composure; she had expected at least some kickback.

"Like I told the other detective, I am not involved in Jason's business dealings. I'm certainly not covering for him. I would never cover up for a murderer if what you're saying is right." Kirsty took a sip of her coffee. Andrea watched her intently, reluctantly accepting that Kirsty was not about to blow Jason out of the water. But she felt obliged to give it one last try.

"You've got a lavish lifestyle Kirsty, it can't come cheap. Did Jason buy you the salons?" Kirsty didn't answer, and she shook her head with disdain, "We will be all over Jason's finances with a fine-tooth comb. Do you want to risk letting him take you down with him?" Andrea said pausing for a moment. "You say you want to move on with your life Kirsty, and we can help you to do that. We have a state of the art witness protection programme that would keep you safe from Jason. Think about it; no decent person wants to protect a murderer."

Andrea stood up and put her coat on. She placed a business card on the table. "Do the right thing, Kirsty. You don't look like the type of woman who would cope well in prison. It's time to talk; even if you just want to point me in the right direction, nobody needs to find out that you helped me. Thanks for meeting anyway. Think it over. I'm probably your best option right now." Andrea settled the bill at the desk and made her way back to her car.

Kirsty ordered a second coffee and selected Frank Burton from her contacts. The voicemail activated, 'Hello, this is Frank. Leave a message.'

"Hi Frank, it's Kirsty. DI Statham has just visited me. She wants me to grass on Jason, she is saying Jason has committed two murders; Paul Smethurst and Carl Smith. Is that right, Frank? Or is she just playing me?"

DS Pete Higgs turned off the East Lancashire Road towards the golf club. He drove along the gravel track to the car park. Having switched off the engine, Pete remained seated and watched, trance like, as four men assembled at the first tee, ready to start the game. He wished his life was as innocent and straightforward as enjoying a round of golf. Pete couldn't concentrate or focus on work these days. He wasn't coping well with the pressure from the tangled web of deceit. But he didn't feel sorry for himself, he was well aware of the risks when he got involved with Frank Burton's corruption. Passing on restricted police information about other criminals was wrong. But in return, he'd received some credible intelligence on Hamilton's rival gangs, from Burton, which made it easier to find evidence to convict them. In Pete's eyes, it was noble cause corruption. It helped him to convict criminals and keep the public safe. But helping Frank to arrange a hit on DS Lee McCann was a different matter.

He got out of the car and walked into the golf club. The corridor wall was lined with wooden tablets, listing previous club captains and cup winners. It led straight to the lounge, where he saw Frank Burton sitting at a table having lunch with his wife in the bar area. He walked over and stopped by their table. "Good Afternoon, I'm sorry to interrupt your lunch Mrs Burton, but I have some urgent business to discuss with Frank."

"It's not a problem; I'm used to it after all these years." She was not what Pete had expected Frank's wife to look like. She had an average build, grey hair tied into a ponytail, wearing little makeup and dressed in a navy cardigan over a white blouse. She looked bookish, professional and came across as confident and personable, not a downtrodden, bullied wife as he had expected.

"I was just about finished anyway," Frank said in a friendly tone, giving the impression Pete was a good friend, "I was ready for a cigarette too; shall we go outside?" Frank stood up, "I won't be long. I'll grab us another drink on my way back." His wife smiled politely and continued to eat her lunch. Pete and Frank walked to the covered smoking area beyond the main entrance.

"Well, Pete, if you are trying to test my patience, you are certainly succeeding." Frank cupped his hands to his mouth as he lit a cigarette. He exhaled and continued, "My patience will only stretch so far. You really don't want to test it, trust me."

"Don't play 'Mr Big' Frank; it doesn't suit you. You need to get a grip of Jason. This is getting out of control. Lee was just doing his job. It's what he does, getting drug dealers banged up. It was nothing personal. How can you seriously expect me to assist your boys in attacking him?"

"I don't need to play 'Mr Big', Peter. I can create a shit storm for you by just making one phone call. And that's not to your bosses. It looks like it's getting too much for you, Pete. You should have thought about the ramifications before you joined the firm's payroll."

"I've never joined any firm, we had a mutual understanding, and I've done more than pay my dues." Pete was getting more agitated.

"If you say so, Pete." Pete sensed that Frank was enjoying his discomfort.

"You have as much to lose as I do Frank, I'm staggered that you are so complacent about this. Does your wife know what you're up to?"

"Steady on, son, if we are bringing families into this, it will get messy. How old is your daughter now?" Frank sounded menacing. Pete instantly regretted mentioning Frank's wife. It was a naïve move. The silence that followed reflected their shared agreement on that score. Frank continued smoking, looking out towards the fairway.

"All Jason wants from you is some background information on Lee, or whatever his real name is. That's all," Frank said and took a long drag of his cigarette. He looked away from Pete as he exhaled the smoke.

"Surely you are trying to talk him out of this, for Christ's sake?"

"I will do my best, Pete, but getting him to change his mind isn't easy."

"If I did get you some background information for you, I'd want some assurance that my debt is settled," Pete recognised the futility of his request. He could never trust Frank to honour an agreement.

Frank laughed cynically, stubbing out his cigarette on the floor. "Now, I must get back to my lunch. Please stop these little visits, Pete. We really shouldn't be seen together. You wouldn't be pleased if I got some associates to start visiting you and your family," Frank glared at Pete for a moment before walking back into the clubhouse.

Pete strolled to his car. This is like wading through treacle, he thought. Give them some info on Lee, and they let me walk away… but would they? He mused. Pete understood the message from Frank loud and clear. He didn't want his wife and children getting dragged into this mess. I can sort this out, he tried to convince himself. Frank is in no position to call the shots; he has as much to lose as I have, thought Pete, as he got back into his car and started the engine. He needed to get back to the office before his new boss DI Dave Ferguson started to wonder where he was. The hands-free phone alert activated; it was DS Lee McCann. Pete felt a wave of guilt run through him. "Hi Lee, you okay, pal?"

"All good mate, I'm at the training centre, on a health and safety refresher course, are you free to meet in the canteen for a coffee? I need an excuse to get out of here."

"Good timing Lee, I was just about to go back to the office. I'll see you in half an hour." Pete set off to the force training centre.

The canteen was not unlike any other police or hospital canteen, basic with no-frills. Pete bought a coffee and joined Lee at a table in the main dining area. The place was quite empty but for a noisy class of enthusiastic recruits, chatting, wearing their new uniforms. "Thanks for coming, Pete. I needed to get out of that classroom. I hate courses."

Pete smiled politely, "How are you settling in with the team?"

"It's going well. I'm enjoying working for Andrea, and I like her old school approach. She can back up the talk with her experience. I wouldn't want to piss her off, though. I guess she doesn't suffer fools. How's the drugs squad going?"

"A home from home, mate, I'm on the syndicate investigating Jason Hamilton. We've got Wayne Davies under surveillance. He's a switched on fella, and he seems to operate very carefully. But I'm sure he'll drop his guard sooner or later. Have you got your head around the Smethurst and Smith murder cases yet?"

"It's all I've been doing up to now, and it would be great to identify a positive line of enquiry. Keep me up to speed on Wayne Davies, will you?" Pete sensed that Lee was a grafter who could progress the investigation. He had an excellent reputation as a top thief-taker when he was in CID. "The guy in the Manchester United shirt who was running along the canal interests me. He must have seen the shooter," Lee continued.

"Yes, we never managed to track him down. I visited the canal several times in the weeks following the death, hoping he was a regular jogger, but I had no luck," Pete lied.

"It's worth a follow-up. I'll do a bit of leg work and try to identify the jogger," Lee said.

Pete suddenly felt pissed off with Lee. He needed the Jason Hamilton investigation to be filed. Not for Lee to identify a credible witness.

"We need to keep in touch, mate; if we work together, I'm sure we can nail Hamilton and his boys. How's your commute to the new office?" Pete asked.

"It's fine, it never takes more than half an hour, and I'm on the Metro link line too."

"Where are you living these days?" Pete felt assured that his question was within the context of the conversation and didn't sound like he was poking around for information. But it didn't stop him from feeling like low life scum.

"I've got an apartment in Chadderton. It's great, really close to the golf clubs and not far from Manchester."

Even though Pete hadn't decided on his plan of action, it was second nature to dig for the information that he might need at some stage. They finished their drinks and agreed to keep in touch.

Pete mulled over his options as he drove back to the office. Lee could be a problem; if he got stuck into the Smethurst murder case and brought attention back to Hamilton's organised crime group. Pete was in no doubt; if the police turned up the heat on Hamilton, then Burton would turn the heat upon him.

The quagmire was getting deeper. He needed to decide on his next move.

Five

Following slowly behind Dean, Jason trudged up the metal staircase. There was no rush to get back to his cell, and Dean knew not to rush him. The healthcare visit had gone well. He was patiently laying the foundations for his planned escape from custody. Over the last few weeks, he had sought medical assistance under the guise of experiencing blurred vision, dizziness and palpitations. The doctor had suggested it was probably stress-related and offered medication. Jason had declined any medication as part of the ruse to clarify he wasn't just seeking medication or malingering.

He had also worked hard to give the impression of being a model prisoner on the wing. He spent his time reading and was careful not to get drawn into altercations with other inmates. If he needed any dirty work doing, he delegated to his errand boys on the landing. He still volunteered, helping inmates with issues on the peer support project, and would tell any staff who cared to listen that he just wanted to keep his head down and do his time.

He looked around to make sure no one was in earshot as they walked up the stairs. "You need to be in the gym at eight o'clock tonight. One of my boys will drop your steroids off."

"Cheers, Jason, how much do I owe you?"

"Nothing Dean, I look after my boys." Jason felt good that Dean didn't object to being called one of his boys.

"He'll have some cash for you as well; you've earned it mate." What Jason didn't mention was that all handovers were filmed or photographed. It was a good insurance policy if Dean started to get windy and have second thoughts.

"You've paid me enough already, Jason."

"Nonsense, I don't know how you survive on what they pay you here. I like you, Dean. You're a switched-on lad. You're worth every penny of your retainer. Once I'm out of here, I'll have a job for you, with decent wages. Besides, my lads at the gym may need you to give them a lift with things at some stage. Treat you and the wife to a weekend away." Jason waited for any sign of demurral, but nothing was forthcoming. Since Jason had taken Dean under his wing, Dean had received less aggravation from the other inmates. Life was good for Dean, for now. They reached the cell door, "Do you think I convinced the doctor?"

"Yeah, he's one of the few that still give a shit. He's not had his motivation drained from him yet, by the relentless grind."

"Good, don't make it too obvious, but whenever the opportunity arises, make sure you let other staff know of your concerns for my health. If people hear something often enough, they start to believe it. Come the day; nobody will be surprised when I collapse."

"No worries, I'm on with it. I'll lay it on thick with Doctor Choudhry when I see him. We get on well. He's sound."

"Just be careful, Dean, don't lay it on too thick. It's a very fine line. We don't want any of the other screws catching on to our arrangement."

Dean nodded, "Don't worry, I won't," he said before leaving for his lunch break. Jason sat on the edge of his bed. The cacophony created by the other inmates, shouting to each other from cell to cell, drifted into the background. He wanted to exercise but couldn't find the motivation. He was beginning to worry about Dean going over the top when spreading the fake news of his health to other officers. Jason had made it clear, though, which officers to engage with and which to avoid. Some of the older screws had seen it all before and would see right through Dean. They could smell a rat a mile away. Jason would just have to manage him well and keep him at heel.

For the third day in a row, DS Lee McCann was sitting in an unmarked police car parked up next to the canal, near the location where Smethurst was murdered. Lee didn't mind the monotony of observations. Proactive policing had always been worth the effort, and if he was going to identify the jogger witness, he had to be patient. Lee was also keen to make a good impression on his team. If he identified the witness, and as a result, Hamilton was re-arrested, it would be a great start.

Lee got out of the car to stretch his legs and walked over the footbridge to the towpath. He studied the scene, hypothesising how the shooting had unfolded. After walking about two hundred metres, he felt a few drops of rain on his face and so headed back to the car in case it started to lash it down. Lee was just about to cross the footbridge when he saw a jogger approaching, and from the description, he knew that this was probably his man, the football shirt he was wearing, all but confirmed it. "Yes, get in," Lee exclaimed to himself. He waited by the towpath whilst the jogger laboured towards him.

"DS McCann, CID, could I have a quick word, please?" Lee said, holding out his warrant card.

"Is this about the shooting?" The jogger asked breathlessly. Lee couldn't believe his luck. He hadn't even mentioned the shooting. Perhaps this guy wanted to talk.

"Yes, I'm looking for a fella matching your description, who was running here just after the shooting."

"Yep, that was me, but I'm not getting involved, pal." Lee found it difficult not to break into a big smile, well why didn't you keep your mouth shut then? He mused. "I stopped jogging along here for a while. I knew you men would be looking for witnesses."

"I can tell you've had a break from running. You looked like you were struggling back there, mate! Lee laughed, trying to break the ice, "Why don't you want to get involved?" He probed.

"You cheeky bastard, I was on for a personal best before you stopped me! Would you want to get involved if you lived around here?" Lee accepted it was a fair point but wasn't about to agree with him.

"I know where you're coming from, mate, but there are things we can do to look after witnesses these days. It's not like we're talking about a stolen pedal bike, is it?" The rain was getting heavier. The jogger accepted the invitation to sit in the car.

"I didn't see anything happen. I just saw two guys hanging about on the towpath. They looked dodgy as fuck. I knew they were up to no good. They were only there for a minute or two, and then they jogged off down the canal. I had a quick peck in the bushes as I ran by where they had been standing. But there was nothing there. I hoped they might have stashed

50

something. I might have come away with a computer or something. It was when I watched the news later that night that I realised they must have had some involvement in the shooting."

"Was there anything in the bushes?" Lee thought that the jogger might have picked the pistol up and conveniently not mentioned it.

"I didn't see anything. I'm not that lucky."

"Did you recognise them?"

"Off the record, yes, I've seen one of them running along here a few times. I'm not giving a statement, though. I'm not risking getting shot. It's risky enough sitting here talking to you."

"Nobody will see us here. I've not seen another soul until you appeared. But don't be hasty fella; this is serious shit. As I said, we have options available to protect your identity and present your evidence anonymously."

"Look, I'll help you off the record, but I'm not giving evidence. From what I've heard, it was gangsters in a dispute over a drug deal. Shit like that comes with the territory. You can pay informants, can't you?"

"I need a witness; an informant is no use to me." Lee didn't want to push the issue too far at this stage. He needed to give the potential witness time to think and consider his options. Lee started asking more general questions about local gossip and criminal activity in the area. The jogger appeared to be happy to change the subject. Lee took his details and mobile number, they agreed to meet up again, somewhere out of the way. Lee knew he had to earn his trust to get him to loosen up and start talking. He'd made a good start, and now he just had the small matter of convincing him to help identify Hamilton and give evidence at court.

Back at the office, Lee took great pride in updating DI Andrea Statham, but he was careful not to gloat. They were sitting at the meeting table in her office.

"Nice one, Lee, Pete tried tracking him down for ages but got nowhere. That's a great result.

"That's because he was keeping his head down, avoiding the cops. He was avoiding the canal intentionally. I've checked him out. He has some previous form, for nicking cars years ago when he was a kid. Nothing recently, though, or at least he's not been caught. He enjoys talking too. I couldn't shut him up."

"That's a good sign. Do you think he will come across as a witness?"

"I'll have to work on him. It won't be easy, but if I can reassure him of his safety, you never know. Witness protection might be an option. I'm sure he would fit the criteria. If he can pick Hamilton out on a video identification parade, it puts Hamilton at the scene of the crime."

"No pressure then, Lee, we just need to get a streetwise small-time scally to identify Hamilton and give us a statement," Andrea teased.

"Let's see how it goes. I'll do my best. It's Jack Beckett's retirement do in Manchester tonight, are you going for a few beers?" Lee asked.

"Yes, I said I'd meet Pete there for a beer. I'll give you a lift into town if you like, then you can have a beer and celebrate your result with the jogger."

"It's not a result yet. I'll go and do some more research on my potential new star witness. I might discover some interesting associates or feuds he has been involved in lately." Lee returned to the main office and got stuck into the intelligence database.

Andrea and Lee huddled under her brolly whilst walking along Deansgate towards the pub. They turned into the narrow side street, giving them a little more protection from the rain. The pavement and cobbles glistened wet with the rain. As they approached the door, their pace quickened. "Last one there gets the beers in," Andrea said, speeding to a sprint and leaving Lee behind, holding the brolly. Lee shook the umbrella and followed her inside. It was a traditional old fashioned pub; wooden floorboards and dark wood panelling covering the walls. Andrea looked through the crowded bar area and saw Jack and his colleagues at the far end. She liked it here, and it was a popular haunt for the detectives when Bootle Street nick was still open.

"I suppose I'd better get the drinks in then, roadrunner," Lee mockingly grimaced.

"Prosecco for me, please," Andrea said with a smile and squeezed past the other punters towards the far end of the pub, where she joined Pete Higgs standing by the fireplace talking to his new DI, Dave Ferguson. "Great timing Andrea, I was just about to go to the bar; how do you time your entrance so well?"

"Years of practice, Dave, I'm okay thanks, Lee is getting them in." Dave laughed and made his way to the bar.

"Lee's at the bar, is he? You're thick as thieves, you two. He's just your type, Andrea," Pete teased.

Andrea played along, "He's a good looking lad, so if he plays his cards right, you never know Pete. I could do a lot worse," she retorted playfully.

Lee approached them, balancing the glasses precariously to avoid spillages, as he dodged through the crowded bar area. "Hi, Pete, how are you doing?"

"Busy mate. As you know, I've been running the surveillance on Wayne Davies all week. It's early days, but he seems to be spending most of his time at his builders' yard. Any new leads on Hamilton?" Pete asked.

"Nothing, he's like a model prisoner apparently, keeping out of trouble. He's helping other prisoners with peer support, reading and other stuff. I guess he's looking for an early release, for good behaviour. The economic crime team are still investigating his banking activity, looking for money laundering or illicit earnings that we could seize under the Proceeds of Crime Act. They reckon his finances withstand scrutiny; through his legitimate investments. It looks like he's covered his tracks well," Lee replied.

"But it's not all doom and gloom. Lee's had a great result today. He's identified the jogger in the Man United shirt who was on the canal when Smethurst was shot," Andrea said, sounding chuffed.

"Nice one Lee, what's he had to say?" Pete asked.

"He must have just missed the shooting by seconds, only seeing two males making off, and he reckons he can identify one of them," Lee said, sounding upbeat.

Pete interrupted, "Wow, that puts our man at the scene. He'll struggle to explain that away. Good effort, Lee."

"Let's wait and see, eh, I don't want to count my chickens just yet," Lee said.

Dave Ferguson returned from the bar, and Lee repeated the good news for his benefit.

"Looking good, we're picking up some intelligence from the surveillance on Wayne Davies, so it's not over yet. Do you think he'll give a statement Lee?" Dave asked.

"Yeah, he's a savvy character, and he's working out his best options before he agrees to anything."

Dave Ferguson moved the conversation on from the investigation to the shock and horror at the results of the recent promotion boards. The list of newly promoted incumbents always provoked fierce debate and strong opinions. Dave was putting on a brave face, having been unsuccessful once again.

"I'm starving, Lee. I was going to grab a pizza on the way home. Do you fancy pizza?" Andrea didn't want to sound too keen but was hoping he'd say yes. She was enjoying the evening, and in no rush to get home.

"I'd prefer a curry, after a few more beers."

"I'll get them in then," Andrea said.

After a few more drinks, they made their way to Lee's favourite Indian restaurant. A gold coloured Buddha effigy, illuminated with spotlights, dominated the entrance. The waiter invited them in and led them to a booth.

"I've not been here before. I love these booths; they give you a little more privacy," Andrea said, taking in the surroundings.

"It's been open for about three years now. It used to be an Italian. I had my promotion do here."

The waiter brought their drinks and poppadums, which they devoured whilst reading the menu. The Indian Krishna pipe music and low lighting gave the place a traditional, peaceful feel. They both watched as the waiter walked by, pushing a serving trolley with Tandoori chicken sizzling on a hot platter.

"That looks gorgeous and smells good too. I think I might have that."

"I'll be adventurous and stick with my usual, chicken madras," Lee said.

"I enjoyed it at the pub, and it was good to see some of the retired guys who turned out. They had some tales to tell. It was a good turnout for Jack. I'll miss him, and he's a cracking detective."

"Yeah, it's always good catching up with people you've not seen for ages. Pete didn't look too impressed about us identifying the jogger. Do you think his nose has been put out of joint because he didn't identify him?"

"No, Pete's not like that; he's a team player. He was probably mulling over where it takes us, evidentially, in the bigger picture. I think he's having second thoughts about leaving the team."

"I was surprised he left, you two have worked on the squads together, and it's a great team. Plus, he's only got a few years until he retires, hasn't he?" Before Andrea could reply, the waiter approached with a trolley and delivered their meals to the table.

"I hope this tastes as good as it smells; those spices smell gorgeous," Andrea said as they started on the main course.

After the meal, Andrea drove out of Manchester along Oldham Road towards Chadderton. They chatted about films they'd seen recently, recommending 'must watch' titles to one another. Lee directed Andrea to his apartment.

"It looks like a nice estate Lee, what are the neighbours like?" Andrea asked.

"I hardly see them, perfect for me, the gym and the golf courses aren't far away, that's all I need. I can't complain at all." As Lee unfastened his seatbelt, Andrea was hoping she might be invited in for coffee. "Thanks for the lift Andrea, I'll drive next time."

"Yeah, it's been a good night, thanks Lee, I had a great time."

Lee got out of the car and closed the door. Andrea watched him walk towards the apartment building. No coffee then, probably for the best, she thought. Lee was making a good impression on her, and her intentions weren't altogether work-related.

Six

Pete lifted his head off the pillow, the thudding headache of a hangover hit him immediately. His mouth was dry, and he needed a drink. He crept towards the bedroom door, hoping not to wake his wife.

"Hangover from hell? I can't say I'm surprised; you were well pissed last night when you got in, Pete. I thought you were off the booze for a while," Rachel said.

"I don't feel too bad. I'll be okay once I've had a glass of water. You know what retirement parties are like." Pete was struggling to convince himself, never mind his wife. He stepped gingerly out of the room and down to the kitchen, where he knocked back two pints of water and some paracetamol.

He sent a text to DI Dave Ferguson to inform him that he intended to take the day off; if Dave didn't need him at the office. He made a coffee and sat down at the dining table to collect his thoughts. I need to get onside with Frank Burton. It's the best chance I have of keeping a lid on things. I'm better working with him than against him. Pete knew he needed to get a grip and stop things from spiralling out of control. His thoughts were interrupted by Rachel joining him in the kitchen.

"Ouch, you look rough," she said as she clicked the kettle switch back on.

"It wasn't too late when I got in, and you can't have been in bed for that long," He said. watching her making a brew. She was wearing the white towel robe he had bought her as a present during their stay at a spa hotel in the Lake District. Her long black hair was all over the place. She looked sexy, he still loved her to bits even after years of marriage and the strife of raising their kids. The peaceful domestic moment was in total contrast to the other side of Pete's life and the mess he had created by getting involved with Frank Burton and his cronies. He couldn't even contemplate the idea of Rachel finding out. She'd go ballistic.

"I'll do the school run. I've taken the day off work. I'll go and get a shower and get ready."

"Won't you still be over the limit?" Rachel asked. Pete had already left the kitchen and pretended not to have heard her. He had more important things on his mind. By the time Pete returned to the kitchen, Rachel had finished getting the kids ready for school.

"Daddy's taking you to school today, be good for him. He's feeling a bit delicate this morning after drinking dirty beer last night." Charlie and his younger sister Louise ran towards their dad and gave him a big hug.

"Let's go, Dad. It's football today. I don't want to be late," Charlie pleaded, holding a football under his arm. It was his final year at primary school. The eldest by two years, Louise hung onto his every word. They were well-behaved children and loved school.

"Right, let me give your mum a hug, and then we're off." Pete placed his arms around Rachel's waist and gave her a peck on the cheek. "Love you, Rachel Higgs, we've not had a weekend away in ages. Choose a nice spa hotel somewhere, and I'll pay. My treat."

"What with? we're pretty skint at the moment… You've not been gambling again, have you? Jesus, Pete, when will you learn," she said looking troubled.

"No, no, it's okay, I haven't. Honestly. It's all the overtime pay I've been raking in," Pete pleaded. Rachel raised her eyebrows, casting doubt.

"Come on, Dad," Charlie shouted from the hallway.

"Seriously, those days are gone. I'm over it." Pete gave her another kiss before heading for the door.

Pete parked the car away from the zig-zag markings on the road. The car had barely stopped before Charlie jumped out and ran ahead carrying his football and packed lunch, "See you tonight, Dad," he shouted.

Pete held Louise's hand as they walked to the playground entrance. He kissed Louise and watched her walk to the playground to join her friends. Pete watched her chatting for a moment, then walked back to the car, passing other parents talking and catching up on local gossip. He savoured the moment as he got into the car. Pete loved doing the school run, quality time with the children. He decided to drive the long way home and call at Tree Tops café in the Country Park for an Americano. He felt overwhelmed and needed to take time out to think things through. Pete took a seat and ordered a drink. He looked beyond the gravel car park to the dense woodland. As a young kid, Pete climbed the trees and collected conkers in there during autumn half-term holidays. But he also had a darker memory, a more recent memory from when he had contemplated hanging himself at the height of his gambling troubles. It was the thought of how his children would have reacted that stopped him.

He had sat in the rain, soaked to the bone, cold, shivering with a length of rope hanging from above him, despising himself for not having the guts to go through with it. It was his love for his family that saved him.

He shook away the memory and made a call, "Frank, it's Pete. Are you free to talk?"

"Good Morning, Pete, or at least it was. What do you want?"

"Listen, pal; I'm sorry for the recent hassle I've been giving you. I've got a lot on my plate. You know the score."

"I certainly do, Pete, apology accepted. Where does that leave you now? I take it you no longer want to walk away with your nice house, nice car and savings book that we gave you?"

"We need to work together, Frank, and watch each other's backs. But for the record, I think attacking Lee is madness. It will only end in tears for Hamilton. But worse than that, mate, he'll take us two down with him if we let him, and he won't give a toss about us. You need to talk him out of it.

"That's easier said than done, Pete, but I will do my best. If he is hell-bent on killing Lee, it's probably in our interest to ensure he covers his tracks and doesn't mess up again."

"We would come out of it worst. We have more to lose, I don't know about you, but I don't intend doing time in prison. Things are running smoothly; why rock the boat?"

"I hear you loud and clear, Pete, and you're talking sense, but I'm not sure Hamilton would agree."

"I'll get Lee's address for you, but surely, intimidation and threats have got to be better than assaulting him? Hamilton could make his life a living hell for a while, and it wouldn't be as risky."

"Leave it with me, Pete; these things tend to work out for the best in the end. I'll speak to you soon," Frank said, about to end the call, but Pete continued.

"Besides anything else, the cops are working hard to convict him of the other murders; Wayne Davies is still under surveillance, they are putting pressure on Kirsty to grass him up, and they have now identified a witness to the Smethurst murder." Pete had saved the best until last, and he knew this would make Frank sit up and listen.

"Who's that then?" Frank said, sounding surprised and intrigued. He no longer sounded like he wanted to get off the phone as quickly.

"The guy in the Man United shirt, who was jogging along the canal. If he identifies Hamilton as being at the scene, your man will be charged and looking at another long stretch inside," Pete said confidently.

"Do you have the name of this witness? We need to shut him up pretty quickly," Frank said.

"I don't think Kirsty will talk, do you, Frank?" Pete asked, recognising Frank's new found concern, and mischievously changing the subject.

"Not at the moment. I'm managing Jason with kid gloves on that score. The split is amicable, and it needs to stay that way. She won't be intimidated by your colleagues by the way. She's made of stronger stuff. Anyway, do we have a name for the jogger witness?" Frank said getting back to the point.

"He's a local fella, Michael May, it's unlikely he will give the police a statement, but a word to the wise, in his ears, won't do any harm."

Pete gave Frank the name and address of the jogger witness. He felt sick to the stomach as he did it, but didn't know which other way to turn. "Frank, I've given you that on the understanding that he is not hurt. Just persuaded not to give evidence, ruffed up a bit at worst."

"That sounds like a reasonable request Pete, leave it with me."

"What I said before makes even more sense now, Frank. We've got to work together and watch each other's backs. I've shown my commitment by giving up Lee and the jogger witness to you. You need to show me some respect too." A silence followed.

"I'll be in touch." Frank ended the call and pressed stop on the voice recorder. He rewound it and confirmed the recording was fine when he heard Pete's voice. He reached for his whisky bottle and cursed when he saw it was almost empty.

Pete drank the last of his coffee and looked out towards the trees. He felt gullible and naive that he was trusting Frank to form an alliance. On the other hand, it was a high-risk strategy that might just pay dividends for him. Surely, Frank didn't want his life to implode either. The nagging guilt of helping Hamilton to take revenge against Lee, a fellow cop, wasn't easy to live with, though. If this ever got out, he was ruined. Pete was under no illusion of where he stood, and he also accepted there was no going back. But this increased his resolve to take control and come out of this nightmare unscathed, even though it meant getting sucked further into the criminal underworld with Frank Burton.

There was a knock at Franks door. His office junior passed him a carrier bag containing a bottle of whiskey.

"Thank you, Nathan. Have you finished those reports for court tomorrow?"

"Yes, all done and dusted. Do you think you'll prevent a custodial sentence?"

"I think we'll need to grease the wheels a bit, but yes, I'm pretty confident. You head off home if you've finished. Leave the reports on your desk. I'll see you at the court tomorrow."

Frank placed the bottle in the bottom drawer of his desk and lit a cigarette. He took out his mobile and selected Wayne from the contacts.

"How's it going, Wayne?"

"Can't complain, Frank. I've just set up our biggest shipment yet. We should all be able to retire in a year or two, as long as you don't let Jason run amok and take us all down with him."

"I'm going to speak with him sometime this week. I've just had confirmation that you are still under surveillance. Have you seen any signs of the cops following you?"

"Yes, a few times, they're pretty good but a bit predictable. I've played along with them but not took the piss; otherwise, they'd realise I'd seen them.

"I've had a bit of disturbing news from my bent cop..." Frank went on to tell Wayne about the identification of the jogger at the Smethurst murder scene.

"I'm not too worried Frank, I remember seeing him. He was a good distance away. It was all over by the time he saw us."

"He recognised one of you from jogging on the canal regularly," Frank responded.

"Well, that will be Jason then, won't it. Fucking hell Frank, we could do without this. Don't tell Jason, for Christ's sake; he'll want us to kill him. Leave it with me, I'll speak to Jason and I'll get a couple of the boys to visit him.

"Yes, that should sort it; I believe he's unlikely to want to get involved anyway."

"So, your bent cop is still coming up with the goods, nice one, Frank. Definitely a useful asset."

"He's more than that, Wayne. He's transferred departments to influence the management of your surveillance. He's worth his weight in gold. And there's no way out for him. He's up to his neck in it. He's with us for the long term.

Seven

DI Andrea Statham was usually first into the office and was therefore surprised on arrival to see the lights on and a tired-looking DS Lee McCann, sitting at his desk.

"What time did you get in, Lee? I know you want to make a good impression, but this is above and beyond the call of duty!" Lee forced a smile, he didn't look happy. He looked worried. Andrea sensed something was wrong.

"I don't feel like I've been home. I'll bring you up to speed, and it's not good news. Have you been called in early as well?"

"No, I needed some time to prepare for the management meeting with the boss today." Andrea was curious. If Lee suspected that she might have been summonsed, it must be serious. "You'd better fill me in; let's go to my office." Lee got up from his chair wearily and followed Andrea.

"I took a phone call at three o'clock this morning from our jogger witness."

"Oh shit." Andrea was already anticipating what was coming next. She sat down in her chair, ready for hearing the worst.

"His house was petrol bombed in the early hours. Don't worry; nobody was injured. He managed to get his wife and kids out before the fire took a proper hold. The fire service turned out, and uniform police patrols attended, but he refused to speak to them. I'm the only cop he would talk to, so they rang me, and I turned out to the scene."

Andrea was working through the possibilities. The fire was unlikely to be a coincidence. Either; the witness had blabbed to others, or he'd been seen talking to Lee, or the worst-case scenario, the perpetrators had been tipped off about him talking to Lee.

"Did he see the offenders?" She asked.

"No, he heard the windows go in and jumped out of bed but didn't see anyone from his bedroom window. Get this, for audacity, after he had moved his car off the drive and parked it around the corner, two heavies confronted him. He described them as proper intimidating bruisers. They told him they knew he had spoken to the cops about the canal shooting. They warned him off and threatened that things would get nastier next time, for the whole family."

"That's brazen, cheeky bastards. They obviously weren't fazed by the police presence at the scene, around the corner. Would he recognise them again?" Andrea asked.

"No chance, he's not interested. We've lost him. He wouldn't even give me a description of the two males." Andrea could see that Lee looked deflated.

"He's bound to feel like that at the moment. The poor sod is probably still in shock. Let's give him some space, and then talk to him again in a few days," Andrea said this hoping to lift Lee's spirits rather than in realistic expectation.

"I wouldn't get your hopes up. I've sorted out emergency re-housing with the council, and I've completed a threat-to-life risk assessment. I now need to do some research and find out how they identified him and his address. He's adamant that he didn't tell a soul. I'll start with a trawl for CCTV evidence; if we can get footage of the two males and identify them, it's game on."

Andrea went to the kitchen and made them both a coffee. She then left Lee to it and returned to her office. She had an unsettling gut feeling about this. The Michael May's house had been petrol bombed only days after speaking to Lee. He hadn't even agreed to assist the police. Andrea was worried that Hamilton's boys had received a tip-off from within the police. She was in no doubt; the fire was down to Hamilton's gang. She opened the computer incident log and read through the sequence of events. There was nothing more to glean than what Lee had briefed her already. She sat back and sipped at her coffee. If the witness's details had been given to Hamilton, who was the rat? She was determined to find out. Only a small, limited number of people had access to the database, and that was auditable. It was outrageous behaviour for a cop to sabotage an investigation intentionally. Who the hell would have done it, and why?

Lee knocked on her door, carrying his coat, "I'm going back to the scene to check for any CCTV on the routes into the estate. I didn't see any in the immediate vicinity, but I'll arrange for some house-to-house enquiries to be undertaken later. They can double-check with the occupants."

"I'll arrange for an audit to find out who has accessed the information."

"It's worth doing, but news of the identification of the witness has probably been shared in management meetings, operational briefings, and well-intentioned conversations with other departments. I'm pretty sure nobody saw me talking to him in the car, though."

Frank placed his key into the front door lock. He'd had a few drinks at the pub on his way home after a hectic day in court. He walked into the hallway and slung his jacket over the end of the stair rail. "Sorry I'm late; the court was a right circus today," He bellowed as he walked into the kitchen.

"Just as well I was delayed making dinner; it will be ready in ten minutes," his wife replied. Frank walked into the lounge and poured himself a large Scotch. He sat on the sofa and savoured the single malt, his first quiet moment of the day.

His mobile started to ring, he saw the caller was Pete Higgs, so he touched the red, reject call button, taking another drink of Scotch. The phone started to ring again almost immediately. He cursed and walked into the study by the front door. The house was a new build five-bedroom home on an executive development. The study was the deal breaker for the purchase, when they first viewed the house. His inner sanctum. "Evening Pete, what is it that won't wait until after dinner?"

"Frank, what the hell is going on? The witness I told you about had his house torched last night and was threatened by two bruisers. The retribution was taken too soon. I thought we agreed you were going to wait and see how things panned out with him? He may have decided not to make a statement to the police by his own accord, negating the need for Hamilton burning his house down."

"That was the plan, Pete, but I'm not the boss. I can only try to influence and give advice to Hamilton."

"That's not good enough, Frank. Andrea Statham is no mug. She will not miss a connection as obvious as that. She will suspect there is a leak in her team now. That was a naive move; you're a bunch of chancers.

No wonder Hamilton is banged up inside. You lot make the cop's job easy for them."

"Point taken, Pete, but will she suspect you?"

"Who knows, Frank, but I'm going to have to keep my head down as a cautionary measure. Get a grip of the dickhead who sanctioned it," Pete said, suspecting it was probably Hamilton. There was a knock on the study door.

"Dinners ready, Frank."

"I've got to go, Pete. Thanks for the call. Leave it with me." Frank was hungry and looking forward to dinner, and anything else could wait for now.

After coffee, Frank returned to his study on the pretext of preparing court papers. Mrs Burton didn't object; she was busy herself, knitting a cardigan for her niece. Frank reflected on Pete's call. Mutual trust was forming between them, albeit based on the understanding that they had a common purpose, to avoid prison. Pete was becoming a welcome voice of reason amongst the big egos in the crime gang.

Frank placed his burner phone on the desk in preparation for his nine o'clock call. Sure enough, minutes later, the mobile phone started to vibrate.

"Hello." He answered cautiously, as always. Frank feared hearing an unknown voice, which would indicate the prison staff had seized Jason's phone.

"Did the house get torched?" Jason asked, skipping any pleasantries.

"Yes, last night. But the agreement was to wait a while, so as not to risk our source."

"Why risk the wait? We needed to shut him up asap. The lads Wayne sent are top drawer operators. They'll have put the fear of god up him. I can guarantee we won't hear a further peep from him."

"But it also puts my bent cop at risk of being exposed. Not many cops had access to the information. It narrows down the number of suspects if they start an internal investigation looking for a grass."

"Fucking Hell, Frank, we pay him enough to cover his tracks," Jason said in a heated, raised voice.

"I know Jason, but he's a valuable asset. He's not only feeding us information but he's also got himself a transfer to the drugs squad and is making sure the surveillance on Wayne fails. Not only that, if he was identified as the source of the link, I'm sure he would take us down with him to mitigate his sentence."

"Chill out, Frank. That's why I had the place firebombed. We didn't injure him or kill him." Jason was irritating Frank; his reckless streak was becoming a massive liability.

"Anyway, let's not make it easy for the cops?" Frank suggested diplomatically.

"Onto more important matters. It's clear the cops still want a bigger piece of me. They're harassing Kirsty and still searching for evidence. So, I can't sit in here whilst they put a case together. I thought they would have moved on by now. You need to get me out of here. The sooner, the better."

"That's a big decision to make," replied Frank, "You'll be out in three to four years. Being on the run won't be easy with all of the technical surveillance the cops have access to these days." It wasn't what Frank wanted to hear, but experience told him that Jason had made his decision.

"Easy for you to say, Frank, would you want to do three years whilst the cops were trying to stick more charges on you? I can't risk it. I need to get out. Speak to Wayne and get it sorted."

Eight

Jason was on his third lap as he strolled around the exercise yard, talking to Scouse. The morning sun was just about penetrating the high wire metal security fencing. There was a prison officer standing in each of the four corners, and two officers by the entrance door to the wing. Jason stayed close to the perimeter fencing because of the protection it afforded him. Around sixty inmates were mulling around in the yard. It wasn't unusual for festering grievances to be settled or fights to break out during exercise.

"Can you get any more pills brought in this week?" Scouse asked. He didn't look like a stereotypical drug dealer. He was an unassuming, quiet guy, blessed with good looks and a warming, polite disposition. But he did have a darker side, which some discovered to their cost when they mistook his amiable personality as a weakness.

"Yeah, no problem."

"I'm shifting a lot more gear since Ritchie got moved to Wakefield."

"What a nutter, he had a good number dealing on the wing. Why the hell did he assault the screw?"

"It was all over a phone call, he was just about to speak to his girlfriend, and the screw told him to get behind his door. There was more to it, though. The screw had turned his cell over a few times and felt humiliated because he'd not found any drugs. Ritchie then took the piss out of him, in front of the other screws, and the screw took it personally. It took four officers to restrain him and even more to move him to the segregation unit. He went fucking ballistic," Scouse said smirking.

"That screw had it coming to him. He was a bully. Great result for you, though; your main rival has gone, courtesy of Her Majesty's prison service. Less competition and better gear, have you upped your prices?" Jason asked, not missing a business opportunity.

"Only on the brown, that last kilo you brought in was well good, top quality stuff that."

"I'll keep it coming as fast as you can move it. No worries there."

"Nice one."

"Anything else you need, just let me know. You're the main dealer on the wing now. Make hay whilst the sun shines. Are there any issues I need to know about?" Jason asked.

"No, just the usual staff shortages, making some of the screws a bit tetchier. But it's good for us, and it keeps them busy with the basics, they don't have time to watch us properly. Oh yeah, that druggie you asked me to jug is out of healthcare. His face is a right mess; apparently, his skin was coming off his face like orange peel. I didn't hang around to see the results."

"Hamilton," shouted the prison officer at the exit gate.

"My pizzas ready," Jason mocked, "Catch you later, Scouse." Jason liked Scouse, but more importantly, he trusted him. Not long after arriving on the wing, Jason undercut Scouse's supplier and gave him quality drugs, not the usual over-cut crap for desperate cons. In return, Scouse and his boys provided Jason with security.

Jason sauntered around the exercise yard to the exit, where Dean was waiting. He followed him to the office, which was more like an old broom cupboard, used for the prisoner peer support project.

"There's only three on the list today, all new arrivals, struggling to settle into the routine. One of them is being bullied and can't handle it."

"Is he a local lad?"

"Yeah, he's from Salford. He had too much to say for himself on arrival and is now paying the price."

"I'll see if he's up to dealing for Scouse in return for some protection."

"Tell the lads at the gym, Scouse was chuffed with that last batch of H, but we need more pills."

"I need to be careful; the more runs I do, the more chance they have of catching me," Dean said hesitantly.

"Fucking man-up, Dean, you're getting paid good money. Do I pay you well?"

"Yeah, of course you do, I didn't mean it that way. I was just saying."

"Do as I said, submit a few intelligence reports to security, telling them that the silent screw is bent, take the heat off you. Worst case scenario, they sack you, and you earn good money on the outside working for me," Jason laughed at Dean's obvious discomfort.

There was a knock at the door. It was an officer from C Wing escorting the bullied inmate. "Just take a seat for a minute pal, we're just getting the room ready."

"Might as well crack on Dean, tell him to come in." Dean waited outside with the other officer.

The lad was in with Jason for just under an hour. If he had been a mouthy gobshite, the bullying had resulted in the desired effect. He'd wound his neck in and appeared timid.

"Tell the screw the meeting was helpful, and book again for next week. Do as I've told you, and you'll be fine. One of the boys will be in touch with you. Don't fuck up."

"I won't. I won't let you down," he said and left the office as Dean returned.

"The other two inmates have cancelled," Dean said.

"Good, I've got my plan sorted for getting out of this shit hole. I can work on that," Jason said.

"When are you going for it?" Dean asked.

"You will have to wait until nearer the time to find out; that way, your reaction will be more natural."

"You will find me in my cell on the floor. You'll set the emergency alarm for the medical orderlies to attend. Your story will be that you found me unconscious and unresponsive on the cell floor. Tell them that you had to clear my airway because I'd swallowed my tongue and that you could only feel a weak, slow pulse. Once you'd put me in the recovery position, I started to cough and splutter. You then raised the alarm."

"The medics will see that your pulse is normal, though," Dean pointed out.

"That's not for you to worry about; just focus on getting your bit right. Before then, you'll be picking up some medication and fetching it in for me. That's not the end of it. You've then got to do your best to make sure the medics send me to Accident and Emergency rather than the prison hospital wing. If you can swing it, accompany me in the ambulance. You need to ram home the fact that I was unconscious, not breathing and had probably suffered a bang to the head. The escape is your big test Dean, let's see if you can deliver the goods."

"Fucking Hell, Jason, this is serious shit." Jason sensed that Dean looked shell shocked, as the reality of his involvement was now starting to sink in.

"Dean, you're one of us now. You've got to think like one of us. Don't think about it as a prison officer. You're a fucking con with keys now, mate."

"What if they find out that we planned it together?"

"They won't, how can they? There's only you and me who know the score. I'm not going to grass on you, am I? They won't have any evidence to prove your involvement." Jason felt relieved that Dean looked more comfortable after his initial reaction. "So, are you confident you can pull this off for me, Dean?"

"Yeah, of course. What happens if the medics move you to the hospital wing?"

"That means you failed… and I need to start preparing a Plan B. But you won't allow that to happen, will you Dean?" Jason started laughing at Dean's concerned-looking face. Dean smiled nervously.

"You need to keep running over the scenario through your mind over the next few weeks. Cover all eventualities of what you think could happen. You need to consider any problems in advance, so it runs like clockwork on the day."

"What happens once you're in the ambulance?"

"You don't need to know that; just be yourself and make sure you and the other screw don't do anything stupid to put yourselves in danger. One other thing, once you sound the alarm, the lads on the wing will start kicking off, accusing the screws of assaulting me and getting angry because it's delaying their association time. This mayhem will make the Senior Officer just want rid of me."

DS Pete Higgs walked along the corridor and opened the back door to the car park. DI Andrea Statham and DS Lee McCann were chatting to one of the detectives who was on his way out.

"Don't be holding him up; he's got work to do," Pete joked. "Good to see you both. Come in, and I'll get the kettle on."

"Are you sure you know where the kettle is, Pete?" Andrea teased.

"Who's got out of bed on the wrong side this morning?" Pete retorted, "Go through to the office; Dave's waiting there for you.

"Morning, Dave."

"Morning, come in, grab a seat. Good to see you. Is Pete making a brew?"

"Yes, I hope he has biscuits too," Lee replied

The office was less clinical and corporate than Andrea's office at Force Headquarters. The drugs unit were located in an old Lancashire County Police Station, built in the early nineteen hundreds. The desk and chairs were wooden, having seen better days. The wooden, glass-fronted book cabinet contained procedure and contingency manuals from times gone by, a pre-digital era of policing.

"It's the first time I've been here. It's like a scene from Life on Mars. I'm surprised I didn't see Gene Hunt's Cortina in the backyard," Lee laughed.

"It's great, isn't it? Very nostalgic," Dave said, "They'll have to drag us kicking and screaming from here."

"Get the scotch out of your bottom drawer Dave," Andrea joked.

"There's too much frivolity going on in here," Pete said, arriving with the drinks and a plate of chocolate biscuits. Pete handed the drinks out and took a seat.

"Right, down to business. I'll update you with where we're at with the surveillance. Wayne Davies appears to be very hands-off, from the day to day criminality. We discovered his new address. His most frequented places are; his builders' yard, Tim's Gym, and the Northern Quarter in the city centre. Unfortunately, he has not been anywhere of real interest. He has not visited Hamilton at Strangeways, though, he has met with Frank Burton, Hamilton's brief, and probably Davies's lawyer too."

"He's very surveillance conscious, which makes sense. This organised crime group have been operating under our radar successfully for a good while," Pete said, diverting the lack of surveillance success from his subterfuge.

"It's just a matter of patience; we are on the right track. It's just a matter of time before he drops his guard, or we get lucky," Andrea said, "Are you okay to keep running on him, Dave?"

"For now, we are, until the force tasking group give us a higher priority target to follow. How are your telephony enquiries going, Andrea?"

"Slowly, I'm in no doubt they use burner phones with good discipline, but we're making headway. We've got lots of numbers and data to process," Andrea replied.

Pete felt vulnerable. A wave of fear accompanied a sudden thought that he may have got sloppy and used his personal phone by mistake. Or had they matched one of his burners to the locations he had frequented. It was a routine telephony investigation. If he got sloppy, they'd be onto him. And worse, was Burton savvy with his burner phone discipline? Pete fought himself to stop overthinking about eventualities.

"Do you have any new leads which would be useful for hitting the surveillance from a different angle?" Pete asked, "I saw the incident log for the torched house. I guessed that was the jogger from the canal you told me about at Jack's leaving party?"

"I think we've lost him, Pete. If he did have any intention of helping us, which was a long shot, to begin with, his bottle has gone for certain now. It's like Hamilton's boys are a step ahead of us. How did they identify him so quickly?... Did the Informant Management Unit discover how Carl Smith's details were leaked? It would answer a lot of questions and make sense if it was down to a bent cop on the inside," Lee said.

"I can't see it, Lee; bent cops are in the arena of television dramas. When was the last time you came across a bent cop? Especially one involved in this level of criminality. Let's be honest, Hamilton's men are feared; they will have their ears to the ground everywhere. Where did you meet the witness, Lee?" Pete had plotted his line of questioning and knew where he was going with it.

Lee shifted uncomfortably in his chair, looking sheepish, "Good point, once I'd spotted him on the canal, we sat and talked in my car, but…"

Pete interrupted, "I'm not being funny, mate, but it makes more sense to me that somebody saw him

79

talking to you," Pete twisted the knife to ensure the discussion was focused on Lee's actions. He noticed Lee leant further forward, looking pissed off.

"I wasn't reckless; I checked the vicinity and can be ninety-nine per cent sure that people didn't see us," Lee countered, looking over to Pete as if to throw down the gauntlet. Pete raised his eyebrows, looking in Andrea's direction. He was in no doubt that Lee would be pissed off with his opinions, but all was fair in love and war. He could see that he had hit a nerve with Lee.

"It's pretty unlikely that somebody saw him talking to Lee. It could have got to Hamilton via several avenues. Let's keep an open mind to all possibilities," Andrea said, sensing the tension building between the two sergeants. Pete felt annoyed that she had stepped in as the voice of reason. He was beginning to enjoy watching Lee squirm.

DI Dave Ferguson broke a short, uncomfortable silence, "That was a useful meeting. We will continue with Wayne Davies as our target. Pete, you keep in touch with Lee and consider any other options we could use. Andrea, if our surveillance teams are re-deployed at any time, we can still provide a limited-service until they are fully available. In the meantime, our intelligence cells and telephony officers can keep in touch to exploit any new intelligence."

Pete started to collect the empty coffee mugs and place them back onto the tray, "Lee, I'll come and see you next week. It's probably worth reviewing the sequence of events, from you meeting the witness to him getting his house torched. We may have missed a connection or something." Pete felt confident he had done all he could to cover his tracks. His thoughts were confirmed by the glare he received from Lee. Although he couldn't be sure for definite, Pete thought Andrea discretely stood between them, sensing the growing antagonism. Pete left the room with the tray, contented; a job well done.

Nine

"Good morning, Wayne, fancy catching up over breakfast?" Frank asked, walking down the steps at Minshull Street Crown Court.

"It's too risky, Frank. I think we need to stick to the burner phones for now. Have you forgotten, I'm under surveillance?"

"Obviously not, but Higgsy keeps me informed of their activity." Frank felt a rush of blood; he realised he had inadvertently let Pete's name slip out. Shit, I need to swear him to secrecy; no point, he might not have clocked it, he reasoned to himself.

"I'm not risking it, Frank, don't get too complacent. Have you ever considered that your bent cop might be playing both sides against each other? What did you want anyway?" It was not a good time to have called Wayne, mused Frank.

"Christ, I've rattled your cage. I do apologise," Frank said with mock sincerity.

"No worries, I'm always a grumpy bastard first thing in the morning," Wayne laughed. He smelled burning toast whilst putting the kettle on. "Shit, hang on a minute, Frank." He retrieved the burnt toast and threw it into the bin. "Go on, Frank."

"I was on the phone with Jason last night. He wants out of Strangeways within the next four weeks or so."

"He'd better start digging a tunnel then," Wayne laughed.

"Thanks for that, Wayne, most helpful. He is planning on the staff taking him to the hospital by ambulance. He says he has that part of the escape sorted. He needs you to follow the ambulance and spring him from there."

"That sounds straightforward unless the ambulance has a police escort?"

"He's done his homework, and that shouldn't happen. We would just have to monitor the situation and adapt the plan. It's more likely to be two prison officers escorting him in a taxi." Frank took a seat on a bench at the Metro link station in Piccadilly Gardens.

"Okay… is this so he can kill the cop?"

"No, thankfully, his need for revenge is on the backburner for now. Over time he may change his mind completely, which would be better for all of us. Things are looking up, and the police surveillance is failing miserably. They will probably get redeployed onto another case at some stage. Plus, the boys did a good job on the canal witness, so he won't be making a statement any time soon."

"Don't you forget the obvious thing here, they will be launching a manhunt for Jason if he escapes, and they will be all over us like a rash." Wayne sat down on the sofa and took a drink of coffee, then stood up straight away and placed some bread into the toaster.

"Fair enough, initially they will be. But the police usually descale operations like that pretty quickly, then rely on border control and intelligence. We will just have to weather the storm. They don't have sufficient resources these days."

"What's his plan for when he's out?"

"Funny, you should ask. Jason needs you to make plans with the Dutch boys. He wants to sail from the North East coast and head on through the Baltics to Turkey. He'll keep his head down at that end of our supply chain. He's even talking about travelling out to Columbia at some stage. The Columbians have been inviting him often enough. But that's all further down the line. He just wants out of Europe fast."

"I like the sound of it, and it will make my life easier having him back on the ground. It will be pretty useful having him sort things at that end of the supply chain too. I'm warming to this plan, Frank."

"Good, let me know how you get on with the Dutch guys. It will be a walk in the park for Dirk," Frank said, looking up at the tram arrivals screen. Frank felt the morning chill and pulled his coat in tightly around himself.

"I might give Ryan a bell. I'll test the water to see if he is getting bored in the sunshine. I can't afford to be hands-on during the escape for obvious reasons. But I suppose I'd be a good decoy and take the surveillance teams on a magical mystery tour. Ryan would be perfect for overseeing the job."

"Good luck with that one; I think we've seen the last of Ryan."

"I'm not too sure. If Ryan assists with getting Jason out of Strangeways, then surely, Jason will leave him alone. I'd say that would settle his debt."

"How long have you known Jason? People don't get away with crossing him. It's a matter of principle." Frank was surprised at Wayne's optimism.

"Fair point Frank, but things have to change sooner or later. If I'm going to do the job right, I need the right people. I'll get in touch with Dirk and start the ball rolling."

Wayne ended the call and immediately rang Kirsty.

"Hi Wayne, long time no hear, how are you doing?"

"I'm good, thanks, how are you? Is it good to be back?"

"Yeah, it's always good to get back, Spain was a nice break, but this is home."

Wayne took the reference to Spain as a natural lead towards the reason he called, "Do you think Ryan will stay out there?"

"Yes, I think he will. He's convinced that Jason still wants to kill him. He's probably right too. He's settled out there; why would he come back?"

"I might be able to help him there. I'm struggling with the workload. I think it's time Jason gave him the all-clear. I could do with him back here. Do you think he would be interested if Frank got an assurance of his safety from Jason?"

"He'd probably think he was being ambushed again, and you couldn't blame him; after all that's gone on. He doesn't deserve it, Wayne."

"I know, but he didn't help himself either. I'll give him a bell. It would be great to have him back. Oh, one other thing. Can you remember the name of the cop that came to your house?"

"There's been two of them; a right bossy cow, Andrea Statham, I think her name is, and a man called Higgs, why?"

"I think Higgs might be bent. What was he like?"

"He was straight up, just a normal nosy copper, more than I can say for Statham, she won't leave me alone. She turned up at the salon, then asked to meet me in the Trafford Centre. She wants me to grass on Jason. I sent her packing. She must be desperate to think I'd do that; she threatened me with proceeds of crime legislation. But it's like Frank said, if she had anything on me, the police would have arrested me already."

"Nice one, Kirsty; Frank's right; they've not got anything on you, so don't worry."

"Easier said than done, Wayne. I'll give you a call if she contacts me again. Or I might be tempted to take a flight back to Marbella."

"Maybe not a bad idea. I'll give Ryan a bell. Let me know if you need anything."

"Okay, two new hairstylists would be great. The salons are booming," Kirsty laughed.

"Apart from stylists," Wayne laughed, "Catch up soon." The chances of Ryan coming back were slim, but who could blame him? There was only one way to find out.

"Hey, Ryan lad, how you doing?"

"Have you won the lottery, Wayne, and calling me to share it?" Ryan laughed. He paused from collecting the glasses and sat down at a table.

"Just having a good day, mate. Thought I'd share some sunshine."

"That means you want something from me, in my experience."

"I've just been chatting with Kirsty, so I thought I'd see how you were doing out there."

"Living the dream, mate." Ryan lent back, enjoying the warmth of the sun on his face.

"I could do with you back here pal, it's all running smoothly, but I could do with some help. I'd increase your pay too, make it worth your while. You must be ready for coming home by now?"

"What about psycho... No thanks?"

"Jason's over it now, and his new nemesis is the undercover cop. You're safe, seriously. Especially if you help out with a specific job."

"What's that then?"

"Jason has hatched a plan to escape from Strangeways. I've got some boys in mind to do the job, but I can't be there. I'm under surveillance from the cops. That's where you'd come in." Wayne was satisfied with his sales pitch. It must be tempting for Ryan, and there's only so much Sangria you can drink before getting bored, he reasoned.

"Would it not make life easier if you informed the prison service of his intentions? They'd heighten his security and make it impossible for him to get out."

"Jeez, don't be thinking of doing that, mate. You'll mess my plans up. You've got to trust me on this. I'm running the show now. Jason will have to leave the country and keep his head down. You'll be working for me, and I've got big plans. Besides, if he didn't escape, he'd be out in three or four years, without the need to flee the country."

"I could be tempted by the right terms. I'll give it some thought; when is it happening?"

"Soon, seriously though, mate, don't jeopardise it by grassing him up."

"Okay, let me think it over,"

Wayne knew it was a risk, telling Ryan about the escape plan, but it also helped to develop the trust between them and make his return to Manchester tempting. He was satisfied Ryan wouldn't inform the authorities… but there was always an element of doubt.

Ten

Jason was feeling confident about his escape plan. He had been over it in detail meticulously, and it was his best chance of getting out. His patience had so far paid off, and the preparation stage had gone well. He was under the radar of the prison officers, a quiet inmate, keeping his head down. He had laid down solid foundations of a troubling medical issue with the doctors and nurses, which would hopefully influence them to make the right decision on the day.

Dean had been indispensable, not only smuggling contraband into the prison but helping to embed Jason's image with the other officers. That was just the start for Dean, and he had to be convincing at the main event and ensure Jason was dispatched to the hospital rather than the prison healthcare wing. Jason was lying on his bed, watching the world go by on the landing. He was confident that Dean would put on a good performance. He'd groomed him well.

A short time later Jason awoke with a start. "Having a siesta Jason?"

"Shit, I must have fallen asleep; I wasn't intending having a kip." Jason placed his stocks and shares investment book on his bed and quickly glanced around his cell; everything was in its place. He had let his guard down. He usually only slept during the lockdown. Dean looked back onto the landing before putting his hand down the front of his trousers.

"Fucking hell, Dean, steady on there. You need to go to the nonce wing for that kind of shit."

"I brought these in underneath my takeaway pizza." He took out a small plastic snap bag containing tablets and handed them to Jason, once again checking over his shoulder. Jason undid the bag, looked them over, and handed them back to Dean.

"You had me worried for a minute Dean, thank Christ it was only tablets that you pulled out. You keep hold of them; for the time being, I'll give you the nod when I need them. It's safer that way." Jason felt elated; the planning phase was almost complete, his freedom was about to become a reality.

"Spider, at the gym, said you were mental taking them. The medication could do you some serious harm."

"I need to be ill. I've got to convince the medics. Or the plan fails at square one. What the fuck were you and Spider doing talking about the escape anyway?"

"There was no one else there; that's all he said when he gave me the tablets, but what if they decide to put you on the health care wing?"

"They won't, not with the BAFTA award winning performance you're going to put on."

"Christ, Jason, heap the pressure on, why don't you? I'm just a screw. What do I know about medical stuff?"

Jason jumped off the bed and pushed the cell door closed, almost in one continuous motion. He shoved Dean against the wall by his throat and went toe to toe, right in his face. What he saw there, was fear.

"Listen to me, Dean. Don't you fucking dare bottle out on me," Jason spat the words out menacingly; his face contorted with anger. Dean looked like a rabbit in the headlights. "I've not come this far for you to fuck it all up. You've got a job to do. Now fucking man up and fucking do it. Have you got a problem with that?" Jason turned around and walked towards the window, fists clenched. He looked like a boxer pacing around, ready to fight. He turned back towards Dean, who looked shell shocked and made a poor attempt at composing himself.

"I was only saying… fuck me, Jason," His voice trembled slightly, giving away his fear.

"I never said it was going to be easy, Dean. You've got to be convincing and make it happen. Why do you think I pay you good money? Welcome to Man town. Now get focused, show me some fucking confidence. You will make it happen."

"Fucking hell, Jason, you know I'm right behind you," Dean stuttered.

"And by the way, tell Spider to keep his mouth shut." Dean looked flustered. He opened the door and walked out onto the landing. Jason couldn't hold back from smirking to himself. Dean had almost shit himself. Jason's outburst had had the desired effect. If Dean hadn't been taking this seriously, he certainly was now.

As Dean left the cell, the quiet prison officer was walking towards him on the landing. He gave Dean a knowing look but didn't say a word as usual. Dean headed for the staff room for some respite.

Wayne had been talking on the phone with Dirk for nearly an hour. He would have preferred to have gone to Amsterdam and met with him face to face, but it was too risky. Wayne prided himself on being meticulous with security and covering his tracks. A deep-seated trait he had acquired from his army days. He was relieved now that Jason wasn't going to seek revenge on the copper. He was confident of getting Jason over to France or Holland but would leave the chosen destination to Dirk. In all honesty, it didn't interest him.

He took a drink of his pint and looked towards the door as two old boys walked in. Both were familiar locals, and he let onto them with a nod, which was reciprocated. He'd not been in the Wagon and Horses since the day of the shooting on the canal. It was a safe haven for him. The two old boys settled at the bar, unfolding their racing papers, studying the horses form. The landlord dutifully selected the horse racing channel on the wall-mounted television. Wayne took another drink, then picked his mobile up.

"Frank, have you got five minutes?"

Frank was at home, "Just a minute Wayne." He got up, grimaced and pointed to his phone. Leaving his wife sitting at the dining table, he walked to his study, closed the door and took his seat at the desk. "How are the arrangements coming along?" Frank asked, slightly out of breath.

"I've not stopped over the last few days. It's a pain making arrangements on the mobile. Meeting face to face is much better. It's all sorted. It should go like clockwork, just another day at the office for Dirk. I'll be honest with you, Frank; I'm much happier now that he's not going after the cop. That would have created a shitstorm." Wayne was starting to feel distracted and irritated by the two old boys quarrelling at the bar.

"I'm guessing I don't need to know the detail of the arrangements?" Frank asked.

"Spot on, Frank, it's the way I work; you should know that by now. It wouldn't do any harm for you to follow suit."

"I'm careful enough, but thanks for the advice, all the same," Frank couldn't help sounding put out.

Wayne lowered his phone from his ear and glared towards the bar, "Will you two keep the fucking noise down, please? I can't hear myself think. Get them a pint each, on me." The landlord nodded and selected two pint glasses from the shelf above the bar. The two old boys took a break from their betting dispute.

Wayne shook his head and got back to his conversation, "I've picked the team to get him out of the ambulance. I'm hoping to have Ryan on board to oversee that phase…"

Frank interrupted, "Are you sure that's a good idea?"

"It will be fine. Jason won't know he's involved. But when he finds out later, it might influence him to give Ryan a break. The only thing on Jason's mind will be escaping, and he won't give a shit about who is helping him. I need Ryan back; the decision will be on my shoulders," Wayne sounded assured and confident.

"What have you got planned? I'll need to tell Jason something?" Frank plugged for more information.

"We don't need to go into detail. We will get Jason out of Manchester straight away and change cars a few times on the way to the North East. I've got accommodation sorted up there. Once we get the nod from Dirk, the Dutch boys will pick him up from the coast."

"Excellent, Jason is phoning me tonight. I'll try and establish when all this will take place," Frank said pouring himself a whiskey from the dregs of a bottle he'd just remembered was in the drawer.

"Dirk did offer an alternative plan which I liked. The Columbian was willing to take Jason in one of his narco submarines from Galicia in Spain across the Atlantic."

"No way," Frank said in disbelief.

"Yes, they've upped their game and put a lot of money into them. A lot of the cocaine comes into Europe that way now. It's always there as an option. It wouldn't be pleasant, and they're living on top of each other. Mind you; I bet that would be second nature to him now after being in Strangeways."

"Let's stick with the Baltic route to Turkey, eh?" Frank chuckled.

"I love the thought of it, though, Jason in a sardine tin with some skanky drug mules for a week a so. We could even video the journey. It would make great reality television." They both laughed at the thought.

"Push Jason for the date, Frank, and then I can arrange the fine detail with Dirk."

"Okay, I'll be in touch."

Wayne took his empty glass to the bar, "Same again, mate, and whatever these two are having."

"What's your tip, fellas? I'm feeling lucky." Wayne asked, and the quarrelling resumed. "Fuck me, why did I ask?" Wayne asked the barman.

Frank remained in his office, working on court papers for the following day. It had gone nine o'clock, and he was just beginning to wonder whether Jason was going to bother calling or not. Frank stood up from the chair to pour himself a nightcap. Just as he left the study, his mobile phone started to ring. He walked back into the office, picked it up from the desk and wearily slouched back into his chair.

"Are we good to go, Frank?"

"Evening, Jason, I've just spoken to Wayne, and everything is good to go. Do you have a date in mind?"

"It's going to be this Monday. I shall be on the road to the hospital mid-morning if all goes to plan. You need to ensure everyone is up to speed and ready to go, Frank. I won't tolerate any fuck ups. Heads will roll; make sure that everyone knows, Frank."

Jason heard a metallic click from the cell door hatch. He slipped the phone under his leg just as the hatch opened. The hatch closed will a clunk, observation completed, the officer continued on his rounds. Jason felt relieved and retrieved his phone.

"I certainly will Jason, I think everyone is aware of what is at stake. Wayne will drive you up to the North East. He has secured a safe house. From there, you will sail across the North Sea as planned, then onto Turkey... Are you still there, Jason?"

"Yeah, I'm here. Double-check all the small stuff, Frank, make sure they've got it covered. Hair dye, glasses and clothing. I need Dirk to sort the passport." Jason enjoyed giving the instructions, and it made him feel closer to regaining his freedom."

"One thing you need to know. Wayne has enlisted the help of Ryan. He has been struggling on his own and needs the help." Frank had considered the disclosure and decided Jason needed to know.

"Well, let's see how he performs, shall we. I will reserve judgement until I'm safely in Turkey." Ryan was still fair game to Jason and still needed punishing. "Are the cops still watching Wayne?"

"They are, but they suspect Wayne's onto them; they are scaling the observations down. My man on the inside has done us proud. We need to look after him when all this is over. He is one of us now."

"Fuck off, Frank, you've always been a soft touch. We've paid him enough. Keep him on his toes for now. We don't want him to get complacent. Fear is the best motivator. You should know that, Frank." Jason felt anger rising within him. He lifted himself and sat on the edge of the bed in the darkness.

"Okay, unless I hear otherwise from you, we will proceed as planned on Monday," Frank confirmed.

"Make it happen, Frank… No fuck ups or excuses will be tolerated."

"One last thing, Jason, it would be remiss of me not to point this out. You do know that the cocktail of drugs you intend to take could kill you." A short silence followed.

"Not me, Frank, it would take more than a few tablets to kill me. I'm getting out of here, pal. If the cops have their way, they'll extend my stay at Strangeways, and I'm not going to sit here and let that happen." Jason ended the call and lay back down again.

Earlier that evening, DI Andrea Statham and DS Lee McCann had driven to Reddish Vale Country Park to meet with the jogger witness, Michael May. They sat in Andrea's car in a remote corner of one of the smaller car parks. It gave them the privacy and security they needed, surrounded by woodland.

"We should do this more often after a stressful day at work," Lee said.

"It's a peaceful place. I love the outdoors. It's the fractals, you know, the recurring patterns in trees and plants. Good for de-stressing and relaxing."

"Listen to you, tree-hugger, every day is a school day. It's twenty past; I don't think he's coming, do you?" Lee sounded disappointed.

"He'll be here. He was okay on the phone when I spoke to him."

"I'll just have a quick pee in the woods whilst we're waiting."

"Again? You've not stopped peeing today."

"I've not had my bagels this morning; if I have bagels for breakfast, I don't need to go as often."

Andrea laughed, "Bagels! How do they stop you from peeing? Yeah, right, more likely it's all the coffee you've been drinking."

"It's true. I read it on the internet and gave it a try; it works. I don't know why!" They both laughed as Lee got out of the car and disappeared into the trees.

Andrea chuckled to herself. She enjoyed Lee's company, and the chemistry had clicked between them. They managed to have a laugh whilst getting the job done professionally. He had indeed filled the gap left by Pete Higgs. Her thoughts were interrupted by the car door opening. Lee got back into the car.

"That's better. No sign of May yet. Let's give it another ten minutes, and then I'll buy you a beer on the way home."

"You'd better get some bagels too."

A battered white van appeared from the track and parked alongside Andrea's car. Michael May got out of the driver seat and strode to the back of his van, out of sight. When he emerged, he had two French bulldogs on leads. He walked to the driver window and looked around the vicinity nervously as if he was expecting some gangsters to emerge from the bushes. Andrea got out of the car.

"Thanks for coming Michael, we should be okay here. How's the new house?"

"It's not been petrol bombed yet, so it's a good start."

"How would you feel about a proper relocation? Out of the area, I've checked with our witness protection people, and it's feasible if you were to give us a statement because of the risk to your life."

"No, it's not happening. Just show me the photographs, and I'll tell you off the record if that is your man. I'm not getting involved. It's your job to nail him. The best way I can avoid risking my life, is by not getting involved."

Lee had got out of the car and was now standing by Andrea's door. He made a fuss of the dogs, stroking and petting them, and then joined in the conversation.

"I know where you're coming from, Michael, but if you make a statement, we'll make sure you're safe. It's a murder we're talking about; we don't want murderers walking the streets if we can help it. We need the help of witnesses to put them away."

"Look, I know you're only doing your job, but we're talking about drug dealers who knew the risk of what they were getting into. Live by the sword, and all that. It's an occupational hazard for them. I'm not putting myself and my family in harm's way; you saw what they did to my house. Where are the photographs? Do you want me to look at them or not?"

Given his stance, Andrea decided not to show him any photographs. There was a slim chance he may change his mind, so she didn't want to risk any possible flaws in identification evidence, should he change his mind. They discussed his account of events once again to make sure they'd not missed anything relevant.

"It's okay, Michael, we'll leave the photographs for now. But if you do change your mind, give me a bell."

"I won't be meeting you again. It's not worth the risk. Don't call me again. That's it now." Michael walked away down a path and let his dogs off the leads.

"He couldn't have made that any clearer," Andrea concluded.

"Shall we show him the photos? He ain't going to change his mind?" Lee asked.

"I suppose so, there's nothing to lose now. We'll have to make a written record of it."

"If he doesn't pick out Hamilton, we will have to disclose it to the defence in the unused material schedule because it may assist their case, or undermine ours, we could apply for public interest immunity to protect his identity," Lee said, as if show-casing his knowledge of procedure.

Michael May soon reappeared with his dogs, "You two still here?"

"Will you look at the photos?" Lee asked.

"Okay, it's off the record, and that's the end of it, yes?"

Lee took his bag from the car boot and removed a selection of photographs mounted in a plastic folder. He placed it on the bonnet of the car.

"Michael, the person you saw on the canal, may or may not be present in this album..." Lee continued through the procedural legal preliminaries required before the viewing. No sooner had he finished,

Michael pointed to a photograph without hesitation, "That's him."

Lee looked at Andrea, and she raised her eyebrows, knowingly, "Thanks, Michael, much appreciated. If you need us for anything, give us a call."

"I won't," Michael said as he got into his van.

"I think we deserve a drink," Lee suggested, unable to hide his disappointment.

Andrea came back from the bar with two drinks. She sat down and took a sip of her prosecco. "So, he didn't pick out Hamilton or any of his cronies."

"No surprises there, he didn't even look properly; he picked the first photo he saw. Making sure it wasn't Hamilton. He just wants us off his back. Their intimidation has had the desired effect."

"Even so, I don't think he would have given evidence if he had picked him out. At best, it would have confirmed our suspicion of Hamilton or maybe an accomplice."

"Maybe he knew that if he did make a positive identification, we could summons him to court as a reluctant witness."

"I've never had any joy with that legislation. More often than not, they satisfy the court that they fear reprisals and make no comment. The court is subsequently reluctant to take any action against them, certainly not sending them down. He'd only need to mention his house being torched, and they'd stand him down from the box immediately."

"We'll never know for sure, Lee. He might not have recognised him. How did the bastards get to him so quickly?"

"I think someone tipped them off, and I smell a rat. It's too much of a coincidence to happen so quickly."

"We need to set a rat trap."

"I'll meet up with the HOLMES Unit, and they will be able to audit anyone who has accessed relevant documents on the database. Which is mostly our team and the Drugs Unit."

"I'll be surprised if one of our team has let it slip."

"It sometimes happens, canteen talk or management meetings. It's a good reminder to tighten our operational security."

Eleven

DS Pete Higgs headed across Crown Square, picking up his pace as he had noticed the queue to enter Manchester Crown Court was growing by the minute. It was an imposing, yet anonymous-looking building, finished in a light coloured stone, stretching right across the square at the far end. The authoritative Royal Coat of Arms chiselled in stone above the entrance was one of the few signs which distinguished it as a court of law. Even the original grand ceremonial entrance, complete with an elaborate canopy, was no longer in use.

Pete entered the main reception area and emptied his pockets of coins, mobile phones and keys. Placing these in the grey plastic tray, he walked through the security scanner. There was a time when he could flash his warrant card and gain entry. Not anymore. The security threat level meant that entering buildings such as this was akin to passing airport security. Everyone was a potential threat. Having passed through security he headed for the wide staircase and entered the long, imposing concourse that gave access to the individual courtrooms.

The concourse was bustling, with lawyers dressed in their black robes and traditional wigs, milling around or huddled together with witnesses and solicitors discussing their cases. Victims, defendants and witnesses sat in the secured metal and plastic seating, some looking nervous like they'd rather be anywhere else. Others were treating the experience with disdain and joviality, showing no respect for the setting or the rule of law. To them, appearing here was just an occupational hazard. A uniformed officer was flicking through her pocket notebook, refreshing her memory, before being called to give evidence. It could be an intimidating place for the uninitiated.

DS Pete Higgs saw Frank Burton talking on his mobile phone, almost hidden in an alcove at the far end of the concourse. Pete was warming to Frank, whom he now sought to be his associate, rather than an adversary. Pete approached him and gave an acknowledging nod of the head; Frank smiled back and gave a thumbs up.

Pete looked out of the court building whilst he waited for Frank to finish his call. An unusual window display opposite caught his attention. It consisted of an extensive collection of antique sewing machines, and he wondered what the business was and why he'd failed to notice something so eye-catching before now.

"Sorry about that Pete, I'm trying to get hold of a witness who should have been here an hour ago. How are you?"

"I'm fine, thanks, busy trying to convince the gaffer to redeploy our surveillance teams away from Wayne Davies and onto some other targets. He'll probably agree to it sooner or later, it's a results-based game these days, and we're getting nowhere fast with Davies."

"That's down to your good work Pete, well-done." Pete felt a wrench in his gut. He was sabotaging the surveillance to save his skin. It still didn't sit right with him; Pete still felt ambivalent about his actions. But he knew it was a needs-must, a self-preservation exercise, to get himself out of this mess.

"What can I do for you, Frank?"

"You've just part answered my issue. I have a last request. Albeit personally, I'd rather you continue to work with the firm, we would make it worth your while."

"Go on, what's the latest last request?"

"Wayne and his boys will be busy on Monday. You need to cancel the surveillance for certain. Can you ensure that?"

"Yes, that's an easy one, then my debt is settled, again?" Pete said mockingly.

"If that's what you want. Keep your ear to the ground on Monday, and let me know if you hear of any police activity targeting our firm. Be ready to take a call from me; I might need your assistance."

"Please tell me Hamilton isn't sending his boys to attack Lee McCann?" Pete felt alarmed. Even just raising the subject made it difficult to reconcile his guilt for selling Lee down the river.

"No need to worry on that score. I have helped Jason to see sense, and he has no plans to go after Lee. Your colleague is safe for now, and I can give you a nod further down the line should Jason present a danger to him. If you stay with the firm, we can make sure Lee is safe between us." Pete felt like a weight had suddenly been lifted from his shoulders.

"Did you pass on Lee's address to him?"

"No, I didn't need to," Frank lied, "I think he's made the right decision. He's now gained enhanced prisoner status and is keeping his head down. It's feasible that he could be transferred to a Category C or D prison in a year or so. It would be ludicrous for him to take out a contract to kill anybody. Why risk further incarceration?"

"That sounds good enough to me. In return for Monday, what're the chances of a payment?" Pete looked at the floor, he hated himself for asking and therefore perpetuating the arrangement.

"Oh dear, Pete, have you been back on the tables? I thought you were over that now," Frank condescended.

"I got pissed at a leaving party the other night and ended up at the casino. I felt lucky. But wasn't."

"It sounds to me like you still need us, just as much as we need you."

"I only need about ten grand," Pete tried not to sound too desperate.

"That's short notice, Pete. I'll tell you what; I'll pay you a few grand today and the remainder on Tuesday after you've disrupted the surveillance operation."

"Cheers, Frank." Pete needed the money desperately. He had no other choice but to accept the terms.

"Right, I need to be back in court. Catch up soon, Pete. I'm going to be busy next week for obvious reasons. Let me know if you struggle to cancel the surveillance," Frank said over his shoulder as he headed back towards the court.

Whilst talking, Pete hadn't noticed DS Lee McCann leaving courtroom two. Lee had a look of relief about him. He'd been given a tough time during cross-examination by the defence barrister, who was trying to muddy the waters. Proceedings had been dragging on for over a year and had been adjourned again at the behest of the defence. Lee had been surprised to see Pete on the concourse and was about to approach him but had thought better of interrupting his conversation. Besides, he had lots to do on his return to the station.

Leaving court, Frank paused and lit a cigarette, inhaling the nicotine as if his life depended upon it. He checked his watch whilst exhaling the smoke. Excellent, time for a pint or two. He was glad to be out of court and even happier now, walking to the pub. He crossed over Deansgate and turned right into John Dalton Street, where after a short walk, he arrived at the pub. The bar was on the far side away from the entrance. He walked by the empty tables and stood at the bar alongside the handful of office workers chatting noisily. He ordered a pint of ale and a double-whiskey chaser, which he necked right away. He picked up a copy of the local paper and started to read it at the bar whilst drinking. His phone vibrated in his trouser pocket. He ignored it and ordered the same again.

After a few more whiskies, Frank reluctantly left the pub and headed back to his office. He hung his jacket up. The alcohol made him feel tired, so he made a strong coffee and sat at his desk, fighting off the weariness he was experiencing. He lit a cigarette and took a sip of coffee. Frank saw the text he had received at the pub was from Wayne. He pressed the speed dial.

"Hello, Wayne, have you had a good day?"

"Not bad. Are we still on for Monday?" Wayne asked.

"Yes, Jason reckons there is more chance of the staff sending him to hospital on a Monday. They have less staff on at the weekend and would be more inclined to put him on the healthcare wing rather than tie up officers escorting him to hospital."

"I've got everything organised from my side. I still think it's a bad idea, but if it's what Jason wants, so be it."

"I've spoken with my man on the inside. He has managed to divert your surveillance on Monday, so the cops won't be following you."

"Frank, are you bloody mad! You've told a cop our plans, monumental schoolboy error, what the fuck were you thinking?"

"Easy Wayne, steady on, it's in his best interests to work with us. He has nothing to gain by thwarting our plans. And for the record, I didn't tell him what was happening, just that something was happening. We need him on board. He's got rid of the surveillance and will warn us of any police activity on the day. He's a valuable asset."

"Be it on your head Frank, but at the end of the day, he's filth. Who knows what he will do? I'm not happy with it."

"Trust me, Wayne, I wouldn't use him if I had any reservations. It will be fine."

"You'd better be right, Frank. It's okay for you. It will be me who gets lifted if he tips his colleagues off."

"He isn't going to cross us, Wayne." Suddenly, Frank felt a prick of doubt. Then he recalled his conversation with Pete, which Frank had discreetly recorded. Thank the lord for Pete's love of the tables.

Twelve

Jason had been tossing and turning for most of the night. He lay awake and was running through his escape plan. It was early morning, and the landing had been silent until now, but noises from outside his door indicated it was slowly coming to life. Eager to get going, he realised now more than ever how his incarceration had induced him into a state of comatose. The thought of being free again in a matter of hours was exhilarating. He could manage the risk of overdosing on the medication, and it was a risk worth taking. Jason had always exercised hard, looking after his health. He believed his body could cope with anything. Intrinsically he was confident that it wasn't his time to die yet.

Jason detested the idea of being dependant on others, but he had no choice. Dean, Frank, and Wayne had better deliver, he brooded. They were all fully aware of the consequences should they let him down. It was time for action. Jason stood up and placed his hands on the washbasin, leaning forward, composing himself. He looked at his reflection in the stainless steel mirror, willing himself to be strong. Jason stood up straight, turned on the tap and filled his plastic cup with water. He then began swallowing the final batch of digoxin and warfarin tablets from the clingfilm wrap, feeling a surge of adrenaline, elation and fear. A satisfying mental state, life was meant to be lived on the edge. He'd never felt so alive.

Jason headbutted the mirror as hard as he could, resulting in a sickening thud. Shockwaves of pain drilled through his head; he felt dizzy and nauseous, gripping the edge of the sink tightly, so he didn't lose his balance. He felt the wet sensation of blood running down his face whilst his blurred reflection in the mirror revealed a wide gash on his forehead. He felt an urge to get on all fours, then lie down, prone on the cell floor. Jason realised he was bleeding heavily and felt worse than he had imagined he would, fucking hell, Dean, hurry up, he murmured. An unfamiliar feeling of fear was creeping into his thoughts.

Dean was opening doors on one side of the landing whilst another officer sorted out the other side. Prisoners were leaving their cells and milling about on the landing. Banter and chatter were resumed from where they left it the night before. The smell of gel and soap drifted onto the landing from the shower room. The stillness of the night was over, and the cacophony of life on the wing indicated the start of another day; chatter, shouting, radios, and televisions. But it didn't feel like a routine morning to Dean. It was no Groundhog Day for him. He felt anxious to the pit of his stomach. He had a feeling of impatience that he just wanted to get the next few hours over with as soon as possible. He knew this would be a day like no other, and he felt a weight of immense pressure. He was in complete fear of failing, and he couldn't even begin to consider what the consequences would be.

He undid the hatch and peered into the cell next door to Jason's. The inmate was lying on his bed. He was a short, weedy old lag, who served most of his time sleeping, hardly ever leaving his cell.

Dean opened Jason's hatch, concentrating on maintaining an air of normality. But he didn't even look through the hatch in his eagerness to get on with the plan. He inserted the door key and pushed open the door.

"Shit, oh fucking hell," he shouted almost involuntarily; it was no play-act, just sheer gut reaction to what he saw before him. He felt a surge of nervous energy. He wanted to run, and keep running, out of the prison and never to come back. But he knew he couldn't.

He saw Jason lay face down on the floor of his cell. Dean stared at the significant pooling of blood surrounding Jason's head. Shit, he's pissing blood. What's gone wrong? There was blood everywhere. Jason was lying with his head towards the door. Dean knelt by Jason's side, being careful not to kneel in the blood. It was a crimson red colour in a macabre contrast to the dirty grey linoleum floor.

"Jason, can you hear me?" There was no reply. He repeated himself, again receiving no response.

He grabbed at Jason's arm and leg and struggled to turn him onto his back in the cramped space between the bed and the cupboard. Jason's hair mopped up some of the blood as Dean rolled him over, becoming instantly matted and congealed. Is he breathing? Pulse? Get a grip, Dean's mind ran through the situation.

"Jason, can you hear me?" Dean shouted several times but again, he got no response. Jason's eyes were closed. Shit, he's unconscious. It's gone wrong. Fucking hell. Dean managed to shift him into the recovery position.

"It's Dean, code blue, code blue, cell 15, Hamilton's unconscious and bleeding from a head wound. Assistance, assistance," Dean shouted into his radio.

"Is he breathing?" enquired Cynthia, an experienced prison officer, as she entered the cell and knelt alongside Jason, squeezing into the limited space. Dean breathlessly briefed her on his discovery. If Dean had worried about being convincing, he needn't have bothered.

"I used a barrier device for mouth-to-mouth; he wasn't breathing. He spluttered and coughed, then started to breathe. I think I got here just in time," Dean said, slowly regaining some composure after the arrival of his colleague.

"This isn't good; his pulse is very weak." Cynthia was holding Jason's wrist. Two other prison officers appeared at the cell door.

"Where are the medics? Get the inmates behind their doors," instructed Cynthia. The two officers disappeared from the door. Dean had grabbed a T-shirt from the bed and was using it to apply direct pressure to the wound on Jason's forehead.

"Jason, can you hear me? It's Dean. You're going to be okay, pal." Dean saw the shadow of someone at the door. He looked up; it was Doctor Irving with one of the nurses. Dean hurriedly briefed the doctor on the circumstances of finding Jason. He was grateful to see it was Doctor Irving, a locum who showed no compassion to prisoners. It was a commonly held opinion that the doctor treated them with disdain. Dean guessed he would just want Jason shipped out and be rid of any responsibility. Most of the prisoners detested Irving and some of the officers too. Irving's off-hand manner riled the prisoners and created an unnecessary hassle for the officers. Dean thought Irving was an arrogant bastard; either he was on a power trip or just a bully.

"Okay, move aside, let us in," instructed Irving. He was encouraging the nurse to take over the application of direct pressure. Dean and Cynthia got to their feet and shuffled towards the door. Dean's white shirt was now covered in blood. He heard the commotion on the wing as he left the cell. Prisoners protested at being banged up, and officers barked out instructions, demanding they return to their cells. Some inmates who hadn't been let out of their cells were hammering on their doors. A prisoner appeared behind Dean, shouting, "Is he dead?" Another officer appeared and led the prisoner away, who was repeatedly shouting to whoever was listening, "Hamilton's dead. The screws have fucking killed him."

Dean watched as Irving went about his examination of the patient. The nurse watched on whilst applying direct pressure to the wound, "He's bled an awful lot. It looks like he cracked his head on the sink basin when he fell," she said, removing the t-shirt from the wound momentarily to take another look, "The bleeding isn't stopping Doctor Irving."

"I've requested an ambulance; it shouldn't be too long now," Cynthia said to the nurse.

"Well, you shouldn't have done; that's my call," Irving interjected, getting to his feet. "I'm concerned about his pulse; it's very weak and irregular," Irving said to no one in particular.

"Hamilton's not been well for a while; he's been to healthcare several times over the last month or so. He's been experiencing vision problems, bad headaches, dizziness and passing out. I knew he was in a bad way," Dean proclaimed.

"Diagnosing isn't your job. It's mine. I think we will get the prisoner down to healthcare and get him stitched up, for starters," Doctor Irving said.

"Are you sure, Doc? That sounds like a big risk to take. He's stopped breathing once, and that's a nasty head injury. Plus, we don't know what drugs he's been taking. The paramedics will be here soon anyway," Dean worked hard at planting the seeds of doubt in Doctor Irving's head, "You'll be going to the Governors de-brief after this, so you don't want to have his death on your hands."

"He's right, Doc," Cynthia agreed, "healthcare won't appreciate his admission either."

Nice one Cynthia, thought Dean. He didn't want to be the voice in the wilderness, championing for a hospital transfer. Cynthia's support took the spotlight off him, but Doctor Irving appeared to be ignoring them both, perhaps making an arrogant mistake; Cynthia's wise counsel was usually taken on board by most others.

"He seems to be breathing easier, his pulse is still erratic, and this bleeding isn't stopping," the nurse reported. She knew better than tell the doctor how to do his job. But it was clear which side of the fence she was sat on. Dean was feeling flustered. The pressure was unbelievable, he had to make sure Jason was taken to hospital, but he didn't want to overdo it.

The paramedics arrived at the cell door; the female entered the cell and knelt by the nurse examining Jason whilst Doctor Irving briefed them of the circumstances.

"Let's get him onto the trolley and into the ambulance. We can patch him up and get him on the monitor. He's going to need an MRI scan with his history," the paramedic suggested. Dean felt like punching his fist into the air in celebration. His work was done. He was watching Doctor Irving for his reaction, he seemed content to agree with the paramedic.

Dean and Cynthia helped the paramedics to get Jason onto the stretcher. One of the paramedics applied temporary strips and bandage dressing to the head wound. Jason's eyes flickered, and he started mumbling incoherently. The paramedic reassured him and informed him he had collapsed and was being taken to hospital.

The wing supervising officer was standing by the door overseeing events. Once Jason was placed on the stretcher, he approached Dean and Cynthia. "Are you two okay to escort him in the ambulance?"

Cynthia looked at Dean and nodded. "It makes sense, you're his personal officer Dean and you both can answer any questions from the medical staff at the hospital," the supervisor reasoned.

"I'll go and get the handcuffs and change my shirt," Dean said. He made his way to the office. He felt euphoric; the initial trepidation and shock were gone. I've done it! Dean celebrated silently, chuffed with his performance. When he emerged from the office, the paramedics and Cynthia were waiting outside for him. He cuffed his left wrist to Jason's right wrist and walked alongside the stretcher, out of the building to the ambulance. Cons were shouting from their windows and throwing whatever debris they could squeeze between the bars down towards the entourage.

Dean wished Cynthia hadn't volunteered for the escort duty. He respected her and didn't want to put her in harm's way. But there was nothing Dean could do now. If he tried to have her reallocated, it would

113

look suspicious at any future incident review. She had worked at the prison service for many years and was close to her retirement date. She was a trusted and respected officer, even by the cons, who never gave her any grief and had a quiet word with any newcomer that did.

One of the paramedics got into the driver seat, the other one, a young woman in her twenties, climbed into the back with Dean and Cynthia. The paramedic set up the ECG and monitored Jason closely as the ambulance left the prison.

"It gets us off the landing for a few hours," Cynthia said to break the silence.

"Yeah, perhaps a good thing, they're pissed off with being put behind their doors. Hopefully, it will have calmed down by the time we get back," Dean said whilst watching Jason. He was becoming genuinely fearful for Jason; he didn't look good at all.

The paramedic busied herself, putting up a line and monitoring the ECG screen.

"Don't worry, Jason, you'll be fine. These guys will sort you out," Cynthia said, patting his arm.

Dean felt exhausted, and he hadn't even started to prepare himself for what was about to happen next.

Thirteen

Wayne opened his eyes at six o'clock; on the dot, as usual, he rolled off his mattress and jumped up from a squat position. Apart from the mattress on the floor, the only other item in the bedroom was a large suitcase which lay opened, strewn with his clothing. His mind immediately focused on the day ahead. He felt apprehensive about the jailbreak; he was more than confident of success but saw it as an unnecessary risk. He went through a mental checklist whilst cleaning his teeth, finally satisfied that everything was in place.

A shipment of cocaine was arriving in Liverpool in three days, which was their biggest yet. He felt niggled at being distracted from overseeing the delivery whilst helping Jason to do a runner. If Jason had any sense, he would keep his head down and do his time, mused Wayne.

He stepped out of the shower, feeling refreshed and ready for action. Reluctantly accepting that Jason had the final say, although he felt irked by Jason's reckless behaviour of late.

He had to make sure he wasn't under surveillance. Wayne trusted Frank, but he didn't trust the bent cop. He sat down on the sofa and checked his CCTV home security video recordings. There was nothing of concern, no activity on the recording. He put his trainers on, ready for his counter-surveillance run. He cautiously exited his back door and squeezed down the side of his shed. He climbed over the back wooden overlap fencing and dropped into the space between the fence and his neighbour's conifer hedge. Struggling along the gap, he cursed as the irritating branches jabbed into him. He scaled the brick wall at the end and lowered himself into the alleyway. So far, so good, he reflected. Jogging through the rabbit warren paths on the estate gave him good cover and excellent vantage points for him to spot the cops before they clocked him.

Twenty minutes later, he was satisfied that the coast was clear. He continued his run from the estate to a nearby terraced street, dodging the wheelie bins as he approached his hire car. He got in, opened the glove box, and checked over the car rental papers and fake driving licence. He familiarised himself with his false identity for the day and set off for coffee and breakfast. He adhered to an old military habit; eat when the opportunity presents itself, the next chance might not be for a good while.

Wayne finished the bacon sandwich and sat sipping his hot coffee in the layby next to the burger van. He knew the food was good here, truckers' were always queueing. He wiped his mouth on the tissue and picked up his new burner phone.

"Morning, Frank, is this madness still going ahead? Please tell me I imagined it all?"

"No, it's happening, Wayne. I've had confirmation that the surveillance teams have been deployed elsewhere today. We are good to go, my friend. Is everything okay at your end?"

"Yeah, I would have preferred Ryan to be involved, but he wasn't up for it."

"I'm waiting for a call from Jason's friendly screw at Strangeways to confirm when he's leaving the prison."

"I told you we didn't need him to call, Frank. It's just another unnecessary risk. My boys are keeping watch. They'll see the ambulance going in and out of the prison."

"It's always worth having a backup, Wayne. Any changes to the plan?"

Frank's question irritated Wayne, he didn't need to know the detail, but it wasn't worth creating a bad feeling. Wayne gave him the edited version.

"I've got some lads on Great Ducie Street and Southall Street. It's most likely that the ambulance will go down Waterloo Road. We'll spring Jason out in Cheetham Hill. One of our cars will be ditched and set on fire at Boggart Hole Clough as a decoy to keep the local dibble busy." Wayne purposefully didn't give his position away.

"Give me a bell if you need me. Otherwise, I'll call you when the ambulance moves."

"It's not when, and it's a big 'if' the ambulance appears. Jason will probably just get moved to the healthcare wing; hopefully, then we can all get back to business doing something useful," Wayne said.

"Now, now, let's not have dissension in the ranks," Frank laughed. Wayne ended the call and checked in with his lads on watch at Strangeways. They were in position and ready to move. Wayne drained the last of his coffee and drove towards Heaton Park.

The heavy security gates opened slowly, and the ambulance emerged from the prison, turning into Ducie Street. It proceeded to the traffic lights at Cheetham Hill Road. A stolen white van was manoeuvred into the traffic, one car behind the ambulance, as it started to gain speed. The occupants of the stolen van were Ninja, riding shotgun, and the driver, Deggsy, who was talking, hands-free with Wayne.

"It's gone the other way, Wayne, we're at the traffic lights, and it's not indicating. It looks like they might be taking him to Manchester Royal, driving through town? Bit weird." Wayne didn't answer; he just waited. "Nope, it's left; we're passing Manchester Arena, heading up Cheetham Hill Road, mate. They must be heading to North Manchester hospital," Deggsy suggested.

"No worries. Let's get Jason out near to Waterloo Road," Wayne said calmly, studying the map on his lap.

Ninja relayed the information to the other team. "We're driving up Cheetham Hill Road. We'll get him out of the ambulance at the junction with Waterloo Road."

"Okay, we're almost there. We'll block the ambulance at the traffic lights. We won't ram it unless we have to," Faz said, starting up the flat back scaffolding truck.

"What the hell? Where's it going now? It's turning right. Shit, do they know we're onto them?" Deggsy sounded flustered, reporting back to Wayne.

"Turning right into Shirley Road, Faz, can you cut him off from the other end?" Ninja asked into the walkie talkie.

"Yep, no worries. That'll probably be easier." Came the reply. Wayne remained silent, just listening. He trusted his lads to adapt the plan to the changing circumstances and make it happen at this late stage. Wayne had a disturbing premonition that the ambulance didn't have a casualty on board, but a team of armed cops in the back. He considered calling the strike off for a split moment, then concluded he was just being paranoid about the bent cop.

The Ambulance continued along Shirley Road. It was a stereotypical Manchester suburban street. Redbrick terraced housing on either side. With too many cars parked on either side, restricting the flow of traffic. It was an excellent shortcut for the ambulance drivers, helping them to avoid the congested roads. The ambulance slowed down to a halt to allow a flat back truck to pass through parked cars coming from the opposite direction.

Deggsy stopped his van at the rear of the ambulance. "We're going to get him, Wayne. Let's go, Ninja," Deggsy yelled excitedly.

They pulled their balaclavas over their heads and got out of the van, sprinting the short distance to the ambulance.

"You could have got a bit closer." Ninja complained as they reached the rear doors of the ambulance. Deggsy yanked the door open, the two prison officers and the paramedic looked at him with a mixture of shock and fear. Deggsy pointed the gun towards them with outstretched arms.

"Take the fucking cuffs off him now," he shouted aggressively.

"Okay, okay, we'll do as you say. Nobody needs to get hurt," Dean said fumbling for the keys on his utility belt." He had made sure he was sitting closest to the rear door. "You two stay back," Deggsy barked at Cynthia and the young paramedic.

"Fucking hurry up, or I'll shoot you," Deggsy shouted. Dean responded quickly unlocking the cuff on Jason's wrist and stood back with the others, leaving the empty bracelet swinging from his wrist.

"It's off, let's all stay calm, everybody stay calm," Dean stammered, attempting to convince himself as much as the others. He was in genuine fear, and in no way did he feel part of the plan. He was scared, not only for himself but the others too.

"Shut the fuck up and back off, with them two, turn around all of you," Deggsy shouted. Deggsy and Ninja got Jason to his feet from the stretcher and put an arm each over their shoulders.

"No fucking heroes, just stay there until the cops turn up." They manhandled Jason out of the ambulance and slammed the door shut behind them.

"Hurry up, Ninja, we've not got all day," Deggsy gasped breathlessly whilst dragging Jason faster.

"You slow down, or you'll make us drop him. What the fuck have you been eating inside, Jason? Pizzas and doughnuts," Ninja laughed at his joke.

They skimmed Jason into the back of the van unceremoniously, and he landed with a thud. Deggsy felt relieved to release his dead weight. He grabbed Jason's legs and spun them around so that he could close the rear door.

"Are you okay, Jason?" Ninja asked as Deggsy slammed the doors shut. They jumped into the front seats, looking around at the deserted street.

"I can't believe nobody has come out of their houses," Ninja said.

"Would you? You bell end?" They both burst out laughing, no doubt releasing the pent up nervous energy.

Deggsy reversed the van at speed, causing Ninja to grab hold of the dashboard to maintain his balance. Deggsy slammed it into first gear and wheel spun left, into a side street, accelerating away at speed; the tyres screeched, leaving behind the smell of burning rubber.

Ninja looked over his shoulder into the back of the van, "Christ; he looks like he's in a bad way." Struggling to be heard over the high revs of the engine. Jason was lying on his side, in an almost foetal position. The only sign of life was his groaning and coughing.

"Jason, it's Deggsy. Can you hear me mate?"

"Just fuckin' drive," Jason groaned almost ineligibly, unable to be heard in the front.

"That was a piece of piss. Let's get you out of here," Deggsy shouted, pressing down harder on the accelerator. Whilst ignoring the blast of a horn from an aggrieved bus driver, who he'd caused to brake harshly. The momentum of the van thrust Jason about in the back. It was all about speed, not comfort.

"Don't move, just wait, Cynthia. They don't pay us enough to deal with shit like this," Dean said. Cynthia was leaning forward, holding her head in her hands. The young paramedic looked shell shocked but relieved, "Shit, thank god that's over." Were the only words she could summons.

"I'm not going anywhere, that's it, I'm retiring, I'm getting too old for this," Cynthia sounded like she was about to cry.

The ambulance driver stepped into the back of the ambulance, "Are you all okay? I didn't shout it in on the radio because the gunman would have heard me." He was met by a stunned silence of relief.

Dean sat down on the stretcher, placing his head in his hands. His hands started to tremble involuntarily, he replaced them from his head to under his thighs, so it looked like he was keeping it together. Cynthia moved closer to him and put her arm around him.

"Well done, Dean, that was brave. You did the right thing and stopped anyone from getting hurt."

"I know that, but I also let a prisoner escape," Dean said, staring at the floor. He felt out of his depth and confused, a mixture of relief at not messing up, with an overwhelming feeling of fear and guilt. He felt like he was having an out of body experience, looking down from above.

"They were going to take him, come what may. If you had resisted, they would have shot you and still taken him. It's probably safe enough to get out now. I'm going to have a ciggy," Cynthia said, stepping out of the ambulance.

The two paramedics had retreated into the front of the ambulance. The driver was on his radio requesting police assistance. He looked out of the windscreen; the flat back truck which had caused him to stop was no longer there.

DI Andrea Statham and DS Lee McCann arrived at the scene, not far behind the first uniform patrols in attendance. The police had cordoned off the ambulance with crime scene tape. Andrea could see the prison officers sitting in the police van; the side door was open. She stepped inside and took a seat, introducing herself. Lee started the witness trawl, knocking on the house doors that overlooked the scene.

"Can we just run through the descriptions of the offenders again?" Andrea asked.

Dean's guilt brought about an irrational urge to come clean. He dispelled it as quickly as it had emerged and repeated the descriptions to Andrea.

"How well did you know Hamilton?" Andrea probed whilst mentally running the vague descriptions against Hamilton's known associates.

It was a question that Dean had not anticipated,

"I knew him from working on the wing and then finding him unconscious this morning." A surge of panic hit him, and he feared that the detective was onto him, "He was never a problem. He kept his head down and didn't rock the boat. I think the illness was straight up, he wasn't breathing when I found him, and blood was pissing out of his head."

Andrea continued with her questions covering the events of the last week. "I understand prison officers have allocated prisoners. Who was his allocated officer?"

"That will be me."

"Did you notice if he was close to any other officers or staff?"

"No, he didn't give us any cause for concern until now," Dean said, looking at the floor.

"Has there been any recent intelligence that concerned you?"

"No, nothing." Dean had composed himself to provide shorter answers. He feared letting something slip or getting caught in a lie.

"Okay, that will do for now, Dean. I'll get an officer to take a statement from you, and we will speak to you again, no doubt." Andrea stepped out of the police van. She noticed more curious passers-by had assembled nearby, beyond the crime scene tape.

The police helicopter rotor blades produced a loud, thick, thudding noise in the sky above; it reverberated, leaving Andrea feeling uncomfortable. Lee approached her from the other side of the road.

"Any joy with the house to house?" Andrea asked.

"Most were no reply, probably out at work. The lady at 37 saw two men in balaclavas helping Hamilton into the van. That's about it."

"Hamilton's surprised me this time. Why would he want to go on the run? He'd have been able to run his drugs supply from inside. There must be a specific reason that's made him do this. What's he got planned, do you think?"

"He has unfinished business with Ryan Young," Lee replied.

"He could task a hit on Ryan Young from inside prison," Andrea said, not convinced. Hamilton wouldn't have taken this decision lightly. Andrea was curious about his intentions. She called back to the office, requesting fast track enquiries to be undertaken at the prison and a CCTV trawl along the route. Lee went to arrange for the ambulance to be recovered. He caught up with Andrea back at the car. Andrea was talking on her mobile phone, and as she finished the call, it rang again straight away. Lee started the engine and set off to the nick.

"That was communications. A white wan has been dumped and burnt out at Boggart Hole Clough. Let's have a look on our way back to the station. They probably switched vehicles there. We've had no further sightings of the van or flatback, so it will be down to CCTV cameras," Lee said.

"The paramedics said he wasn't looking well; weak pulse, irregular heartbeat and a lot of blood loss. They said it's unlikely he could have been faking it.

It sounds like he is still in need of medical assistance. I'll get some alerts set up at the hospitals." Andrea got back onto her mobile.

Having arrived at Boggart Hall Clough they stood looking at the skeletal like, black remnants of a van, which was still smouldering.

"There's nothing of evidential value for us. It's burnt out," The crime scene examiner said, taking his gloves off. Andrea nodded her acceptance. From the state of the vehicle, it was plain for anyone to see.

The fire crew turned off the hose and began to pack up their gear.

Andrea and Lee walked back to the car through the saturated soil, which squelched underfoot.

"There's someone I need to speak to who may be able to help us. Let's go to Urmston; Kirsty must have known this was going to happen," Andrea suggested.

"Probably not a good idea for me to come with you on this enquiry. Kirsty's probably still a bit raw from my infiltration. My presence might light the blue touch paper," Lee replied.

"Good point, but on the other hand, it might get a reaction too. Let's go back to the station and brief the team. I can call and see Kirsty on my way home later."

Fourteen

The rain began to drum lightly on the car roof. It had a calming meditative effect, in contrast to Wayne's current activities. He didn't bother turning the wipers on; he just watched the water trickle down the windscreen. He waited patiently, parked on a layby, next to the red brick wall of Heaton Park, near to the motorway junction. He was hidden away behind the cover of a cluster of trees, listening to the events unfold on the open phone line and walkie talkie, his fingers tapping on the steering wheel.

Deggsy and Ninja were on their way to meet him with Jason. Wayne couldn't help but feel this would be his last relaxing moment for the next few days. Normality resuming, once he had despatched Jason, onto his journey across the North Sea. He was jolted from his ruminations by his mobile phone ringtone.

"We'll be with you in five minutes boss, we've switched into the black people carrier as planned. We got away pretty sharpish, and I'm happy we're not being followed. It's all going to plan," Ninja said excitedly, still riding high on a surge of adrenaline.

"Nice one, Ninja, what state is the cargo in?" Wayne probed, still not convinced that the cocktail of drugs was Jason's brightest idea.

"He's coming around a bit now; we were worried at first. Watching him drink the salted water was funny. He's busy throwing up his guts. It stinks of puke in here now; it's a nightmare."

"When you get here, park between my car and the wall. I'll jump into your vehicle and have a look at him. See you in five minutes." Wayne ended the call and checked the contents of his man bag, which comprised of; vials, syringes and other medical equipment.

Wayne watched as Deggsy turned off the main road and reversed alongside his car. He observed the other traffic, leaving his car once he was satisfied Deggsy wasn't being followed. Sliding the side door open, the smell of acidic vomit was overpowering.

"Ugh, that's rancid; you weren't kidding, it stinks in here!" Wayne flinched, turning away momentarily, delaying getting into the backseat whilst fighting a gagging reflex. Deggsy and Ninja laughed loudly at his obvious discomfort, they'd become accustomed to the vile stench.

"You're not wrong. I'm glad I'm not cleaning this out," Ninja declared.

"Yeah, leave the door open," Deggsy begged mockingly.

Wayne got inside and sat alongside Jason.

"He looks out of it. Jason; can you hear me?" Jason was hunched over, with his face buried into a carrier bag, bulging precariously with vomit. Wayne lifted Jason's head and looked into the sombre, dilated eyes of a sick man. "I've seen worse in Afghan. You should be okay."

"I feel like shit," Jason mumbled incoherently, "Get the injections done."

"I've got them here. Hang on a minute." Wayne took out the vitamin K and drew it up into the syringe.

"Give me your arm Jason." Jason was busy retching, so Wayne took hold of his arm and injected it into the muscle. "That's one done; you've got another two of them for later."

Jason made a retching noise and dipped his head back down towards the bag. He was struggling to get anything else up, just saliva.

Wayne waited, positioning his head towards the fresh air outside, then administered the last vitamin K injection.

"This is the antidote for the warfarin. Keep still, for Christ's sake."

Jason mumbled that he was feeling better already.

"You've emptied your stomach, so you should be fine for now. Let's hope there's no lasting damage to your internal organs, you mad bastard."

"I just need to get my head down. Let's get going."

"Okay, let's get you into my car." Jason slid across the back seat, oblivious to any spilt vomit, whilst Wayne helped support him.

Wayne helped him as he slumped into the front passenger seat.

"Here, there's a bucket, just in case. I don't think you'll need it." Jason placed the plastic bucket in the footwell. Wayne's attention was taken by Ninja laughing at Jason's predicament. He looked up at them, "What are you two still doing here, piss off, and get rid of the carrier." Deggsy didn't need to be asked twice, and he headed for the motorway with all the windows open.

Wayne took in the surroundings, a steady flow of traffic passing by. No one was taking any interest in their activities. He was aware of the pressing need to get going and bent down looking at Jason.
"There's some fresh bottled water in the footwell; keep drinking as much as you can, then try and get some kip." Wayne was satisfied he'd done all he could for now.

"Fuck me, mate, it's good to be out. I ain't going back in there." Jason said, he adjusted himself and leant his head against the window, cushioned by his hoody.

"Here, let me fasten your seat belt." Wayne clicked in the clip.

Wayne had a final check around, then drove the car onto Middleton Road and headed north. He glanced across at Jason, who appeared to be fast asleep already. At least Wayne hoped so and that Jason hadn't taken a turn for the worse. Wayne's thoughts took a dark turn, and he contemplated that maybe it wouldn't be a bad outcome if Jason had taken a downward turn. It was a shock to his system, seeing Jason appearing so vulnerable and pathetic.

Kirsty's hair salon had the appearance of being closed and locked up for the day. DI Andrea Statham pushed to gain access anyway, and to her surprise, the door swung open. The shop looked empty for a moment before Kirsty emerged from the back storage room, sweeping brush in hand.

"What do you want now? Don't you believe me? I don't know anything about what's gone on," Kirsty said, exasperated.

"Wind your neck in and stick the kettle on Kirsty, black coffee, no sugar, please," Andrea said disarmingly.

"There's no need to get on your high horse," Kirsty replied, shaking her head at the cheek of it. She ditched the brush and flicked the switch on the kettle. Her back was towards Andrea whilst she made the drinks, but Andrea could see her face in the mirror, watching her closely, weighing her up. Did she know about Hamilton's escape or not? Kirsty walked over with two coffees and handed one to Andrea.

"I'm guessing you've not come for a cut and blow-dry or are you thinking of a new colour?" Kirsty smiled then took a sip of coffee, "Let's sit in the waiting area."

Andrea followed her. She begrudgingly respected Kirsty. Under different circumstances, they would probably get along fine. She wasn't the typical gangster's moll, or if she was, she hid it very well.

"Kirsty, I know this is a difficult time for you. I can only imagine what you are going through. But work with me, trust me, and I will see you are looked after and kept safe."

"Let's consider for a moment that you are right, and I do know what Jason has been up to; I'd be an absolute idiot to testify against him. You've seen what he is capable of, going after Ryan Young, for starters."

"When we start charging people, you'd prefer to be sitting in the witness box rather than the dock. Trust me, Kirsty, I'm trying to help you here." Andrea reluctantly accepted that Kirsty wasn't going to give evidence nor provide any off the record intelligence. She decided to wrap it up for now.

"If I find out you are assisting an escaped prisoner, I will be obliged to throw the book at you. It's much better for all of us if you cooperate, Kirsty."

"What… has Jason escaped from prison?" Kirsty started laughing, "And of course, I've let him hide in the back storeroom. You must be grasping at straws… me hiding him… really! Feel free, have a look in the broom cupboard," Kirsty laughed sardonically. Her response looked genuine; Andrea was satisfied that Kirsty was being truthful about the escape.

"I believe you, Kirsty. I suspect you wouldn't risk going to prison. But it's not out of the realms of possibility that someone has told you something." Andrea could see Kirsty's face glowing redder; she looked like she was getting flustered. Andrea felt confident that she was getting to her; she needed to keep applying the pressure.

"Tell me where he is; he will not find out you have spoken to us. Do the right thing, Kirsty."

"Do the right thing. You're lecturing the wrong person. Why don't you ask your mate DS Higgs where Jason is? He knows more than me," Kirsty muttered.

There followed a moment of silence. Kirsty picked up the brush and started sweeping the floor as if she was trying to compose herself. It was Andrea's turn to feel surprised.

"Why did you say that Kirsty, why should DS Higgs know where he is?"

"You just made me angry; I said it in a temper. He's the cop who wanted to speak to Jason at the start of all this. Look, I don't know where he is, and I'm not interested, get out and leave me alone. I'm not saying anything else. Just leave me alone. If you want to ask me any more questions, go through Frank Burton. I've had enough, will you leave, please.

Andrea glared at Kirsty. Why did she call out Pete Higgs, then start retracting her words? What did she know? Was she playing games? Andrea accepted that she was not going to grass on Jason, whether through fear or misguided loyalty.

She had been taken aback and caught her off guard when Pete's name was thrown in the mix. Pressing Kirsty's buttons had worked, but in a way, she hadn't anticipated.

Andrea felt perplexed and decided that was enough for now. She walked over to the door. Surely to god, Pete isn't involved with Hamilton. Her mind was racing over the comment, but she accepted that trying to push Kirsty on it any further would take her nowhere…for now.

She turned back to Kirsty, "Look, Kirsty, I'm only doing my job. I need to find Jason soonest; it's in everyone's best interest, especially Ryan's. He must be in fear, looking over his shoulder now that Jason's out. Think it through and give me a bell. I need your help." Playing the Ryan card was her last attempt…for today.

"I've told you, go through Frank Burton," Kirsty replied.

Andrea walked back to her car; her gut feeling was that there was more to the Pete Higgs accusation, she wasn't satisfied with Kirsty's innocent explanation.

Fifteen

Jason's snoring was driving Wayne to distraction. He pulled over from the dual carriageway into a tree-lined layby and stopped the car harshly with a heavy foot on the brake. The jolt of the car seemed to stop Jason from snoring. He switched the engine off and looked over at him. He was still sound asleep, but more importantly, still breathing. Wayne got out of the car and stretched his legs; he felt stiff and tense. He walked along the layby to exercise his legs and take in some fresh air. There were no missed calls or texts on his mobile. He opened the phone casing and took the sim card out. After throwing the phone into the shrubbery, he flicked the sim card into a litter bin.

Wayne sat down on a bench, closed his eyes and enjoyed a moment of peace. He'd made good time and reached York quicker than he had expected. He took his new burner from his jacket pocket.

"It's me, Frank. It's a new number."

"Good to hear from you, Wayne. Are you out of Manchester yet?" Frank put his pen down on the desk and rubbed his eyes.

"Yeah, I've made good progress. I've just passed York."

"Good, it's been on the local television news already, along with Jason's photo. To be expected, I suppose. How is he?"

"He's sleeping like a baby. I gave him the injections and tried force-feeding him water. By the amount of vomiting, there can't be much left in him. I'll give him the last of the injections when we arrive. I should be there in an hour or so. Which photo did they show on television? Was it the one with his beard?"

"Yes, it was the custody photo from when he was arrested."

"Excellent, that makes life easier. After his makeover, he'll look nothing like that. Have the cops been in touch with you yet?" Wayne stood up and started strolling back towards the car.

"No, not yet. DI Statham has paid Kirsty another visit, though. From what Kirsty told me, it sounds like things got a bit heated."

"I'm surprised they haven't locked Kirsty up to put a bit more pressure on us," Wayne said, arriving back at the car.

"There's time yet, Wayne, but I'm sure she'd be fine with my representation."

"I'm sure she would Frank, anyway, I'm going to crack on. I'll phone you later.

Wayne got back into the car. Jason began to grumble about being cold. Wayne tried to persuade him to drink some more water, but he turned to his side, away from Wayne.

He's not thrown up for over an hour; that must be a good sign, thought Wayne. He started the car engine and turned the radio volume up in anticipation of the snoring. The rest of the journey passed by pretty quickly. He knew the route well from previous visits.

Wayne drove along the single track service road until the holiday lodges came into view. He entered the one-way system, passing the site office and the family entertainment centre. The smell of fried food, hot dogs, burgers and chips wafted into the car from the Snack Shack, where families were sitting outside dining by the kid's playground. The sound of children playing woke Jason up, "Are we there yet?"

Wayne laughed, "You're obviously feeling better, normal whinging resumed."

He parked up in the main car park. South Shore, Bridlington was an unlikely destination; he had a good feeling that they'd be safe here. He got out of the car and immediately felt the fresh sea breeze on his face. For a moment, it took him back to when he was a kid, arriving at the caravan with his mum and dad. The seagulls were just as noisy now as they were then.

The lodge looked perfect for what they needed. There was a wooden decked area fenced off at the front. It contained a metal table and four chairs. The lodge had been finished in dark wooden boards, contrasting against the white patio doors and windows. Wayne clicked the latch on the gate and entered the decked area. He tapped the code into the keypress, took out a set of keys, and looked at the fob, 'Welcome to Bridlington.' I wish it were a tad warmer, he thought, unlocking the door and stepping into the lounge area. A huge five-seater L shaped sofa dominated the room, facing a wall-mounted fifty-inch television screen. The floor was pine laminate wood throughout. He glanced into the tiny galley kitchen and then the two small bedrooms.

Wayne heard the patio door slide open and looked around to see Jason stumbling inside. "Put the fire on, man; I'm fucking freezing."

Wayne started laughing, "I'll get you a duvet."

Jason tried to laugh but broke out into a coughing fit and crashed out on the enormous sofa. Wayne threw the duvet over him.

"Don't you worry, mate, I'll go and fetch our bags." Wayne returned to the car to get the holdalls and carrier bags of groceries. He took a moment on the decking to look at the sea. The lodge was in a prime location, a corner plot, set at an angle from the other chalets and lodges in the row. Bonus, we won't get into garden fence chatter with the neighbours, mused Wayne. He placed the bags in the lounge, then opened a can of lager, taking a drink on the decking.

"Where's the water, mate?" Jason was standing at the patio doors.

"I thought you were fast asleep. It's still in the car; give me a minute, and I'll fetch it. Christ, Jason, you look rough. You look like an extra from Dawn of the Dead." Wayne walked to the car laughing, leaving Jason feeling sorry for himself. A short while later he returned to the lounge and handed Jason a bottle of water.

"Get that down your neck, and then I'll give you the last of the injections. I hope it's been worth it," Wayne said, shaking his head.

"It's a no brainer. I'm not doing time again. If Statham had managed to get something on me for the shooting, I'd have never got out. I wasn't risking that. Give it a few years, and I'll be yesterday's news."

Wayne took a seat on the sofa and looked over towards Jason, "How are you feeling?"

"Just tired, mate, I'll be right after a good sleep. So, when am I being picked up?" Jason re-stacked his pillows to raise himself.

"Two or three days. Dirk will give us the nod when they're ready. It's all down to high tides and nautical stuff. You can recuperate and get your energy back whilst we wait."

"I'm not staying there long; I'm going to Turkey at the earliest opportunity. Once I get my feet under the table there, we'll cut Dirk loose and operate directly from the source. Cut out the middle man. It will save us a fortune."

"Or it will cause world war three! Dirk isn't going to stand for that without a fight. He'll take it as an insult, seeing it as you've done the dirty on him. Besides, how do you know you can trust the Turks? We're struggling to launder the amount of cash we make now. Are you sure it is worth the risk? I think it's a bad move." Wayne felt exasperated. It was becoming one thing after another.

"You see, Wayne, that's the difference between you and me. I'm a risk-taker, a leader, and that's why we've been so successful. You're a follower, so maybe it's best if you leave these things to me." Jason turned on his side and closed his eyes. Wayne was fuming, but he bit his lip. He knew this was a battle to be fought another time. Wayne took another can from the fridge and sat out on the decking. He needed some space to gather his thoughts and plan his next move carefully. Jason seemed to be on a relentless mission of self-destruction.

DI Andrea Statham returned from her meeting at the economic crime unit. She sat down at her desk and switched on her laptop. The main detective office was empty but for the usual early evening stragglers and HOLMES indexers battling against their ever growing in-trays. Lee left his desk and followed her in, taking a seat near to the window.

"How did yesterday's meeting with Kirsty go?"

"I tried a bit of the bad cop routine, and I mentioned the proceeds of crime and the possibility of her being implicated. It didn't work. She's probably received legal advice that we would have locked her up already if we had anything on her. She doesn't seem bothered by us anymore."

"Does Kirsty know where he is?"

"I don't think so. She seemed genuinely surprised. But who knows?"

"You're probably right. It wouldn't make sense for her to be involved."

"Did you have any luck tracing any of the vehicles, Lee?" Andrea changed the subject. She was beating herself up for failing to get Kirsty to talk. But she was in no doubt that if the money laundering trail led to the salons, Kirsty wouldn't be as confident, sitting in a cell. She wanted to forget Kirsty…for now.

"No, the van at Boggart Hole Clough was burnt out. They probably swapped cars there."

Andrea wanted to tell Lee of her concerns about DS Pete Higgs, but she decided to keep it under her hat for now. It wasn't that she couldn't trust Lee; she just wanted to be sure she was on the right track. The last thing she wanted to do was create an unjustified distraction. Albeit a second opinion would be helpful.

"Do you fancy calling for a kebab and beer on the way home?" Lee asked.

"Sounds good to me. Are you buying?"

"Again… it's no wonder you're loaded, Ma'am."

"Piss off. I got the beers last time," Andrea retorted jokingly. Lee got up and walked out of her office laughing.

"Ouch, I touched a nerve there," Lee shouted back, laughing.

Andrea found her eyes following him as he walked to his desk. She selected DI Dave Ferguson from her contacts.

"Hi, Dave, are you still at work?"

"I'm driving home. You're okay, though, I've got you on handsfree. Are you attending the strategy meeting in the morning?"

"Yeah, I'll see you there; it's pretty handy for attending meetings, working from force headquarters."

Andrea felt that was enough of the pleasantries, time to move on. She needed to do some digging without making it obvious. It was far too early to share her concerns with Dave. There might be nothing to worry about, after all.

"It's sod's law that you didn't have Wayne Davies under surveillance. He must have had some involvement with Hamilton's escape. I've had the teams out looking for him today. That would have been a result if you had them under surveillance."

"I'm sorry, Andrea, it always seems to be the case. We'd been running observations on him for ten days prior to this. Pete Higgs asked for them to be redeployed to one of our other jobs, having received some intelligence." Andrea's ears pricked up, and she experienced a sickening feeling in her gut. Dave continued, "We were drawing a blank with Wayne Davies up until then. You couldn't write it. The day we leave Davies, this happens." Andrea sensed Dave was genuinely gutted and wondered if he regretted allowing Pete to make the switch.

"And now we don't know where he is, so we're unable to resume the observations," Andrea reflected.

"We have to switch jobs quite often to meet new priorities, and it's a calculated risk we need to take these days. Limited resources, working smarter and all that. Pete's gutted, nine times out of ten, we get away with it, but this time we got bit on the ass."

"Was Pete's request justifiable?" Andrea knew her question would come over as being potentially critical.

"Yes, I wouldn't have authorised it otherwise," Dave answered defensively. Andrea knew that would be the obvious answer, but she'd succeeded in planting a seed, should Dave have any private reservations in hindsight.

"I know that came over a bit like a criticism, Dave, sorry, but I needed to ask."

"No worries, I was just surprised you may have doubted Pete's judgement."

"Just covering all bases, Dave. I'll see you at the strategy meeting tomorrow. We can crank up this manhunt."

Andrea wasn't naïve, and she knew these things happened; it was often the case that the suspects had more than their fair share of luck. But she couldn't get rid of the gnawing anxiety eating away at her. It seemed too coincidental. The thought of DS Pete Higgs compromising the investigation rocked her to her core. Considering the possibility made her feel guilty like she was stabbing him in the back. But her gut feeling didn't usually let her down. Pete hadn't been himself for some time, and his request for a move soon after was a surprise. Kirsty appeared to have inadvertently let his name slip before backtracking? And now this…

Sixteen

Jason opened his eyes, squinting in the bright sunshine that shone into the room. He was lying on the sofa covered by a duvet. He felt as if he was wrapped in cotton wool, which was a welcome contrast to his prison bed. Albeit he still felt cold and weak, and the head fog hadn't lifted. It was exacerbated by a dull headache, making him feel reluctant to move from the comfort of his makeshift bed.

"Wayne," he shouted, his voice sounded croaky. He coughed and spluttered, wishing he'd not bothered shouting. Fearing he was going to vomit again, he reached for the yellow plastic bucket, but nothing came up. The duvet slid to the floor as he slowly sat up on the sofa; his knee joints felt like they had seized up. The lodge was silent but for the seagulls screeching manically outside. He got up and stepped the short distance to the kitchen. The sun was shining onto the white wall cabinets, and the brightness hurt his sensitive eyes. "Where the hell's Wayne," he muttered to himself. Having quenched his thirst with a pint glass of water, he gave up searching for painkillers and retreated to the relative comfort of the sofa empty-handed, falling into a troubled sleep within minutes.

He was awoken by the front patio door sliding open. He looked up to see Wayne entering the chalet.

"Have you got some pain killers, Wayne? I feel wrecked like I've aged thirty years."

"You don't look good. It's a bit early for Halloween, which is a shame because you wouldn't need to dress up. You'd scare the kids to death as you are," Wayne said walking into the kitchen laughing. Jason sensed that Wayne was cockier than usual. It irritated him; he resolved to put him straight once he felt better. He was feeling too rough to challenge him at the moment. Wayne returned with a pint of water.

"Here, there's some codeine that should do the trick."

"Cheers, pal," Jason said knocking the tablets back, whilst fighting the impulse to throw up. "Have you been running?" Jason asked.

"Yeah, I love a run along the beach in the morning. It's great here. It reminded me of the summer holidays when I was a kid."

"I'd rather forget about childhood holidays. It was always Blackpool for me, sat outside a pub with a packet of crisps and a bottle of fizzy pop. I'd be there for hours whilst my mum and dad were getting pissed inside. Then back to the shit-hole they called a bed and breakfast, lay in bed listening to my mum crying after my dad had knocked her about."

"What a tosser he was," Wayne said.

"He sure was; I got him back when I was sixteen, he was up to his usual tricks, so I ran downstairs and leathered him with a cricket bat. We never saw the fucker again after that."

"Good on you pal, you've never told me about that before."

"It's something I try to forget."

Wayne shook his head, looking at the floor, he despised bullies.

"We need to get on with changing your appearance. Your mug shot has been on the local news. You need to shave the beard off, and I've got some peroxide; you need to go blonde."

"Slow down, Wayne, I've only just woken up… We could do with Kirsty up here and get her to do a professional job."

"Too risky, mate… Where do you two stand now?" Wayne said, taking the opportunity to find out more.

"Are you trying to wind me up? The last I heard, she was shagging Ryan in Spain. I think it's pretty obvious where we stand now, don't you?" Jason stood up and hobbled to the kitchen. He looked out of the window whilst restraining himself from launching a tirade at Wayne. Jason expected better of Wayne and wondered why he was asking stupid questions.

"Nobody knows for sure; Ryan has a girlfriend out there," Wayne said before accepting he'd have been better keeping his mouth shut.

"Fuck off, Wayne, it's pretty obvious, we're finished. I hadn't even got through reception at Strangeways before Ryan made his move. He's a fucking snake, that lad. Ryan knew that Kirsty was in a bad place and made his move." Jason's knuckles were white as he gripped the handle on the kettle. Fighting the urge to launch it towards Wayne.

"I can see where you're coming from, mate, but you did give Ryan a hard time. It's no wonder he kicked back at you, and then you took out the contract on him. Don't forget you were shagging Kirsty before she left Ryan." Wayne walked outside onto the decking. Jason slammed the kettle down on the worktop and followed Wayne outside, struggling not to punch him in the face.

"When are Dirk's boys picking me up?" Jason spat out, abruptly, leaving Wayne in no doubt that the previous conversation was over.

"I rang him last night to confirm you were out. He's looking forward to seeing you. They will pick you up at Hull docks or nearby. I think it's a fishing boat, but I'm not sure about the detail. Then you'll be spending a few days at a farmhouse outside Rotterdam whilst they sort your papers out."

"I want to get to Turkey asap." Jason was impatient and didn't want to be hanging around.

"We know that, and you will be. It's all in place. Dirk thinks it would be a good time for you to visit Columbia too."

"It will be safer there, I suppose." Jason felt the codeine kicking in, giving him some welcome respite from his zombie-like state.

"Unless the American DEA takes an interest in you, then you'd be fucked. They've got proper prisons over there and proper sentences. I'll bring you up to speed with business later. We have our dealers back in Bristol, and I've got us into the market around Portsmouth. We can't get enough gear into Glasgow, and that's becoming our biggest market now. Having you in Turkey will be a good move, so you can work on cutting our wholesale prices."

"So, when am I leaving?"

"In the next few days, just waiting on a call from Dirk," Wayne said, picking up the carrier bag and emptying the contents onto the sofa; Electric hair shaver, peroxide, disposable gloves and towel. "I think we'll give you a number four, a bit longer than a skinhead. And dye it blonde; you'll look totally different. Let's get it done, and then we can go for a

144

walk on the beach. You look like you need some fresh air."

"Yeah, you can bring me up to speed with business, whilst we walk," Jason said, asserting his control.

"You're not serious about cutting Dirk out, are you?"

"Of course, I'm serious. It's the only way Wayne, it's how we've got to where we are now. We can't afford to stagnate; more power means more money." Jason sensed a reluctance to progress in Wayne's attitude; he didn't look happy, "Are you okay with that, Wayne?" Jason said derisively, seeking a reaction.

"Of course, I am; I just think it's a big risk. Making enemies unnecessarily." Wayne's empty show didn't convince Jason of his commitment to the cause.

DI Andrea Statham sat down at her desk, the greasy smell of the kebabs from the night before still lingering in the office. They had worked late, reviewing the Hamilton case from start to finish. Their hard work was outlined on the whiteboard, which provided a summary flow chart of where they were and what they needed to do next. She carried her wastepaper bin through the empty office to the kitchen and disposed of the kebab wrappers before making a coffee. The team were on a rest day, but Andrea was on-call senior detective, covering for a colleague.

She sat down, holding the cup with both hands and took a sip of the hot coffee. Her mind returned to Pete Higgs, as it repeatedly had over the last few days. She quietly hoped her investigations would come to nothing, but unfortunately, her gut feeling suggested otherwise. Either way, she was determined to get to the bottom of Pete's clandestine activities.

Andrea had steered the conversation with Lee the night before towards how unlucky they had been when the surveillance was switched from Wayne Davies. Andrea also mentioned her chat with DI Dave Ferguson concerning the circumstances surrounding the switch. Her attempts to tease out any concerning opinions Lee may have held proved fruitless. But Lee did mention seeing Pete at court a week earlier. Her ears pricked up at this comment because the team had no cases being heard before the court. She finished her coffee and headed for her car.

Andrea parked in one of the city centre multi-storeys and walked the short distance along Deansgate to the Crown Court at Crown Square, picking up some cakes along the way.

Once through security screening, she approached the court management office and tapped on the door. A grumpy looking man in his mid-sixties, with unruly grey hair, opened the door. He had a ruddy, weathered face, probably enhanced by fags and booze. A big smile replaced his grumpy expression instantly when he saw Andrea.

"Hello, stranger, good to see you. I thought you'd forgotten all about me and moved on with the whizz kids."

"How could I ever forget about you? You taught me all I know, stick the kettle on Jeff, I've brought your favourite cakes." Jeff was a retired career detective now working three days a week at the court security lodge. They had worked a lot of cases together and been through many scrapes. Jeff was Andrea's tutor detective when she was a trainee detective. To say Jeff was old school was an understatement.

"How are Barbara and Sophie?"

"Barbara's still working at the hospital. I want her to retire, but she says it's the only respite she gets away from me. Sadly, I don't think she's joking," Jeff said, deadpan, "We're off on a cruise next week in the Norwegian Fjords, all-inclusive." Jeff stirred the coffees and placed them on his desk. They both sat down. Andrea got the cakes out of her bag.

"Victoria sponge," she announced.

Jeff nodded his approval of her choice, "Sophie is doing fine, and she's a ward sister now. No sign of grandkids yet; Barbara is starting to fret. She's eager to be a grandparent."

"Be careful what you wish for Jeff, or you'll be babysitting instead of cruising the world and drinking cocktails." A silence followed whilst they ate the Victoria sponge. Jeff took a drink of his coffee and looked towards Andrea, "Have you found Mr Right yet?"

"Don't be silly; you know me." Andrea ignored the image of Lee that flashed into her mind.

"You're too bloody fussy; that's your problem. That solicitor you went out with was a good catch. He seemed like a good lad, the one you brought to the Christmas Party; what was his name?"

"Tom, yeah, you're probably right, but I was too young then, and the long shifts probably helped to ruin any chance we had. Jeff shook his head mockingly. Andrea hated talking about her boyfriend situation and quickly changed the subject. It seemed everyone she knew was obsessed with getting her fixed up.

"I need a favour," Andrea said quietly.

"Of course, you do. You don't fetch me a cake for the first time in months for no reason," Jeff laughed, breaking into a smoker's cough.

"I need the court listings for the fourteenth and a look at the security footage outside of Court Three between ten and eleven o'clock."

"And the reason? Or have you forgotten about the data protection act and all that?" Jeff looked at her, his eyes focused, as shrewd as ever.

"Murder investigation," Andrea replied, unsure of whether he was just teasing.

"Sounds like a reasonable request to me." Jeff started tapping away at his keyboard. Then the printer clicked and whirled into action. Jeff handed her the printout. "That's the listings. We need to go to the CCTV suite for the footage.

They sat down at a monitor. It was a standard CCTV security room. A security guard sat at a desk facing five screens on the wall in front of her. It must have been a quiet day, and she had been enjoying a game of solitaire, which she switched off hurriedly when they entered the room. Apart from saying hello to Jeff, she showed no interest in their arrival at the office.

Jeff selected the file then fast-forwarded the footage to ten o'clock.

"Here you are, just use the mouse to fast forward." Jeff slid the mouse to Andrea. Just after ten o'clock, she saw Pete enter the frame and walk towards another male talking on a mobile. Andrea recognised him straight away. It was Jason Hamilton's lawyer, Frank Burton. After a moment, they walked towards each other and started talking. Andrea felt a rush of blood. It was not what she had wanted to see. What the hell was Pete doing?

"Is that Pete Higgs there?" Jeff's voice brought her back to the moment.

"It is Pete, yes," Andrea replied.

"Pete 'Hold-Em-High" Higgs," Jeff laughed, "Not seen him in ages. How's he doing?"

"Hold-Em-High?"

"Enjoys his poker does Pete. The trouble is, contrary to popular belief, he isn't very good at it."

"I thought he'd made a few quid over the years?"

"No, he's average at best. He lost a fortune on his CID course and had to sell his car to settle his debts."

Andrea didn't want to look too interested in Jeff's disclosure. She didn't know how close he was to Pete. But she recognised the significance of what he was saying; officers with debt problems were vulnerable to corruption.

"He's fine; he's just gone on attachment to the drugs unit. I'll give him your regards if you like. Listen, Jeff, please keep this visit to yourself. It's a bit of a sensitive enquiry."

"Enough said Andrea, as long as you don't leave it too long until your next visit. Maybe some Bakewell tart with custard next time?" They both laughed.

"It's a deal."

Back at the office, Andrea reviewed the court listings. Pete was not a witness in any of the cases before the court that day. I suppose he could have been there to swear out a warrant, Andrea reasoned, although not convincing herself. That would be easy enough to check later.

She slid the disc into the dvd player and watched the footage again. At any other time, she would be satisfied it was just a run of the mill conversation, but

149

it wasn't under the circumstances. It looked pre-arranged; the implications were concerning.

Seventeen

Jason felt refreshed and much better after a good sleep. He looked at his reflection in the mirror whilst cleaning his teeth. He cringed at his new blonde hair; he hated it, but it was a needs must, that he looked totally different and unrecognisable from the mugshot shown on the local television news. He finished off in the bathroom and walked through to the lounge.

"Lovely hair, you need to join a boy band, mate," Wayne said, laughing.

"You need to fuck off," Jason replied with a scowl.

"I wonder if Dirk can get you some work on stage, in one of his bars, in Amsterdam?" Wayne said with a mocking smirk.

"Yeah, yeah, enjoy it whilst you can, you tosser," Jason said, putting the kettle on. Wayne was irritating Jason, but he didn't want Wayne to know he was getting under his skin; he bit his lip, keeping his powder dry.

"Hopefully, we'll hear from Dirk today and get you out of here."

"Give him a call Wayne, chase him up. He needs to pull his finger out. I thought he'd have this sorted by now. You should be on top of this," Jason couldn't resist having a dig.

"I'm going for a run along the beach, and then I'll call him when I get back. Do you fancy a run, get your system back to normal?" Wayne finished tying up his training shoes and picked up his water bottle.

"No, I'm not feeling right yet. I won't push it." Jason followed Wayne outside and sat at the table on the decking. He watched as Wayne ran towards the beach.

"At least put some effort in, for fucks sake," Jason shouted after him, but he didn't get a rise out of Wayne. He laughed out loud, satisfied that Wayne had heard him.

He took a drink of his coffee and relaxed back into the chair. The salty sea breeze wafted on his face, whilst the sound of the seagulls felt comforting. It made him feel determined not to go back inside. He finished his coffee and walked back into the lodge, straight to Wayne's bedroom. He picked up the car keys from the bedside table and headed back to his own bedroom. He threw what little clothing he had into a bag. He was feeling energised and much better; the effects of the medication had almost gone.

Jason left the patio door unlocked just in case Wayne hadn't taken a key. Jason walked towards the car park; a family was walking towards him. The two little girls looked excited, carrying red plastic buckets and spades. The father was laden down with a windbreak, dingy and picnic bag.

"Beautiful weather; we chose a good week," Jason said.

"The girls love it here. The beach is gorgeous; if only the weather was always like this," replied the mother.

Jason continued walking. It was one of his first interactions with people since he'd got out. It felt good. He reached the car and opened the hatchback, pulling the cover aside to look under the spare wheel. He opened the black canvas bag and looked around to make sure no one was watching. He took out the 8mm Baikal pistol and checked the magazine. It was fully loaded. He cocked the weapon and made it ready to fire. He replaced it and checked the other canvas pouch, which contained rounds of ammunition.

"Let's get this show on the road," Jason said to himself as he got into the car and headed off.

As Jason turned onto the A614, Wayne exerted a final burst of energy with a sprint finish to the lodge. He reached the decking and leant on the fencing, breathing heavily. He was surprised that Jason hadn't come outside to take the piss out of him, but then he guessed he'd probably be sleeping. Wayne walked to the bathroom and took a shower. He was enjoying his time here; it was nostalgic. He dressed, made a coffee and sat out on the decking. Leaning back, he closed his eyes and enjoyed the heat of the sun. A ringtone broke his moment of solitude.

"Good morning Dirk, how are you?"

"All is good in Amsterdam, as always, Wayne. How are your punters enjoying that last shipment?"

"They can't get enough. It's selling like hotcakes."

"Hotcakes? Are you smoking the wacky-backy, Wayne?" Dirk didn't get it.

"Just a local saying, mate, it means it's selling well. Seriously we're going to have to bring the November shipment forward, definitely for the 'H' that was good stuff."

"The Heroin was from a new source in Afghanistan."

"It's a good source. Let's stick with them," Wayne suggested.

"How is Jason's recovery progressing?"

"He's recovering slowly, he's still a mad bastard, though. The medication he took could easily have killed him. We had to break into a residential care home to get our hands on it; it's prescription only. He looked like a zombie when we got him out. He's lost a lot of weight."

"Is he okay for tomorrow?" Dirk asked getting to the point.

"Yes, pal, he's eager to be on the move. He's all over the place at the minute. Do you still want to rendezvous in Hull?"

"No, change of plan. Go to the lighthouse on the south jetty at the harbour in Whitby. You will see that there is a concrete platform just below the lighthouse. He needs to be there at 4 am on Thursday. Unless you hear anything different from me, that is the plan."

"Excellent; once we've got this sorted, I'll get over the water to see you." Wayne took every opportunity to develop his bond with Dirk, even if it was to the detriment of Jason. It was a cutthroat business, and Wayne had no intention of being a victim.

"I look forward to it, my friend," Dirk said.

"Before you go, I need to call you later on tonight. Will you be available?" Wayne said, looking towards the patio doors; there was still no sign of Jason.

"Yes, can't we talk now?" Dirk asked, puzzled.

"No, it's a sensitive matter. I need to run something by you."

"Okay, speak later Wayne, you Mancs are crazy." Wayne placed his mobile on the table, feeling satisfied with the developments so far. He was hungry after his run and needed some lunch. He went inside and tapped lightly on Jason's door, "You awake, pal?" He enquired, there was no answer. Wayne got a pen and scribbled a note, gone to get us some pizza. He placed the note under the television remote control on the sofa.

The car keys weren't on his bedside table. He checked his coat pockets and looked around the lodge but couldn't find them. He returned to Jason's room and quietly opened the door; Jason wasn't there. What the hell, maybe he's gone for a walk, Wayne reasoned.

He walked to the car park but knew what to expect before he got there. The empty parking space confirmed what he suspected. The car was gone.

Frank Burton was sitting at his desk when he was interrupted from his reading by the desk phone.

"Burton and Co."

"Good morning, could I speak to Mr Burton, please?"

"Speaking."

"It's DI Andrea Statham," Andrea had expected a secretary to answer. "I need to speak with you regarding your client Jason Hamilton absconding from custody."

"When were you thinking?" Burton said, buying time to process the best way to deal with the unexpected request.

"I could be at your office within the hour. It is an important matter and time-critical."

"How about two o'clock?" Burton suggested. He ended the call, walked over to his office window and lit a cigarette.

Frank's burner phone started to vibrate in his pocket. He found some space in the ashtray amid the growing pile of butts to stub out his cigarette, failing miserably to prevent ash spilling onto his desk.

"Good morning Wayne, how is sunny, Bridlington?"

"Not good, Frank."

"Oh Christ, what's up now?" Frank sat back down in his chair.

"I went for a run this morning, and when I got back, Jason was nowhere to be seen," Wayne said downbeat.

"He'll be back. He's probably walking on the beach," Frank said reassuringly.

"I don't think so Frank, he's taken his stuff, and our car's gone. I was hoping he may have phoned you?"

"Afraid not. When is he sailing?"

"All set for the early hours," Wayne couldn't hide his disappointment.

"What the hell is he playing at here? I take it you've phoned him?" Frank asked.

"It just goes straight to voicemail; I've left messages. If he's heading back to Manchester, I'm done with him, Frank."

"I'm sure he'll be back. You stay at the lodge, and I'll put a call into him. There's no way he'd risk coming back to Manchester. He's probably out enjoying some freedom; don't forget he's been inside for months. Keep in touch, Wayne. We'll get him on the boat tomorrow come what may."

"I hope so, Frank. He's doing my head in at the moment."

Frank placed his burner phone back in his pocket and rubbed his temples. He sensed there was trouble ahead; his reassurance to Wayne had been optimistic, to say the least. Frank lit another cigarette and stood looking out of his window, deep in thought. He saw

DI Andrea Statham walking up the street towards his office. She walked like a woman on a mission.

"She's keen. She must have been in town when she phoned," He said to himself. Frank waited for the intercom buzzer to be activated.

"Hello Inspector, come in, up the stairs to the top floor, there's only one door."

"Thank you."

Andrea entered the office out of breath from the climb up the stairs. Frank Burton appeared from behind the door opposite.

"Good afternoon Inspector."

"Good afternoon. Thank you for seeing me at short notice, sorry I'm a bit early."

"No problem, I've just made some coffee. Would you like one?" Frank's fake sincerity made her skin crawl.

"Yes, please, black, no sugar." Andrea walked over to the window and looked out, whilst Frank poured the drinks, "Nice view you've got here Frank, how long have you been here?"

"It's just temporary," Frank answered evasively. He placed the drinks on the desk. They both took a seat,

"I guess you know why I'm here; I need to locate your client. Why has he gone on the run?" Probed Andrea.

"Good question. I wish I knew the answer. Jason took me by surprise with this crazy move. I had a legal visit booked for tomorrow morning."

"Has he been in touch with you?" Andrea asked, observing his response closely.

"I wish he had. I could have tried to talk some sense into him. If he does, I will certainly try to get him to do the right thing." Andrea almost laughed aloud at Frank's mock sincerity. Spare me the bullshit, she mused.

"The investigation is progressing well. We have some highly rated intelligence which should lead to arrests being made," Andrea lied, again watching for Frank's reaction. Frank didn't flinch, "Do you represent his partner, Kirsty?" Andrea continued mischievously.

"I don't think she would require my representation, Inspector. She has done nothing wrong," Frank said with confidence.

"I'll be the judge of that. It doesn't look as clear cut to me," Andrea retorted.

Frank moved on, "Unfortunately, I can't help you. I was led to believe he was keeping his head down and serving his time. He was a model prisoner, from what I was told. He certainly gave me no indication of his intention to do a runner."

"Hardly doing a runner, Frank, two of his cronies threatened the prison officers and ambulance crew with a pistol," Andrea almost spat her words out.

"Well, I assure you, Inspector, if he makes contact, I will advise him to accompany me to the police station. You have my word. Was there anything else, Inspector?"

"No, not for now. I'll leave you my card… Oh yes, there was one other thing. Do you remember DS Pete Higgs?" Andrea was sure she saw a reaction of surprise at her mentioning of Pete's name. Frank hesitated for a moment.   "Yes, he was the interviewing officer when Jason was in custody." Andrea paused, hoping to create an uncomfortable silence. She picked up her mobile phone and looked at the screen.

"Sorry Frank, I'm expecting an important text... Where was I?"

"DS Pete Higgs," Frank didn't look flustered or wrong-footed, but Andrea sensed something that she couldn't quite put her finger on.

"Oh yes, just to let you know, he's moved on. You can deal directly with me if you hear anything." Andrea thought Frank looked relieved that it was nothing more serious.

"Do you know Pete?" Andrea decided to push her luck and probe a little further.

"Should I?" Frank said with a puzzled expression.

"I was just wondering. You've both been on the circuit for a good while. I thought your paths might have crossed."

"Not that I recall, but it's possible, I suppose. I've represented many clients over the years, but the police officers seem to move on quicker these days." Andrea didn't respond right away. She left the conversation hanging there. The conversation she had watched them having on the CCTV just took on a whole new sinister connotation.

"He knows quite a lot of the local briefs. He's been a tier five trained interviewer for some time, so he has a lot of contact on disclosures and the like."

"In that case, we probably have crossed paths. Is it important to you?"

"Just curious, Frank, that's all."

Andrea thanked Frank for his time and left the office. She hoped to have spooked him with her vague enquiry about Pete Higgs.

Eighteen

Jason was sitting in the restaurant at the motorway service area on the M62 eating burger and fries. The spicy chilli sauce had a hell of a kick and was almost too hot for his newly acquired prison food palate. He savoured the moment and promised himself he would never take his freedom for granted again. The eating area was open plan, surrounded by shops and fast food outlets, bustling with travellers. The sun felt warm, radiating through the large glass panels. He felt much healthier and was definitely on the road to recovery from the effects of the medication. Life felt good again. He realised he was enjoying the small things whilst living in the moment. It was a new experience that he liked. It made him feel more prepared. His mind was less cluttered.

An involuntarily smile spread across his face as his attention turned to the thought of Wayne arriving back at the lodge and discovering that he'd gone. It was a reminder to Wayne that he was back and running the show. It was great to be in control of his destiny again and not be told when to get behind his door or when to eat. He picked up his phone and dialled a number from memory.

"Hello." He was pleasantly surprised at how good it felt to hear Kirsty's voice.

"Kirsty, it's me. How are you doing?"

"Jason, what the hell have you done? You've been on the local news and in the newspaper." Kirsty laughed nervously, "That bloody Andrea Statham has been on my case again. She's convinced I know where you are and won't take no for an answer. You need to watch her. She's obsessed with putting you back inside."

"She hasn't got a clue, don't worry about her, babe. Are you keeping okay?"

"Apart from Statham's visits to the salon, everything is back to normal. The salons are doing well, fully booked now. Do you want to meet up?"

Jason sensed her desire in the question. It felt good.

"I can't, babe. The cops are probably following you. That's what they'd expect us to do. Once I'm settled somewhere, we can arrange something."

A sudden wave of paranoia hit Jason. Was she trying to set him up? He discounted the thought as quickly as it had surfaced. No chance, not Kirsty; she wouldn't do that.

"It would be good to catch up; there's no reason we can't be friends. We have been through a lot together."

"Yeah, one day at a time, Kirsty. Let's see how things pan out. I'm not being banged up again, that's for sure. What's Ryan up to? Is he still in Spain?" Jason had vowed to himself that he wouldn't talk about Ryan, but the words just came out anyway.

"We've not spoken for a few weeks, but he seems settled out there. He's got a girlfriend and enjoys the lifestyle. Are you still mad with him?"

"I've not given him much thought, to be honest, babe," Jason lied.

"He's a loyal friend Jason, if you want my advice, I'd offer him an olive branch."

"We'll see. I've got more important things to do right now. I'll be in touch. Remember, only use the phones that Frank gives you if you call me."

"You keep your head down, don't create any more trouble for yourself," Kirsty pleaded. Jason said goodbye and ended the call with a feeling of contentment for having spoken with Kirsty. It was good to know she was safe, even though it was unlikely they would get back together.

He was just about to go for another burger when his attention was taken by two police officers walking towards the newsagents. They engaged in conversation with the woman cashier; Jason observed them. He regretted not having his pistol with him but was confident they wouldn't recognise him and enjoyed the buzz of them not having a clue of his presence.

"Fucking keystone cops," He muttered and decided it was probably best to get back on the road.

DI Andrea Statham strolled across the car park at the force training centre with a feeling of trepidation and entered the crime training building. As expected, the building was empty, with it being a weekend. She walked along the deserted corridor, passing classrooms on the right and scenario interview rooms on the left. The lights clicked and flickered into action as she passed under the sensors.

This building had been intrinsic to her career. She had completed her Initial Detective Training course here and later her Intermediate CID course following her promotion to Detective Sergeant. The course she enjoyed most was the Senior Investigating Officer Course. Andrea had learned from some of the best investigators from around the country, who had presented case studies of high profile complex investigations. In more recent times, she had shared her knowledge and experience with the attendees of such courses.

She paused to look at the photographs of colleagues past and present. Looking back at her, from one of the photographs was a slimmer Pete Higgs. It was the Pete Higgs she used to know. It made her feel uneasy about how the next hour or so would pan out.

Andrea was making a coffee when she looked out of the window to the car park below. Pete Higgs had just arrived and was walking across the car park towards the building. He looked up and waved; Andrea waved back, lacking her usual enthusiasm at seeing him. She took a drink of coffee and studied him; if he was nervous, he wasn't showing it. She suspected that Frank Burton had already called him and given him the heads up of her visit to his office.

When she arranged to meet at the training school, Pete hadn't asked why, which she thought was out of character for him. Usually, they would meet and have a coffee or some lunch away from the nick. Over the years, she had trusted Pete without question. Now there was a nagging doubt that she needed to reconcile one way or the other. Andrea heard the fire doors banging shut in the corridor as Pete made his way into the building. She switched the kettle back on and made two coffees.

As Pete appeared in the doorway, she noticed he was out of breath, probably because of the stairs. He didn't seem as upbeat as usual, and he had the demeanour of someone who was anticipating a dressing down.

"I've not been in here for months. I was just looking at the course group photographs in the corridor. It makes me feel old when I look at those. I think the last time I was here, I was attending the Harold Shipman investigation seminar," Pete reminisced. Andrea passed him a coffee; she watched him closely, as she would with a suspect, for any signs of leakage to help her make sense of all this.

"I've been here far too often for my liking, Pete, giving presentations to the trainee detective courses. This place never seems to change. Let's go and sit down next door."

They entered the classroom; the windows adjacent to the corridor ran along the room's length, covered by vertical blinds. On the other side of the room, the windows overlooked the car park. Around twenty chairs formed a horseshoe, facing the whiteboard on the far wall. Andrea was confident they wouldn't be disturbed. The noisy doors on the corridors would give an early warning if anyone were approaching.

"It's like a museum of classroom ancillaries through time; old overhead projectors, flip charts, whiteboards, electric presentation boards and now computer power point feeds. It's just missing a blackboard," Andrea tried to make light of the tense atmosphere. It didn't work; Pete didn't respond with one of his usual witty glib replies.

They took a chair each, leaving an empty chair between them. There was an uneasy silence for a moment until Pete broke it.

"Is something wrong, boss? I'm getting the feeling I've pissed you off," Pete said.

"You tell me, Pete." Andrea took a drink of coffee but maintained eye contact. Her attitude towards Pete, on this occasion, felt alien to her. She was in the role of investigator, not friend or colleague.

"How about giving me a clue?" Pete laughed nervously.

"What the hell have you got involved in, Pete?" Andrea said quietly. Pete was no longer laughing. In fact, he was starting to look anxious. Andrea knew he would be biding his time to discover what she knew. It was a game of poker. Damage limitation being the objective for Pete. She'd have done the same in his position.

"Frank Burton," Andrea said, maintaining her stare. Pete leant forward, placing his elbows on his knees and head in his hands.

"What have you heard?" Pete muttered.

"I'm not playing games here, Pete. We go back too far for that; show me some bloody respect, please. Whatever I've heard doesn't matter; for now, what matters is what you are about to tell me." Andrea stood up from her chair and walked to the window, looking outside. "This isn't going to go away, Pete. Perhaps it's best for you to be explaining this to me, rather than the professional standards branch?" Andrea suddenly felt quite melancholic, "If it's something we can sort out together, all well and good. But you need to be honest with me. I can't let this go without us sorting it out." The fact that Pete hadn't kicked off with her suggested she was on the right lines. Pete stood up too and joined Andrea at the window, both of them looking out.

"I don't want to put you in a position that if I share stuff with you, you will be duty-bound to take it further," Pete said, probably buying more time.

"Just tell me, Pete, I can decide what to do myself."

"I've known Frank Burton on and off over the years whilst he has been representing suspects. When I got wind he represented Hamilton; I decided to lean on him and apply a bit more pressure. Since then, I've been getting bits of intelligence from him. In return, I've given him a bit back, nothing significant and mostly stuff that is already known in the wider criminal community." Pete turned to face Andrea, "You don't need to tell me what a dickhead I've been. I've worked that out for myself."

"Bloody hell Pete, we could be talking miscarriage of justice here."

"No, we're not. He's given me jack shit that would compromise his clients. He's not stupid. He gave me intelligence of unconnected street-level dealing. It's just old school coppering, but I know it won't wash with the bosses these days. I know it's wrong, but he was hardly going to register as an informant formally, was he? I will back off him. Burton isn't going to bring the matter up. It's not in his interests to do so. It doesn't prejudice the case at all."

"What else?" Andrea asked, knowing full well this would be the initial watered-down version of events.

"There is nothing else," Pete said, avoiding eye contact as he sat back down.

Andrea wasn't satisfied, "Bullshit… be straight with me now, or you're on your own."

"What are you going to do?" Pete digressed.

"I've not decided yet. I need to think things over. And I suggest you do the same, now get out of my bloody sight Pete." Andrea surprised herself with the ferocity of her concluding outburst.

"Pete looked sheepish and left the room, leaving Andrea sitting alone in silence. What he had disclosed to her wasn't enough, without further evidence. He would probably get slapped wrists and a formal warning at most. The easy option was to refer him to professional standards and pass the buck to them. Her preferred choice would be to undertake further enquiries and establish the facts.

It would be difficult to prove he had sabotaged the surveillance. The rationale for his policy decision would stand up to scrutiny. That was clear from her conversation with DI Dave Ferguson; if Pete had undermined the investigation intentionally, he had covered his tracks. Had he passed on the details of the canal jogger, Michael May? Andrea mused. She suspected he might have but needed more evidence.

The textbook answer to this problem was to refer it to professional standards...she decided to sleep on it and decide on her next move in the morning.

Nineteen

Jason's eyes felt dry and gritty; he rubbed them, unfortunately making them feel worse. He was tired and hungry as he drove onto the new residential housing estate in Chadderton. It looked like many other new housing estates, a mixture of detached and semi-detached houses with some apartment blocks, complemented by neat and tidy gardens. The properties were tightly squeezed in along narrow winding roads. He drove slowly past the apartment he had come to visit. It was set back from the road, on the ground floor of a three-storey building. It didn't look like anyone was at home from what he could see.

He drove further into the estate past a children's playground and turned the car around. It was, as he suspected, only one access road onto the estate, which limited his escape options. He stopped short of the apartment on the way back, reversing into a parking space surrounded by bushes and trees. He'd decided on this spot as a good vantage point from where he could see the entrance road to the estate, the residents parking area for the apartments and an excellent view to the front window of his target address. Perfect, I just need to take him out by the side of the house, that will give me sufficient cover, thought Jason.

He didn't want to attract unwanted attention, and Lee McCann wasn't expected home for an hour or two, so he left the estate to check out the surrounding area and grab something to eat. He had felt a constant craving for junk food since his recovery.

Jason was gripping the steering wheel tight. Just looking at Lee's home had increased his raw need for revenge. He thought about what he would do to him; Lee was going to endure some severe pain. It was personal, and he was going to revel in taking his revenge.

Pete Higgs was slumped on the sofa watching a football match on television. He wasn't entirely focused on the game; his mind was involuntarily brooding over his meeting with DI Andrea Statham. Pete couldn't stop fretting about how much she knew and what she would do next.

Luckily, he had some space to himself. Rachel had taken the children to the cinema with a group of their friends. Leaving Pete with the house to himself. At half time he took a can of beer from the refrigerator and walked into the garden. He placed his can on the garden table and took out his phone.

"Hi, Frank, are you free to speak?"

"I thought you'd be watching the football?"

"It's half time. We've got a big problem brewing, Frank. Andrea Statham confronted me today… she's onto us, Frank. How many people know about our arrangement? Could somebody on your side have grassed us up?"

"No, I've not told anyone," Frank replied, failing to mention his slip of the tongue to Wayne Davies, "She called at my office too. She was pressing for information on Jason's whereabouts. As if I was going to tell her." Frank chuckled, "She also asked how well I knew you, which makes more sense now," Frank lifted his empty glass in a gesture towards the barman.

"Christ, Frank, why didn't you tell me?" Pete exclaimed.

"I thought nothing of it. Just a routine enquiry which I would have expected, being Jason's lawyer?"

"What did you tell her?" Pete was worried. Andrea hadn't mentioned this visit to him. What else had she not mentioned? He felt physically sick. He couldn't stop his mind ruminating over what Andrea had on him.

"I told her that I hardly knew you, of course." Frank smiled at the barman and handed him a twenty; he took a drink of his pint and leant forward against the bar. "She didn't tell me what information she had or its source. I didn't embarrass myself by asking her either. I would have looked desperate... and guilty. So, I gave the scantest of details I could think of, to explain it away. I had to give her something," Frank explained.

"Which is?" Frank's blasé attitude was beginning to irritate Pete; maybe Frank didn't appreciate the reputation of who they were dealing with, a respected adversary.

"We may have crossed paths, but I didn't recall doing so."

"Great, I said we had known each other on and off for a long time, and I'd been getting bits of unrelated intelligence from you," Pete said. A silence followed.

"How did she react?" Frank sounded like he was beginning to realize the gravity of the situation.

"Hard to tell, Frank, Andrea is a good detective, one of the best. I guess she'll be keeping an open mind at this stage, but she won't leave any stone unturned. I suppose it depends on what she knows already, or more importantly, what she can prove." Pete shifted nervously and took a drink of beer.

170

Pete's next-door neighbour looked over the fence and waved. Pete smiled and waved back, when really, he felt like telling him to bugger off, he reminded himself to keep his voice down.

"I suppose we just have to wait then," Frank said, sounding much less confident than he previously had, "If what you're saying is right, I guess they'll drag you in at some point. At least they should provide you with some disclosure of their suspicions if it's official. Probably making no reply at this stage would be the best way forward." Frank easily slipped into legal representative mode.

"You need to bloody tell me if she gets onto you again. If I go down, you're coming with me," Pete blurted out under the pressure of his growing fear.

"Piss off, Pete, you're the bent public servant. I'm just a naïve back street solicitor, blackmailed by you, a savvy detective. Surely you know I have covered my tracks. It's you they're after; I'm just collateral. In reality, they will probably want me to give evidence against you." It was the first time that Pete had heard such a menacing tone from Frank. Pete suddenly felt very lonely and vulnerable. His thoughts were whirling around, struggling to think straight and make sense of what to do.

Frank continued, "You'd better sit down, Pete. We have another problem to contend with."

"For fucks sake, what now?" Pete was now having a serious wobble.

"I've had a call from one of Jason Hamilton's associates. He has gone missing; they don't know where he is," It was Frank's turn to sound concerned.

"That's nothing new; we already know he's escaped," Pete sounded relieved. He had anticipated far worse.

"But he's reneged on their original plan. He's on his toes from his boys as well as the police. I fear that he's going after Lee McCann, which is not good news. The guy was just doing his job. You need to do something, Pete."

Pete felt deflated; a feeling of panic started to overwhelm him. It just felt like he was experiencing one nightmare after another, with no happy ending in sight. Pete felt like he was never going to escape from this predicament. He was out of his depth, suicide momentarily crossing his mind as a viable option. He dismissed it immediately, knowing full well that he didn't have the bottle to go through with it.

"I'll see what I can find out. Tell me if Statham gets back onto you. If she does, be careful what you say."

"One thing you've not mentioned, Pete, do you have any dirt on Statham which we could use to get her to back off?"

"No chance, she's solid," Pete said, feeling guilty at the thought of stitching Andrea up, "I'll try and do some damage limitation. I think you need to get onto your clients and put Hamilton back inside. It would be the best result for all of us right now."

Pete walked through the lounge, oblivious to the fact that the second half of the football match had started, and he'd missed a goal. He went to the boot of his car and grabbed his spare burner phone. He switched it on and dialled Crimestoppers.

It was the best way he could help Lee McCann, alerting the police of the impending threat, without throwing himself under the bus at the same time. He felt exhausted and just wanted to sleep.

"You need to listen carefully: the life of a serving police officer is in imminent danger. Jason Hamilton has escaped from Strangeways and is on the run. He is looking for DS Lee McCann, as we speak. DS McCann works on the Major Incident Team, Serious Crime Division. DI Andrea Statham is dealing with the case, and you need to make her aware of this asap. Act on this now. There isn't much time," Pete instructed, attempting to disguise his voice. The woman on the other end of the phone started to ask a question. Pete didn't want to delay the dissemination of the intelligence and ended the call. No time for a procedural questionnaire to dot the I's and cross the T's.

Pete got back on to Frank, updating him on the call to Crimestoppers.

"Give me Hamilton's mobile phone number. I can pass it on to Crimestoppers, and then the cops can triangulate it and locate him. We need to cover our tracks. It's self-preservation time. Let's watch each other's backs. We stand a better chance looking out for each other."

"I've not got his number, Pete. He's out there on his own." Pete sensed either fear or regret in Frank's voice.

"Try and get hold of it; one of his cronies must have it. We need to stop him. That's probably our best chance. Give me a bell if you sort anything."

Pete sat down on the sofa; he mulled over what else he could do to help Lee without incriminating himself. He couldn't understand why Frank denied having Jason's number, and he was starting to feel extremely vulnerable.

Frank left the pub and walked back from the Northern Quarter to his office. He found it difficult to continue past the pubs on the way back; following his conversation with Pete, he was very tempted to carry on drinking to block everything out.

Back at the office, he turned the key in his safe. There was a loud metallic clunk as he pressed the heavy brass handle down. His voice recorder was nestled amongst a pile of mobile phones. He sat at his desk, lit a cigarette and listened to his recorded conversations with Pete Higgs.

Four cigarettes later, he placed the voice recorder into his pocket and poured himself a whiskey.

He sat back in his chair, listening to his mobile ringing out until Wayne answered. "Hello, Wayne, has he been in touch."

"No, nothing. Jason's taking the piss now. Not just us but the Dutch boys too. How the hell do I explain the delay to them? They won't be happy with him fucking them about." Wayne said, pacing around the holiday lodge, "It's getting very messy… I don't do messy.

"We need to face facts. Jason's probably gone after the cop. It can't be anything else. Ryan is still in Spain. If it were anything else, he would have returned by now," Frank said, taking a drink of his whiskey before lighting another cigarette.

Wayne was feeling claustrophobic, having been waiting in the lodge for Jason to return. He put his jacket on and left the lodge, heading for the beach, "I thought he was leaving the cop, for now, obviously, that was all talk. He's even planning to undercut Dirk once he meets the Turks. That's a suicidal move?"

"I agree with you, Wayne. If he has gone after the cop, we will hear something sooner or later. It's a waiting game, I'm afraid." Frank took solace in the nicotine hit, exhaling the smoke towards the ceiling.

"But we can't just sit back and watch him fuck everything up… Well, I'm not prepared to do that anyway. I'm going to get some contingencies in place."

Frank believed Wayne was just venting his anger through his last comment. He steered the conversation to Pete.

"My bent cop is stressing out. He's convinced someone has grassed him up to his boss."

"That's all we need. No doubt he'd grass you up to save his skin," Wayne said sitting on a bench, "Fucking hell, this is turning into a clusterfuck. I think I might just get on the boat with Dirk myself and fuck off."

"Don't worry. I'm watertight. I've got recordings of him arranging for me to send him money. I've covered my tracks well," Frank boasted.

"Maybe so, Frank, but I'd guess he probably has things up his sleeve. Maybe recordings too."

Frank felt a shiver; he'd completely overlooked that possibility. He poured himself another glass.

"If needs be, we can make contingencies as you say. Jason would do the same if this were the other way around. We can't tolerate a loose cannon. Let's see what happens over the next few hours and then save what we can from the wreckage. Don't be doing anything hasty, Wayne, we need to work together on this."

Twenty

Jason wiped his lips with a tissue, dropping the food packaging out of the car window. He felt thirsty again after eating the over-salted fries. The queue snaked out onto the road, and there was no way he was joining the line again just for a drink. The woman's strident voice taking the orders at the drive-thru intercom was too loud and repetitive, dulled only by the occasional boy racer over-revving an engine, causing gunshot like bangs from a big boar exhaust. Irritated by the cacophony and eager to get on with the job he'd decided to call Wayne, Jason had enjoyed winding him up by disappearing but decided he might require his help later on.

"You okay, Wayne, you're not still looking for your car, are you? Jason laughed.

"Where the fuck are you, Jason? I've got Dirk's boys all set to pick you up in the early hours of tomorrow morning." Wayne was thankful for the excuse to stop running and get his breath back; he sat down on the sand.

"Unfinished business, mate. I'll be back up there in no time. Take a chill pill, for fucks sake and remember who pays your fucking wages."

"Please tell me you're not going after the cop?"

"What's the matter with you, Wayne? He set me up and put me in Strangeways. He's going to pay for it. Do you expect me to walk away from it? You know it doesn't work like that."

"Maybe not, mate, but what's the rush? Our priority is to get you out of the country. Think it through; it's not worth the risk of getting caught and banged up again? Let's go back to the original plan," Wayne suggested.

"If only it were that easy, he humiliated me. I can't let it go, pal," Jason said, feeling no shame, as he watched a teenage employee wearing a hi-vis jacket picking up his food wrappers with a litter picker. Why was Wayne not getting it? He brooded.

"There's still time to put it on hold. I can arrange for the cop to be dealt with whilst you are out of the country."

Jason sensed that Wayne was starting to sound desperate. He was getting irritated by his faltering.

"You're not fucking listening Wayne, what he did was personal. I'll give you a bell when I'm on my way back." Jason ended the call and set off for the exit. There was a rough sleeper begging at the junction.

"Any spare change, mate," he said, looking up from his cardboard seating on the floor.

"Not for your next bag of heroin, you fucking skank," Jason spat out without looking at him.

He drove onto the housing estate and passed DS Lee McCann's apartment, there was still no sign of his car, and the flat looked like nobody was home. Jason parked up in the same place, on the other side of the road. The dense landscaped bushes provided adequate cover. He unfolded a newspaper and rested it on the steering wheel, giving the impression he was killing time waiting for someone. His plan depended on McCann arriving home at his usual time.

Jason wanted to keep it simple, short and sweet. Once he saw Lee McCann arrive, he would use the bushes as cover and follow him to the side door. He would pull the pistol on him and force him inside the flat. No witnesses, no chance of being disturbed. The cop wouldn't be missed until the following morning when he didn't show up for work. By which time Jason would be crossing the North Sea to safety. He took the pistol from his jacket pocket and gave it a final check. He looked around, and the estate was deserted, a burglars paradise.

Jason began taking steady breaths, in through the nose, out of the mouth. He closed his mind to other distractions and focused on his nemesis. There was no need to motivate himself. The need to revenge this guy was the only motivation he needed.

DI Andrea Statham switched off her computer. The main office was deadly quiet, as she had given her team an early finish. It was Friday afternoon, and they'd had a busy week. Andrea started packing up her things, ready for home. She was looking forward to starting the weekend with Lee in China Town later in the evening. She took a handful of mugs to the kitchen to wash up.

Earlier in the day, she had discreetly made Lee aware that she had no plans for the weekend. Lee came up trumps and suggested they could go out for dinner together.

Andrea wondered if Lee found her attractive or not. They got along well, and Andrea admitted to herself that she was fond of him. However, she wasn't going to rush things and spoil it, neither was he from the look of things.

Andrea was just about to put her coat on as her mobile started to ring. She looked at the display; it was the force intelligence unit. She sighed and answered the call.

"Good afternoon Ma'am, sorry to trouble you. We've just had some concerning intelligence come through. We can't rate it for credibility as it's from an anonymous source, through Crimestoppers."

"Go on," Andrea said, perplexed, as these types of urgent calls always seemed to come through on Friday afternoons when she had a weekend off. He continued to brief her on the intelligence regarding the threat to the life of DS Lee McCann and subsequent checks he'd undertaken on the databases to assess the intelligence.

"Lee's left the office, but he did say he was going home. Will you arrange for an urgent uniform response to his address?" It was an instruction rather than a question, "I will call him and arrange to meet up; then we can assess the threat more thoroughly once we know he's safe."

"Yes, I'll do that now, Ma'am."

"Keep me updated, please." Albeit the source of the intelligence was unknown, Andrea was immediately concerned for Lee's safety. She dialled his mobile, to be greeted with the line busy tone. She grabbed her coat and headed for the car park. Once again, Lee's mobile was engaged. Bloody typical, Andrea cursed.

Andrea telephoned Pete, "I've just received some intelligence. Hamilton is searching for Lee McCann as we speak. Now's the time to be straight with me and tell me if you can shed any light on this?"

"Bloody hell," Pete replied, "Where is Lee? Is he with you?"

"No, I gave him a flyer. He should be home by now. I've got a uniform patrol on their way, and I'm going to make my way there too. I'm taking this threat seriously. I'm going to get Lee accommodated out of the area until we can find Hamilton."

"Have you rung Lee?"

"Of course, I've bloody rang him, his phone is engaged."

"Is it credible intelligence?" Pete asked.

"Anonymous via Crimestoppers."

"I'll get onto Frank Burton. I'll get Hamilton's mobile number, then we can triangulate his phone."

"Phoning a friend Pete?" Andrea couldn't help herself from having a cheap dig. She hung up rather than waiting for an answer. It wasn't the time to get angry with Pete, but she would make him pay if it transpired he was involved in this.

Andrea left headquarters and crawled along in the late Friday afternoon rush hour traffic. Her suspicion of Pete's involvement with Burton was gnawing away at her as she drove. Never in a million years would she have expected Pete to go off the rails. His explanation of running Burton as an unofficial informant was flimsy. It was more likely that he was working with Burton, giving him the heads up on surveillance arrangements to make Hamilton's life easier. The thought of Pete succumbing to corruption made her feel sick.

She was getting impatient and went heavier on the gas, driving down some side streets navigating a well-known rat run. Was Lee not answering because he was already in trouble? She feared. "For god's sake, Pete! What have you done?" She exclaimed as she reached more stationary traffic at a red light, with no viable way to get past.

Twenty One

Jason glanced up from his newspaper as he heard a car approaching. A surge of adrenaline flowed through him. He could see two male figures sitting in the front seats of the SUV. It stopped outside the apartment. Oh shit, someone's dropping him off. Change of plan, I'll have to knock on the door once he's inside. The passenger walked to the rear of the car, then walked to the driver's window. After speaking with the driver, he walked towards the house next door. "It's not him," whispered Jason. The SUV was driven away, further into the estate. Jason slid down into his seat, refocussing his composure and re-inspecting his Baikal pistol once again. It was fully loaded with one in the chamber, ready to go. The same as it was when he checked it twenty minutes ago. He looked up and saw another car approaching the apartment. It turned off the road and reversed into the residents bay. Spontaneously Jason eased himself out of the driver's seat. Using the bushes as cover, he swiftly made his way towards the car and crouched watching, breathing heavily. Jason's heart was pumping fast. He was in the zone. It was time for revenge.

Jason got a glimpse of the driver in the wing mirror. It was him, no doubt about it this time. Come on, get out of the car, Jason urged his victim. Lee remained sitting in the driver's seat. He was talking on his phone. Jason stayed crouched down, watching, self-conscious of his behaviour looking dodgy and attracting unwanted attention. He glanced around, checking for any nosy neighbours. Jason started to feel angry at Lee's inactivity. He felt a primal urge to attack here and now. It was the first time he had been so close to Lee since they were arrested together at the motorway services.

The car door opened, and Lee stepped out, closing the door shut behind him. He was still chatting on his mobile phone, obviously in no rush. He strolled towards his apartment deep in conversation, oblivious to the danger that Jason presented.

Jason watched intently; the feeling of hatred inside him was palpable. He had waited a long time for this moment. He was itching to charge across the road and tackle Lee where he stood, but he had to be patient and wait until Lee reached the cover of the building line. Come on, you bastard, get a move on. The longer that Lee took, chatting and laughing on his phone, the angrier and more restless Jason became. He had the irrational thought that Lee was taking the piss out of him, making him wait. Jason glanced around, making sure there was still nobody around. The coast was clear.

He looked back towards Lee, and his heart nearly skipped a beat. Lee was no longer talking on the phone but staring back at him. Fuck he's seen me. Jason expected Lee to run away, but to his surprise, Lee started striding towards Jason. He looked perplexed. "What the fuck are you doing there?" Lee shouted.

Instinct kicked in, Jason launched himself forward from the edge of bushes, sprinting towards his prey. He experienced a feral surge of energy.

Lee looked shocked, as if the imminent threat had just registered. He shouted again, "What the fuck are you…" He didn't finish the question.

Jason dived into him with instinctive aggression, and they both hit the floor with force. Jason had the advantage of landing on top and started punching Lee repeatedly in the face. Lee looked winded and did his best to regain his composure whilst failing miserably to deflect the incoming blows.

Jason stood up and grabbed Lee's collar. Trying to drag him to his feet, "Get up, fucking get up." Jason fumbled about in his jacket pocket with his free hand. Relieved, he grasped the handle of the pistol and produced it from his pocket, pointing it at Lee's head. "Get up now," Jason shouted. Lee stumbled to his feet; he still looked to be in shock and pain from the sudden unsuspected onslaught.

"You're fucking pathetic, look at you. Open the door, or I'll shoot you here and now." It was an option Jason knew he couldn't risk taking. He needed to get him inside away from prying eyes.

"Fucking hell Jason, it wasn't personal. Have you lost the fucking plot?" Lee spat some blood from his mouth; his upper lip and nose were bleeding too. Jason was about to answer, but his attention was elsewhere, having heard the screeching of tyres. A police patrol car stopped less than twenty yards away. Two uniformed officers bounded out and walked purposefully towards them. Jason's grip on Lees collar tightened instinctively. He raised the pistol and pointed it into the side of Lee's head. He felt confused. It didn't make sense. What the hell were the cops doing here?

"Don't come any closer, or I'll kill him," Jason shouted to the advancing police officers.

"Okay, let's all take a minute; nobody needs to get hurt here," the uniform officer shouted, raising the palms of his hands in a defensive gesture. "Put the pistol down on the floor. We can sort this out peacefully," he continued. The other officer was talking into his radio. Jason suspected he would be requesting armed backup.

Jason surveyed the scene. His car was too far away; even if he could get to it, the cops would follow him and call in the helicopter. His only credible option was to get inside the apartment. The two cops retreated to the cover of their patrol car. One of them was still shouting, but it was just white noise to Jason. His focus was solely on survival.

"Jason, you've got time to getaway. Get out of here whilst you can. It's over. I'm not worth a life sentence," Lee's voice was calm and confident, the voice of reason. Jason looked him in the eyes and laughed.

"Like fuck it's over. I can shoot you and still escape, you coward."

Another police patrol car arrived and stopped behind the first one. Jason saw the officers take cover behind the first patrol car. The same officer as before shouted out again, "Put the pistol on the floor and kneel down. Nobody needs to get hurt here. Don't let this get out of control."

"It makes sense, Jason. It's over. You don't want to spend the rest of your days inside. Put the gun down," Lee pleaded.

"I'm fucked already. I might as well shoot you now." Jason pushed the pistol harder into the side of Lee's head. Lee winced with the additional pain and fear of death. Jason felt the strongest of urges to pull the trigger and then make a run for it. His finger tightened on the trigger. It took all of his willpower not to do so. He released his finger, knowing he couldn't trust himself with the impulse to blow Lee away.

He pushed Lee into the front door, his head almost smashing the glass panel. Lee fumbled with his keys; he had no other option but to open the door. They entered, and Jason slammed it shut behind them.

"I bet I'm the last person you expected to see today," Jason laughed manically, "Great, isn't it, Lee, payback time. Lie face down on the floor," Jason instructed, pushing Lee in the back. Lee fell to his knees then lay face down. Jason pulled some plastic-ties from his pocket and pulled Lee's wrists together. Jason felt euphoric.

"They're too tight; they'll cut off my circulation," Lee complained, grimacing because of the cutting pain in his wrists. His face pressed into the hard laminate flooring.

"That's just for starters." Jason stood back then kicked Lee in the ribs with such force that Jason suspected he'd broken a few. He stood back then kicked him again in the same place. Lee groaned, helpless, unable to defend himself.

Jason walked away and looked outside before closing the curtains. The patrol cars were still in situ, with blue lights flashing. He ruled out killing Lee and making a break for it. He needed to formulate a plan, but one thing was for sure, if he were to be arrested, it wouldn't happen before he'd shot Lee. He yanked Lee's head up by his hair, "You're going to wish you'd never set your eyes on me by the time I've finished with you." Jason sat on the sofa, planning his next move and staring at the pathetic figure lying in front of him.

Twenty Two

DI Andrea Statham was only two miles away, frustrated at the slow movement of traffic ahead of her. Listening to the events unfolding over the police radio had been a shock to her system. She had dealt with many sieges and hostage situations, but not one involving a police colleague as the victim. The initial situation report from the first response team and subsequent requests for armed response patrols, and the ominous presence of a police helicopter highlighted the magnitude of the situation. If only she had been quicker requesting the uniform response. They must have arrived only minutes too late. She couldn't shake off memories of laughing and joking with Lee, having a great time together. Better times, with no worries. Now she was worried sick, almost unable to believe or accept his life was in danger at the hands of Jason Hamilton. How had it come to this?

She turned into the housing estate, halting abruptly at the police crime scene tape stretched across the road from lamp post to lamp post. She got out of the car and approached the uniformed constable, standing at the police cordon. He looked sombre and gave Andrea a courteous nod of his head before lifting the tape for her to walk underneath. Andrea approached the three officers standing in cover behind the patrol car.

"Did you capture anything on your body camera?" Andrea asked.

"Yes, I can play it back for you. We didn't get too close for obvious reasons," the young policewoman said excitably.

Andrea watched in disbelief as the events unfolded. At first, she didn't recognise Hamilton because of his bleached hair, dark rings under his eyes and a pale pallor. He had the sinister look of a man who had spent time behind bars. She then saw Lee with a pistol to his head; his compliant inaction made him look unusually vulnerable. She felt a surge of anger and determination to get him out of there unharmed.

Irrationally she felt guilty about Lee's predicament, mainly as she knew that Hamilton was deranged enough to kill Lee. This predicament was like no other crime-in-action that she had dealt with; the pressure she was feeling was burdensome already.

Andrea turned around; the uniform sergeant was briefing and despatching other officers who had arrived in a personnel carrier. She felt relief at seeing an experienced sergeant who knew what he was doing without the need to be told, the kind of cop she needed on a job like this. Andrea headed towards him, "Long time no see, it's a nasty one, this bastard has got the potential to shoot him," Andrea said, unable to hide her concern.

"A wacko with a pistol, just what we need on a Friday afternoon."

"Have you commenced an evacuation of the houses in the immediate vicinity?"

"Yes, we've nearly finished, we have now secured the scene, and we've set up a visual containment. Someone was seen looking out of the front window and then closing the curtains. Nothing else other than that."

Andrea was just about to take stock and consider her other priority actions when she saw the firearms team arrive at the scene in a military-style 4 x 4. They didn't hang around, deploying to positions around the apartment immediately. The officers had their MP5 submachine guns pointed in readiness as they approached positions around the target address. Andrea felt assured that the uniform and armed officers now contained Hamilton in the property, and the local residents were safe. She wished she could conclude the same about Lee's safety.

Having arranged the armed containment, commencing negotiation with Hamilton was her next priority. She took a seat in the now unoccupied armed response vehicle and selected Lee from her contacts.

"DI Statham," Jason greeted with mocking courtesy, "Lee can't get to his phone right now; he's tied up," Jason laughed, "tied up literally and feeling very sorry himself."

"I need to speak to you, Jason. What's made you do this today?"

"I thought it would be a nice idea to catch up with Lee and kill him. I thought he would have put up a fight, but it's turned out he's a right little snivelling coward."

"Jason, I need you to calm down and consider the situation rationally. Do not harm Lee. I am asking you to sit down for a moment and think this through. There is nothing to be gained from harming Lee. I can offer you safe passage out of the address if you come out now, which is the best option for all of us."

"Yeah, that sounds like a really tempting deal. I'll be back in Strangeways in time for supper. You'll have to do better than that."

"Jason, don't let emotions and revenge influence you to make the wrong decision. You're an intelligent man, and it's your call, end this now and come out."

"I'm getting bored; you sound just the same as this snivelling little shit." Andrea was about to reply when she realised he had ended the call. She pressed re-dial, but the connection went to voicemail.

"Not so brave now, are you, Lee?" Jason sneered, "In fact, you look pretty pathetic right now," he goaded.

"Easy for you to say when you're holding a pistol, Jason." Jason pistol-whipped him against the side of his head. Lee instinctively rolled over onto his side, away from the blow, from his seated cross-legged position.

"God, that felt good. Maybe I should delay shooting you and let you enjoy more pain first." Jason continued to stand over him, pointing the pistol in Lee's direction. "The thing is, Lee, I was going to do the decent thing and just kill you, but things have changed. I wasn't expecting all your buddies to show up. Albeit, they're not much use, are they?" Lee kept his mouth shut tight. He sat still cross-legged and facing the wall.

"Keeping quiet, Lee? You're a quick learner," Jason laughed, "nice place you've got here. Who's the little girl?" Jason had picked up a framed photograph from the television.

"She's my daughter," Lee lied. It was, in fact, his niece. Jason replaced it and sat down in an armchair, running through options.

"Fuck it, let's get this over and done with." Jason walked back over to Lee and pressed the pistol roughly into the back of Lee's head. Lee screwed his eyes up, his body tense in anticipation of death. "Anything you want to say, Lee?"

"Yes, can I write a note to my daughter?"

"Can you fuck."

"If you remember, Jason, I tried to persuade you not to take out a contract on Ryan. We were only investigating you for dealing drugs. You fucked up. It had nothing to do with me. I told you it was a bad idea, but you ignored me."

"Shit, I didn't realise, Lee. I'd better let you go without further delay and self-flagellate myself for my penance."

Jason paced the room; his anxiety was growing as he accepted his chances of getting away were extremely slim. He knew the police would have the place covered. Jason had read about suicide-by-cop in the newspapers. He could kill Lee then point the gun at the police, who would respond to the threat by shooting him. Jason ruled it out, he didn't want to die, but he didn't want a life sentence for killing Lee either. He needed some time to think things through. The room felt like it was shrinking; the walls were closing in on him.

Twenty Three

The insignia on the police major incident vehicle reflected brightly under the yellow glow of the street lighting. It was a large, heavy goods vehicle containing a state of the art, self-contained incident command centre. Its white elephant like presence in its surroundings was imposing, turning a quiet suburban street into a scene from a television drama. It had been parked in a sterile outer cordon area near the junction with the main road. Andrea walked away from the two patrol cars, where ballistic screens now provided safer cover. The curtains of Lee's apartment had remained closed. The lack of contact with Hamilton was increasing the tension. Andrea had called Lee's mobile several times since her conversation with Hamilton, but it had diverted to voicemail each time. On each occasion, she had left a message requesting Jason to contact her, suggesting that they could sort things out without anyone getting hurt. Andrea wasn't surprised that Jason had declined the offer. She guessed he was unsure about his next move and needed time to think.

As she walked towards the major incident vehicle, her attention was taken by a bright light source on the far side of it, just outside the cordon. She could see a television media van with satellite dishes affixed to the roof. By the side of it, a familiar-looking news reporter was talking into a microphone, standing in the bright spotlight of the camera team's lighting equipment, reporting live from the scene. It amazed Andrea how quick the news corporations responded to significant incidents these days. Maybe it was to meet the public's expectation in this day and age of twenty-four hour news coverage. Together with a hunger for news updates came more demanding scrutiny of public authorities and police actions. Andrea knew it wouldn't be long before the force press office called her, requesting her to undertake media interviews. She had already decided to decline and delegate a 'talking head', probably the local Superintendent, to provide the usual textbook media release and assurance to the public. Giving such interviews didn't intimidate her; Andrea had done many. But her time was better utilised focusing on the job at hand, and besides, she detested being in the public spotlight. She nodded to the uniform police officer at the entrance and climbed the steps into the major incident vehicle meeting room.

The Chief Superintendent, Gareth Parkinson, welcomed her, "Good to see you, Andrea, albeit in unfortunate circumstances. Grab a coffee, and we can get started." Parkinson was a very slim, bespectacled, studious looking man with an almost nervous like disposition. He was tapping his pen on his folder, looking anxious to get the meeting started. He reminded Andrea of her old school headmaster at the all-girls grammar school.

"You too, Sir, evening everyone," she replied, looking at the faces around the table, with an apologetic smile. She sensed a tone of impatience in Parkinson's voice. Andrea was the last to arrive for the gold strategy meeting, which wasn't unusual. On this occasion, it was more likely to be tolerated by the others, who understood the demands upon her. She didn't feel the need to apologise. The Tactical Firearms Advisor, Hostage Negotiator Liaison Officer, North West Ambulance Manager and Force Press Officer were already seated.

Andrea placed a spoonful of instant coffee into a disposable paper cup and filled the cup with hot water from the boiler. She sat down next to the Chief Superintendent, the only spare seat available.

With the round of introductions completed, Andrea delivered a briefing of events. She provided a background of Hamilton's Organised Crime Group. From there, she gave a brief summary of the Smethurst and Smith murders, the infiltration operation by undercover officer Lee, and lastly, Hamilton's escape from prison. The gravity of the situation was written on the faces of all those present.

The firearms tactical advisor, Ollie, was next to speak. Andrea thought he looked intimidating and wouldn't want to be on the wrong side of him. He wouldn't have looked out of place in the England Rugby Union team. His short black hair and heavy black stubble matched his quasi-military uniform. He confirmed that there was a full armed containment surrounding the address. His manner brought an assured calmness and control to proceedings. He confirmed that the adjacent addresses in the street had been evacuated and that traffic was now diverted. The scene was now sterile and under police control.

"I'm unaware of any intelligence regarding what firearm he has in his possession. Can you shed any light for me, Andrea?" Ollie asked, looking up from his notes, pen poised.

"The only confirmed weapon is the pistol he was holding to Lee's head. It does seem to be his weapon of choice. We have no other information, sorry."

The Detective on the live-link television monitor introduced herself as DC Nadia Khan from the intelligence cell, based at force headquarters. Nadia confirmed that the negotiators had two active phone lines into the address at present. DS Lee McCann's mobile and his landline number. "I'm working on telephony lines of enquiry to establish the number of Hamilton's mobile phone too," she added.

"Good point, his OCG are ruthless. They successfully got him out of prison and may intend rescuing him from here," Andrea said, dreading the thought of a gun battle in the street.

"I'll get another team allocated to ensure we've got the numbers to cover that eventuality," Ollie responded.

"We have several covert lines of investigation underway to establish any communications between Hamilton and his associates," Nadia added.

"Well, it looks like we have covered all our bases to allow the negotiators to work their magic," Mr Parkinson said, "Let's get DS McCann to safety as soon as possible, team. We will continue with a strategy of negotiation whilst maintaining a contingency of immediate action to undertake an armed entry if required. Ollie, can we speak outside of this meeting regarding the threat of a rescue attempt by his associates." Andrea smiled politely.

Whenever she had worked with Parkinson previously, she had found him to be hard work, hence her nickname for him, FHW. He avoided decision making whenever he could or took the most risk-averse option. His rationale always gave her the impression that his main objective was damage limitation to keep his hands clean and enhance his promotion prospects.

Andrea walked down the steps from the Incident room. Caroline, the Hostage Negotiation Liaison Officer, caught up with her.

"Hey, Andrea, how are you doing?" Andrea watched enviously as Caroline lit a cigarette. The smell wafted over to Andrea like an old friend showing up unexpectedly to help out.

"I'm fine. I hope Lee's okay in there; Hamilton is a right psycho." She looked around in fear of being in earshot of the press pack, relieved to see that the cordon had provided a safe distance from any unwanted eavesdroppers.

"He's gone for it this time. What the hell is he trying to achieve by taking Lee hostage?" Caroline said, "Escaping from prison wasn't enough for him."

"That's what scares me; we now have him backed into a corner. I guess that makes him even more dangerous and unpredictable. He's ruthless enough to shoot him without giving it a second thought." Andrea felt worried sick to the pit of her stomach for Lee, but her professionalism and determination motivated her to keep focused on the task at hand.

"Are you free to come and meet with the negotiators? You can sign off on the strategy if you're happy with it."

"Good idea." They stepped back into the truck and entered the adjoining annexe-room from the main area. It was signed 'No Entry – Negotiation Cell' on the door. Andrea closed the door behind her. She was glad to see Gaz and Becca, two very experienced negotiators with years of investigative experience. The room was prepared and ready to go. Most of the wall space was taken up with notice boards and information, critical to a successful negotiation outcome.

"How's it going?" Andrea asked.

"All good ta, we've just had the latest briefing from the intelligence cell. I've put in a request for DS Pete

Higgs to contact us. He interviewed Hamilton when he was in custody; he might have some useful pointers for us," Gaz said.

"Good thinking," Andrea replied, she hadn't had time to think about her dilemma with Pete, that was on the back burner for now, "I've got the details of Kirsty, his ex-partner and Frank Burton, the solicitor who represents him in case they can be of use." Andrea handed a piece of paper to Caroline.

"We've been putting calls into the address, but he doesn't want to talk at the moment. My priority is to get proof of life for Lee. We've also got a dedicated two-way secure phone which we can deliver to the address if needed," Caroline said.

"It's time for the next call," Becca announced.

"Crack on; I'll stay quiet in the background," Andrea said, taking a seat alongside Caroline at the other side of the room.

"What the fuck do you want now?" Andrea would have recognised that voice anywhere... she despised it. She felt a chill down her spine and a feeling of contempt for him.

"Is that Jason?" Gaz enquired.

"Yeah, who the fuck do you think it is? who the fuck are you?"

"Jason, my name is Gaz. I'm a negotiator, and I want us to sort out this situation together. I understand DS Lee McCann is in there with you. I need to know if he is okay. Can I talk to him, please?"

"You'll have a job unless you're clairvoyant. Lee's dead!" Hamilton laughed menacingly... "You still there, Gaz? You've gone quiet. I guess you've arrived too late this time, pal."

"Jason, what's happened in there? What have you done to him? I need to get paramedics to him if he's injured."

Jason had ended the call. Gaz dialled the number immediately. No answer. He continued to re-dial the number but each time it went to voicemail.

"He's got to be bluffing," Andrea whispered to Caroline, sitting forwards, whilst Gaz was redialling the number. Andrea felt tense; she tried to relax her shoulders and sat back in the chair.

"We'd have heard a gunshot, surely?" Caroline replied.

The phone was answered on the fourth attempt.

"Is that you again, Gaz? You're worse than my fucking Mrs for pecking my head. What do you want now?"

"Jason, have you harmed Lee?"

"No, not yet. I was just fucking with you. Calm yourself down."

"Can I speak to him Jason, I need to know he's okay?"

"Are you okay, Lee?" Shouted Jason.

"I've been better," Lee shouted towards the phone held out by Jason, looking over his shoulder, best he could. A tangible sense of relief filled the negotiation room. Andrea leaned forward and rubbed the back of her neck, soothing the stiffness.

"Thank god for that," Caroline whispered.

"There you go, Gaz, you happy now? Me and Lee are going to settle down and watch Coronation Street. We've got lots to catch up on over a beer. Lee got me sent down, you know? What do they call it Lee? Agent provocateur? He's a fucking snake this one, Gaz. Don't turn your back on him."

"Whatever he's done or not done, hurting him won't help you, Jason. You could walk out now if you chose to. It would be a good move."

"Don't think so Gaz, one last thing, though, don't be thinking of storming this place. If I hear a peep from outside, you will force me to shoot him. Don't back me into a corner." The line went dead from Jason's end. Gaz took a drink of his water, satisfied with his first proper contact.

"He's a right charmer, isn't he?" Becca said to no one in particular whilst writing in her logbook. Andrea walked into the main room and made coffees for the negotiators. She placed an additional spoonful in her drink. Caffeine was the only thing stopping her from succumbing to the growing urge for a cigarette. She could still smell the smoke from Caroline's last cigarette.

Andrea handed out the coffees, "Nice one, Gaz, that was a good start, thank you, mate," she said, and stepped out of the vehicle for some fresh air, where she stood sipping her drink by the steps.

Ollie, the firearms tactical advisor, followed her outside. He had been going over the fine-grain detail and immediate action drills with the Chief Superintendent.

"He's just signed off the firearms authorisation document. He looks like he'd rather be elsewhere," Ollie laughed.

"Wouldn't we all, especially Lee," Andrea replied.

"I've just requested another firearms team to form an additional outer cordon. If Hamilton's cronies have sprung him from prison custody, I wouldn't put it past them to have another go here."

"He's got the connections for sure. I hope Lee's okay in there. The tech guys will be arriving soon.

Once they install some live visual and audio feeds into the apartment, we'll have a better idea of what we're up against," Andrea said, glancing at her watch, feeling like time was flying by.

"I suppose if he wanted him dead, he would have shot him already," Ollie said reassuringly, "Hopefully, he's just dragging it out to be in control and mess us all about for a few days."

"I hope you're right. Lee's a bright copper, and he knows what to do to increase his chances of survival."

Andrea took her empty cup into the trailer and used every ounce of willpower not to ask Caroline for a cigarette.

Twenty Four

"I'm considering going out with a bang Lee. I'm backed into a corner here. Probably best to go out all guns blazing. I could give your colleagues something to have nightmares about, something they'll never forget, no matter how hard they try. I could take you outside and kill you live on television, maybe take out a few cops too. They'll return fire, and I'll be dead. It's got to be a better option than getting banged up again."

"You don't need to kill me, Jason. It's your best option, not to. You'll probably only get a ten stretch for this and serve four if you let me go. If you kill me, you won't see the light of day again. We both know you don't want to die." Lee was still sitting cross-legged on the floor, facing the wall. His voice was low, meek and calm. Jason was sitting on the sofa directly behind him on the other side of the lounge. Jason considered what Lee had said. He sounded as pathetic as he looked. Seeing him in such a sorrowful state diminished Jason's appetite to kill Lee, albeit Jason was thriving on Lee's fear.

"Suicide by cop, it sounds sinister, doesn't it. Live on television, or would it be too graphic to show?" Jason mused aloud.

"We're not that different, you and me. I came out of the army and could have gone the same way as Wayne, working for somebody like you and climbing my way up to the top. I just chose a different team, and we clashed. It was nothing personal for me; I'd never heard of you before. I was just carrying out orders from above. You're no different, Jason; we are both using our skills to get a job done. You have decided who lives and who dies. The lad on the canal and Carl Smith are just two I know of… You must have known the cops would have come after you sooner or later; it's an occupational hazard in your business. You put yourself in Strangeways, not me, nobody else, you."

"Quite philosophical Lee, they say the mind grows in focus and clarity when death is imminent. Are you ex-special forces? Or was that bullshit too? You fucking Walter Mitty." Jason flicked a drinks coaster which hit Lee on the back of his head; Lee didn't flinch.

"Ten years in the Paras," Lee whispered, head tilted down.

"So, you must have trained for shit like this to happen. Being captured by the enemy and paraded on television. Sat wearing an orange boiler suit. Are you working on an escape plan, sussing me out, looking for weaknesses?"

"I've already told you we can both get out. There's no need for either of us to die. I can help you get away."

"And how the fuck do we do that, dig a fucking tunnel?" Jason asked mockingly.

"We create a diversion," Lee didn't miss a beat, then paused, "A distraction which gives you the best chance to slip away whilst the cops are busy focused elsewhere." Jason was curious, and he didn't want to die for sure. His suicide by cop plan was intended as psychological intimidation, nothing more. He was willing to listen but didn't want to look too keen. He was still enjoying the experience of Lee staring into the face of death.

"I need a beer. Have you got any in the fridge?" Jason asked.

"Yeah, help yourself."

"Very kind of you Lee, I think I will. Roll over and lie face down, so I can see you from the kitchen." Lee groaned in pain as he repositioned himself. Jason laughed at his obvious discomfort, "How are your ribs?" Lee didn't answer.

Jason returned from the kitchen to the sofa with a can of lager. He took a mouthful. "Back against the wall, same position as before," he commanded. Lee slowly manoeuvred himself into the crossed leg position.

"So… do we start planning your escape?" Lee suggested.

"I've not decided yet. I might just shoot you in the back of your head and take my chances. You fucked me over, Lee; there's got to be payback. It's the way these things work."

"Have you seen the news on television?" Frank Burton asked before taking a long drag on his cigarette. He exhaled into the dimly lit room, beyond the light from the desk lamp.

"No, I'm out. What's happening?" Wayne could only just hear Burton on his mobile phone due to the noise of the wind on the beach. He was out walking, a welcome distraction to his current predicament.

"There's a siege at the cop's address in Chadderton. I think Jason might have messed up again. They've not released any names or details, but it's got to be him. A witness has been interviewed on television; she says two men were fighting on a driveway. One produced a pistol and dragged the other man into the flat. He's lost the plot good and proper this time. Even by Jason's standards, this is a shit show. How the hell does he expect to get away?" Frank took the last drag and stubbed the cigarette into the ashtray on his desk. He sounded battle weary.

"What the hell. Have you spoken to Jason?" Wayne had turned about spontaneously and headed back towards the lodge; his footsteps in the sand felt heavy.

"No, and I won't be taking any calls either. The cops will be monitoring them," Frank said, wearily, as if distancing himself from Jason's actions.

"That's okay; you're his solicitor. It's legitimate to speak to him."

"I suppose so." Frank realised in hindsight that ditching his burner phone wasn't a good idea. Jason now had no way of contacting him other than by calling his legitimate business phone.

"I'll drive back over to Manchester, just in case he does manage to get out of there in one piece. I'm bored of making sandcastles now, and the takeaways aren't up to much here."

"What about Dirk?"

"That's on hold for now. I didn't want to mess the Dutch boys about. I told Dirk that Jason had taken a turn for the worse."

"Okay, keep in touch." Frank ended the call and lit another cigarette. He walked from his desk to the window and eyed a single streetlight in the deserted street. The peaceful monochrome scene was in stark contrast to his life right now.

Frank walked across the office and took a seat on the red leather Chesterfield sofa. The news channel was now showing the reporter's initial update for the third time. Frank was looking at the television screen but not watching or listening. Just smoking and thinking; would it be a bad thing if Jason got shot? It was a realistic outcome. How else was this going to end? Jason would not fancy another stretch inside for sure. Whatever the outcome, Frank knew he needed to be closer to the action whilst the events unfolded. There was a call he needed to make.

"DI Andrea Statham."

"Hello Inspector, it's Frank Burton. Just a quick call to let you know I've been unable to locate Jason Hamilton. I thought he would have called me by now, but it's a negative result, I'm afraid."

"Are you playing games with me, Frank?" Andrea asked, stepping back into the major incident vehicle.

"What do you mean?" Frank stammered, trying to sound sincere and bewildered.

"Your client is busy holding a hostage at gunpoint. But I'm sure you already know that."

"Steady on Inspector. I've just got back from meetings. What the hell is going on?"

"Switch the news channel on, Frank. It may be worth meeting me here to assist your client. I've got negotiators speaking to him right now." Andrea gave him the address and ended the call.

Frank smiled to himself. He had rattled her cage but also received the invite that he sought. Frank didn't need to watch any more of the news. He left the office and headed for his car. He knew the location of where he was heading already.

Twenty Five

"I'll leave you with it, Andrea. I need to go back to the station. I'm senior command cover today, and I've got quite a few plates spinning already. Give me a call on the mobile if you need me for anything. I think we've got everything covered for now," Chief Superintendent Parkinson stood up, slid his chair under the table and grabbed his green wax jacket from the coat hook. Andrea smiled, relieved that he was on his way, allowing her to crack on with the job.

"No worries, Sir, I'll keep you updated, but I won't call you unless it's necessary." Andrea wasn't sure whether it was just her cynicism, but she sensed Parkinson looked like he couldn't wait to put some distance between himself and the incident room; he certainly had a spring in his step as he left.

"Speak to you later," he called over his shoulder. This time Andrea didn't look up as he left the major incident room. She was engrossed in writing her operational decisions and subsequent actions in her policy book, grabbing a moment whilst she could. She felt a calming effect from the silence of the room. Her notes were almost up to date when DC's Walsh and Nolan, the technical surveillance detectives, arrived.

"Come in, guys, take a seat." The two detectives in plain clothes took a seat at the table. Andrea had worked with them many times over the years and knew she could rely on them.

"This is a nightmare, Ma'am. Have we got any update on DS McCann?" DC Walsh asked earnestly. He was a conscientious and intense detective. Andrea didn't recall ever engaging in small talk with him. He took his glasses off and wiped them with a tissue whilst holding Andrea's gaze.

"He sounded as well as could be expected in the circumstances. It seems calm in there at the moment. Nothing has changed since I briefed you earlier on the telephone. We have permission from the owners of the adjacent flat to use their premises. My priority is for you to install a listening device asap. That's essential for the negotiators and the Firearms commander. Once that is done, a live video feed from inside the flat would be next on my wish list. The sooner, the better, no pressure."

"We're good to go, Ma'am. The surveillance application document has been authorised, and I've agreed on a protocol with the firearms commander for our safe entry to the building," DC Walsh said.

"Could I have a quick look at the surveillance authority?" Andrea asked. DC Walsh handed the papers to her. Andrea was meticulous. She couldn't afford any mistakes; an error in the document could mean critical evidence being ruled inadmissible later down the line at court.

"That's a copy Ma'am; you can keep it for your records. Do we know which room they're in at the moment?"

"I'm not one hundred per cent sure, but I suspect the lounge. The curtains were closed not long after they went in, and someone has looked from behind them a few times," Andrea replied.

"Our van is parked behind the incident command truck. We'll run the live feed to there if that's okay with you. There's room for a member of your staff to monitor the feed if you like."

"Thank you, keep me up to speed, fellas." Andrea felt relieved that they were about to get on with the job. The live feed would provide invaluable insight and assist her with future decision making.

Frank Burton parked his car on the main road, a hundred metres short of the junction. He could see bright lights ahead in the darkness, illuminating a police major incident lorry and other police vehicles parked up nearby. He checked his pockets and made sure the only mobile he had on him was his legitimate business phone. He walked along the roadside until he reached the police cordon tape.

"Good Evening, I'm here to see DI Andrea Statham. I'm Frank Burton, Hamilton's solicitor."

"I'll give her a call," The uniform police officer replied gruffly.

"Hold on; I'm going to have a cigarette first." Burton proffered his packet to the officer, who took a cigarette. Burton lit the officers cigarette, then his own. "Let's hope we can get this sorted; Christ knows what he's thinking," Frank said, shaking his head.

"He needs to give himself up. It's as simple as that," the officer replied.

"I'll do whatever I can to make sure we get the officer out safe and well. I may represent Hamilton, but I don't want to see the officer come to any harm." They smoked their cigarettes in sombre silence.

"What's the latest update from inside the flat?" Frank broke the silence, trying his luck to obtain a bit of inside information.

"Above my pay grade, pal, I'm just the hired security tonight." The officer looked like he had a good few years of experience under his belt. A cigarette wasn't going to influence him into opening up to a defence solicitor.

"Bit of a clusterfuck, Frank," DS Pete Higgs announced as he approached them at the cordon. Burton looked around, surprised to see DS Higgs. "What's this? Smoker's corner," Pete said, wafting his hand before his face.

"Indeed, Peter, clusterfuck is an apt description; the sooner we can sort it out, the better," Frank said. Pete acknowledged the uniform officer with a nod and held out his warrant card for inspection.

"I'll take him through with me." The officer lifted the cordon tape, and they made their way inside the sterile area. Pete stopped short of the Major Incident truck and turned to face Frank Burton. "I'll be honest with you, Frank, I hope he gives the firearms officers justification to shoot him. He's gone way too far this time. Lee McCann was just doing his job, for fucks sake. I thought you said Hamilton was riding off into the sunset?"

"I'm not going to disagree, Peter; it would certainly make life easier for us all if Jason disappeared. It would appear he's gone into self-destruct mode. I'm as shocked as you are, seriously. I thought I had made him see sense."

"We've got to do all we can to make sure Lee comes to no harm. We need to work together here, Frank. We can sort this out and keep ourselves out of trouble whilst we're at it. Don't let Hamilton drag us down with him."

Pete headed up the steps into the incident room, followed by Frank.

"We'll go and get started," DC Nolan said. DS Pete Higgs almost bumped into them at the doorway.

"Fellas, I need to speak to you before you deploy to the address. I'll see you at your van in a minute." DS Higgs said.

"Okay, Pete, don't be long. We need to get moving," DC Walsh said.

Andrea gave the DC's time to leave, "Arriving together gents, very cosy," Andrea intended her words to be as cutting as they sounded. She watched carefully for their reaction. Frank remained deadpan whilst Pete looked at her with disbelief. Andrea couldn't help herself; she wanted them to know that she was onto them, and more importantly, that she wasn't shying away from confronting the issue.

"Close the door, Pete, take a seat, gents. Thanks for coming Frank, I hope we're on the same song sheet here. We need to make sure we get Lee McCann out of this situation unharmed. We need to work together, I don't expect you to compromise your client, but we need your help."

"I will do all that I can to assist Inspector." Andrea's skin crawled, Burton's mock sincerity made her cringe.

"Let's cut to the chase, Frank. What does he want out of this? What is he hoping to achieve? Do you think he intends to kill Lee?"

"Firstly, I didn't have a clue he was planning any type of revenge against the undercover officer. I can't answer any of those questions, I'm afraid," Frank replied eagerly.

"Let's be straight here," Pete interjected, "Of course, he is capable of killing Lee. He's looking at life in prison if he does, and he doesn't want that. He has a point to make. Hamilton doesn't want to lose face, and he will not be in a hurry to come out of there. We need to give the negotiators a chance; it's our best option. I think he would have killed him already if that was his intention," Pete said.

"Frank, would you be willing to speak to the negotiation liaison officer? They will need an idea of what may calm him down or what will wind him up and other personality stuff."

"Yes, of course, happy to help. I'll just have a cigarette first," Frank agreed.

"I'll go and get Caroline," Andrea said as she headed for the negotiation room. Pete seized the opportunity and left the truck, following behind Frank.

Pete joined Frank at the side of the major incident vehicle, in the shadows, out of sight.

"Will they want me to speak to Jason?" Frank asked after exhaling a cloud of smoke.

"I doubt it, but it's an option for later down the line, I suppose. You need to assist the negotiators with information, Frank."

"Are you sure? Life would be a lot easier without Jason here to go off the rails every ten minutes."

"We helped to get Lee McCann into this mess. It's only right to help him out of it."

"Steady on, Peter, my conscience is clear. I talked him out of it, and he made alternative plans with his cronies. This is the last thing I expected him to do."

"You gave him the fucking address."

"Indeed, but only after it was provided to me by your good self," Frank reminded him.

"And that's why we need to help the poor bastard. Anyway, we aren't going to help him going around

210

the houses here. I've got a plan; I'm going off-piste with this one. Andrea will go ballistic when she discovers what I'm up to, but it's worth the risk.

"What the hell are you going to do?"

"No time to explain, Frank. You get back in there and help Caroline. Keep your phone switched on. I may need to call you." Frank stepped back into the major incident room. Caroline was sitting at the table, waiting alongside Andrea.

"Sorry, I just needed a quick cigarette."

"No problem, Frank, I need some background information on Jason." Caroline went on to quiz Frank Burton about his client.

Pete walked over to the technical officer's van. He felt like he was experiencing an out-of-body experience. He was trying to reconcile that his plan of action was the right thing to do and struggling to justify it to himself. All his years of training and experience in the job weighed upon him not to do it. It was a massive personal risk, reckless and certainly against every protocol in the book. If all went to plan, he'd get himself into deep shit. But he had to get Lee out of there, and if he did, that would be his mitigation.

Twenty Six

"Can I change position? My legs have gone dead," Lee groaned, wincing at his discomfort, wriggling about on the floor.

"Same as before, lie face down." Jason stood and pointed the pistol at Lee from a safe distance. He didn't want to take any chances and knew that if the opportunity arose to overpower him, Lee would grab it with both hands. Jason still regarded him as a potential threat, even in his current debilitated state. Lee flinched as he rolled onto his front. Jason removed a pillar case from a sofa cushion and roughly dragged it over Lee's head. Lee lifted his head from the floor, acquiescing without saying a word. Jason knelt on Lee's back and checked the plastic ties; he could see they were digging into his skin, causing a raw redness. He continued to tighten them anyway.

Jason stood and looked around the room. It was minimalist; two brown leather sofas, fireplace, flat-screen television, bookshelves and a cupboard. Jason pulled out an electrical extension lead from behind the television and bound Lee's ankles together.

"That's better. I can relax a little more now."

"I won't be trying anything on Jason; you've got the pistol. I'm not mad." Jason smiled. He suspected Lee was trying to tick all the psychological survival boxes, staying in the conversation, behaving in a non-threatening manner and seeking to create a human bond.

"That's good to hear, Lee, but unfortunately, I can't believe a fucking word you say. You've stitched me up once, remember. You fucking snake."

"Jason, it wasn't personal. How many more times do I need to tell you! I was following orders. It's my job. It's how I pay my mortgage."

"Oh, that's alright then…" Jason was interrupted by the ring tone on Lee's phone.

"Hello."

"Jason, it's Gaz, the negotiator. Are you both okay in there?"

"Nice of you to call and ask Gaz. As it happens, we're fine and dandy. Lee's having a lie-down, and I'm pointing a pistol at his head."

"Jason, please don't point the pistol at him. We can resolve this without anyone getting hurt. Shooting Lee won't help your situation. It's not the answer."

"Maybe not Gaz, but it'll make me feel pretty good. I'll be buzzing."

"Why don't you let Lee leave the flat now? You and I can then discuss the next move, getting you both out safely and unharmed. Letting him out is a game-changer for you and will be looked upon favourably by the courts. Surely you don't want to spend the rest of your days in prison?"

Jason petulantly changed the subject. "Gaz, we're starving in here. Send us some takeaway pizza whilst I think things over." Jason hung up, shaking his head.

"Gaz doesn't want me to shoot you, Lee. Do you know him?"

"No, he's right, though. You've made your point, and we all know you could kill me if you wanted to. But you don't need to, Jason. I don't want to die, and I'm sure you don't want to be inside forever. I'm at your mercy, and I know that… you've made your point."

"Fuck me, Lee, shut up. You're going to have me in tears if you carry on," Jason scoffed.

"I'm talking sense, and you know I am. You need to sort things out with Kirsty. From what I saw, she's your soul mate, and she thinks the world of you. Don't mess that up by killing me. You two could have a great life together."

"I've got to give you credit for your hard sell, but things aren't that easy. What are you suggesting? I put a request into the prison governor for a relocation to the honeymoon suite and move her in?"

"It's down to you, Jason; you can retrieve this situation if you want to. You don't need me to tell you that."

Jason sat back on the sofa. He was thinking about Kirsty. Their enforced sabbatical hadn't been as easy to deal with as he had anticipated. He had even been swaying towards inviting her to Turkey at some point to start a new life. Perhaps she was his soulmate after all. He felt like he couldn't live with her but couldn't live without her either.

The last few days were catching up with him. He felt exhausted. For the first time, he felt regret at not sticking to Wayne's plan to get him out of the country.

"You mentioned a distraction; what sort of distraction did you have in mind?" Jason asked, becoming more curious about what Lee had planned.

"We've got plenty of time to work out the finer detail, and I'm not saying it's going to be easy. If I ran out of the front door making a scene, you could slip out of the utility room door. Whilst the attention is on me. In no time at all, you could get to the electricity substation, which would provide cover. You could then squeeze down the side and into the garden at the back. Then if you're quick enough, you're gone. It's down to you then. Can you arrange for a getaway car to pick you up?"

"Fuck me," Jason laughed sarcastically. I thought you were serious when you said you had a plan. You're having a laugh. I'd be a sitting duck, especially when you tell them which way I've gone."

"But I wouldn't, would I?... If you let me out of here, I'd stay quiet. I'd do that in return for you deciding not to kill me. It's a win-win for both of us, and we'll be quits. I don't want you coming after me again in years to come."

"I'd still be up against it," Jason mused aloud, but the gnawing thought of letting Lee live in return for him getting away was becoming a temptation, his hunger for revenge was dissipating whilst his desire for freedom was growing.

"I know you would, but it is what it is; we're surrounded by armed cops, for Christ's sake. You aren't going to get a helicopter lift out of here, are you? it's not a blockbuster Hollywood movie?"

"How about I just blow your fucking brains out and then threaten the cops, so they shoot me. End of story. That might become a Hollywood blockbuster." Jason felt irritated at Lee's feeble plan. He'd hoped for something better. He could feel his anger rising, "I know what you're trying to do, Lee. I'm not stupid. You're setting me up to fail." Jason didn't want to show his growing enthusiasm for the option of getting out of here. He needed time to consider his options, and he had plenty of time.

"That's not true Jason, just like me, I don't think you're ready to die yet," Lee continued, like a dripping tap, creating more uncertainty for Jason. Jason reflected on the last sentence and reluctantly accepted that Lee was right. Bizarrely he trusted Lee to keep his side of the deal.

"The other option is me going out of the utility room door and you running out of the front door, it's a lot riskier, but you could be inside my car within five seconds," Lee laughed.

"Yes, and shot on sight, you fucking idiot, are you serious?" Jason said seeing the funny side.

"Give the first option some thought. I don't think the cops will have a line of sight at the back of the sub-station. It would be as if you had literally disappeared, and by the time the police worked out what had happened, you'd be long gone. You stand a good chance. It's your only realistic option of escape. Although you still have the option of letting me walk out and you having five years added on to your sentence, you'd be out before you were fifty. We both know you could handle that time and still run your business from inside. You don't need to kill me. You could have a new start with Kirsty once you're released," Lee continued to reason.

Jason knew what Lee was doing. It was all about self-preservation. But even so, Jason was finding his influence hard to ignore. He accepted his original plan to shoot him and get away was history. Jason didn't want to die, but he didn't want to go back inside either. His head was feeling foggy with tiredness.

"Okay, Lee, shut the fuck up, that's enough for now. Don't bore me too much, or I might shoot you out of desperation, just to save my sanity," Jason said standing up and pacing the room. He was feeling tired but restless.

Lee's mobile phone started to ring.

"Jason, it's Gaz. I've managed to arrange a food delivery for you. In return, I'd like to talk some more about helping you to sort this situation out without anyone getting hurt."

"What food have you got?" Jason asked, sidestepping the prompt to discuss releasing Lee.

"Takeaway pizza. When we've finished this call, armed officers will approach the front door and place the food down on the doorstep. They will then leave. Once they are back in cover behind the police cars, I will call you; at that point, you can collect the food."

"Yeah, okay, tell them to hurry up, will you."

"Stay away from the windows and doors. Do not approach the armed officers. If you present a threat, it could result in you getting shot," Gaz confirmed that Jason understood the instructions and ended the call.

"Right, Lee, let's take the pillowcase off your head, stand up. You'll be my cover when I collect the pizza, don't try anything on. I'll be stood right behind you with the pistol. Don't give me the excuse to shoot you. I won't need much persuasion."

Lee followed the instruction. Jason sniggered at the sight of Lee shuffling along with his ankles bound together.

"Fucking hell Lee, I should have filmed that; you look comical. A far cry from your days in the Paras. It would go viral on social media." Lee didn't reply. He paused behind the front door, waiting for the next instruction.

The phone rang, "The food is outside, Jason. I'll give you half an hour to eat, then I'll call you. It's in all our best interests to resolve this peacefully."

"Okay, Gaz, I need you to call my solicitor, Frank Burton. I want him representing me out there. I'll need to speak to him at some stage tonight."

"I'll try to sort it out, Jason," Gaz said and ended the call. Jason opened the door a fraction.

"Stand in the gap," Jason instructed. Lee squeezed into the gap, which Jason kept tight with his foot, the pistol pointing at Lee's head.

Jason looked over Lee's shoulder. He saw armed police officers with MP3 machine guns pointing right at him. He felt intimidated and withdrew further back. The helmets, goggles and ballistic armour gave them a sinister, intimidating appearance. Jason was under no illusion, he knew the armed officers were probably itching for justification to get a headshot and take him out. He had hurt one of their own.

Bright spotlights were pointing towards the apartment. The scene before Jason felt surreal. He felt a mad impulse to open fire on them but knew it would be an act of self-destruction. He removed his finger from the trigger as a precaution to the temptation.

"Jason, you need to release Lee now. Tell him to walk towards us," a voice boomed from behind the ballistic shields.

"I don't fucking think so," Jason shouted back. He crouched down and grabbed the pizza boxes, shoving Lee out of the way. Jason slammed the door shut. The smell of freshly cooked takeaway pizza filled the hallway. Jason began to salivate in anticipation of the feast.

"Right, get back into the lounge, food time," Jason laughed as Lee shuffled ahead of him. He was lapping up Lee's humiliation.

"Back into the same place, you can eat when I've finished, if there's anything left." Lee adopted his seated position facing the wall. Jason sat on the sofa and opened the cardboard box taking out the first piece, snapping the stringy mozzarella cheese free from the other piece. Albeit the pizza was lukewarm, Jason devoured each piece like he'd not eaten for days. Once he'd had enough, he roughly fed Lee a couple of the remaining slices, causing as much discomfort as possible, almost choking him and sniggering at Lee's humiliation.

DS Pete Higgs knocked on the side door of the van. The door slid open, DC's Nolan and Walsh were inside prepping their kit. Pete stepped inside, and DC Nolan slid the door shut. The van vibrated as the door banged closed.

"It's cosy in here. How's it going, fellas?" Pete asked, squeezing in amongst the storage boxes and wall-mounted screens.

"We're good to go, pal. The firearms team are going to escort us in through the gardens from two houses away. We'll get into the flat next door and take it from there. It should be a straightforward job. These new builds make life easy. It's just breeze block and plasterboard we're drilling through," DC Walsh said.

"Excellent, I'll carry some of your kit, if you like? DI Statham wants me to go with you," Pete lied.

"How come? We usually work alone," DC Walsh sounded disgruntled.

"Safety in numbers, I suppose, I will be your eyes and ears whilst you focus on setting up the surveillance kit," Pete replied, not taking any notice of DC Walsh's obvious displeasure.

"Fair enough," DC Nolan shrugged in conciliation; Pete was relieved that Walsh hadn't taken his protest to Andrea. Pete grabbed one of their black cargo bags and led the way to the firearms team rendezvous point. He needed to move fast and get the show on the road before DI Statham got wind of what he was doing.

They walked further down the road, escorted by four firearms officers armed with MP3's. Having passed the next two houses beyond the target address, they walked along the driveway into the rear garden. Pete was feeling a mixture of excitement and anxiety, half of him wanted to abort the mission, but the other half was determined to rescue Lee. He slowly continued behind the defensive huddle of the firearms officers and the tech lads. They stepped through the gaps left by the removed fencing panels and walked slowly and quietly through to the darkness of the next garden. The trees and bushes in the garden formed dark, sinister shapes watching over them. At the far side of the second garden, they reached the rear door of the flat next door to Lee's place.

Two of the firearms officers entered the building, and the remaining two took defensive positions on either side of the door. The tech guys and Pete followed on into the building, joined afterwards by the remaining two firearms officers. The door was closed quietly behind them.

"I know I'm teaching you fellas to suck eggs but maintain total silence, please. We don't want Hamilton to realise we're in here," DC Walsh whispered.

"Okay, we'll go and sit in the kitchen and keep out of your way," The firearms sergeant said in a low voice. The four of them filed out of the lounge and into the kitchen.   Pete Higgs stood back and watched DC Nolan and DC Walsh unpacking their electronic kit out of the black cargo bags. Pete took a seat on the sofa, watching on. There was no conversation. Both went about their business setting up the listening devices and carrying out the necessary checks.

There was little conversation next door either. Jason walked over to the kitchen door. He didn't take his eyes off Lee for a moment as he lay face down with a cushion cover over his head. Jason was experiencing a dilemma; he wondered whether it was safe to make a phone call or would the cops be able to intercept Lee's phone? He decided it was a risk he needed to take.

"Hello, who's this?"

"Wayne, it's me. I can't speak for too long. I'm at the cop's house in Chadderton. Can you get down here pronto?" Jason whispered, "I don't want to miss the boat tonight."

"I'm already on my way; Burton brought me up to speed. What the hell are you doing? You lunatic. The plan was good to go, and you've probably fucked it up."

"Wind your neck in Wayne, I'm taking care of business, that's what. Dirk's boys just need to change the timings. How soon can you get to the cemetery entrance?"

"Twenty minutes or so, I'm not far away."

"Good wait there, it's well hidden from view. No more calls. No change of plan at all, only if you hear from me." Jason ended the call. Getting to the cemetery on foot was achievable. He felt like he was regaining control now. He was creating options for himself.

Twenty Seven

Andrea walked in on Caroline, Gaz and Becca discussing their strategy. Gaz was standing at the whiteboard, writing bullet points. Andrea stood by the door, waiting for them to finish talking. Listening to their plans boosted her confidence in achieving success.

"Caroline, I've got Frank Burton ready for you outside. Get what you can out of him but be careful with him. He's way outside of the circle of trust."

"Okay, it seems quite stable inside the target address at the moment. Hamilton is content enough to engage with us. He isn't as angry now; there's been a noticeable change in his attitude. Burton may be useful."

Andrea and Caroline stepped back into the main office; both Frank Burton and Pete Higgs had left. Andrea accepted that she should go easy on Pete for now, despite her reservations. He was of more use helping her than being ostracised. She joined Caroline sitting at the table.

A moment later, Frank stepped back into the incident room and smiled apologetically.

"Sorry for keeping you waiting, ladies." A waft of cigarette smoke followed him inside.

"No worries, thank you for helping Frank. I'm Caroline. I'm with the negotiation team. Take a seat." Frank pulled out a chair and sat down opposite them, elbows on the desk, hands clasped in front of him, looking eager to answer the first question. "Excuse me for being forthright, but time is of the essence. Can you tell us your perception of Hamilton's character in these circumstances and your opinion of what has driven him to take this action today?" Caroline asked, getting straight to the point.

Frank began waxing lyrical like he would presenting a case for the defence to the court. Caroline quickly interjected, asking Frank to keep to the point. Explaining that time wasn't on their side.

Andrea was enjoying seeing the uncomfortable look on Frank Burton's face. Caroline was a petit woman with a runner's build; she had black hair styled in a bob. She wore a dark blue trouser suit and white blouse. Caroline had a business-like disposition and was intense, entirely focused on the matter at hand. Andrea suspected Frank's attempts at old fashioned charm and wit, with a bit of chauvinism thrown in for good measure, would be wasted. Caroline was having none of it. An excellent spectator sport for Andrea.

"How do you think he would react if we broached his relationship with Kirsty?" Caroline continued with the intensity of questions.

"He's still very fond of her, but the last I heard, they'd split up. I don't think it will wind him up if that's what you're asking. But who knows? Right, I'll take a fag break here if you don't mind?" It was more of a statement of intent than a question. Frank stood up from his seat hastily, with a look of relief on his face.

Frank stepped outside and approached the uniform cop guarding the scene. It was a different officer than the last time. Frank offered her a cigarette, she declined and stepped away, maybe indicating her reluctance to engage in secondary smoking and small talk. Frank sensed her displeasure, "Do you mind?"

he asked, gesturing with the cigarette between his fingers.

"Not at all, as long as you keep your distance," she replied in a tone that implied she didn't want his company.   Frank walked a few paces towards the inner cordon whilst smoking. He looked around for DS Pete Higgs but couldn't see him anywhere. Frank's phone started to ring. He dropped his cigarette to the floor, only half-smoked and stubbed it with his foot.

"What is it, Wayne?"

"I'm back in Manchester. Jason wants me to park up nearby. He wants me to hang around in case I'm needed. What's he planning?"

"I'm not sure. The cops are negotiating with him. Where does he want you to park up?" Frank was also curious about what Jason was planning.

"It's a need-to-know Frank."

"Fine, it makes my life easier if things start going tits- up," Frank couldn't hide sounding like he felt put out, "He's up against it if he's going to escape. The place is swarming with armed cops," Frank added.

"Why are you there, Frank?"

"The cops want me here as an intermediary. I'm just taking a break. They're trying to empty my head of anything that may help them negotiate with Jason. Talking of which, have you heard from Kirsty?"

"No, nothing. Can you speak with Jason and get him to see sense? He's messed us up in good style. He should have been out of the country by now, instead of making our lives difficult. We need this police attention like a hole in the head. We've got enough on our plates without this bloody circus."

"Let's see how it plays out. The cops might shoot him yet," Frank said sensing a pang of guilt at not being too bothered about Jason's possible demise.

"The way I'm feeling at the moment, that may not be a bad outcome. The Dutch fellas must think we're amateurs. It was all planned and ready to go, then he does this. To be honest, Frank, I'm losing my patience with him."

"As I said, Wayne, let's just wait and see what happens." Frank hung up. He felt uncomfortable with Wayne's 'need-to-know' comment. Frank didn't like being outside the circle of trust but accepted it was probably for the best on this occasion. For one thing, he wouldn't inadvertently let anything slip to the cops, but, even more importantly, he wouldn't get dragged into a mission impossible scenario. Frank was still experiencing some guilt over his current thoughts about the whole situation. Would it be a bad thing if Jason got himself killed by the cops? The thought led him back to his curiosity about what Pete Higgs was doing. He admired Pete's nobility for wanting to save Lee McCann, but how the hell was he going to pull that off? On that thought, Frank returned to the irritating but safe sanctuary of his meeting with Caroline.

Having updated her policy decision book, Andrea put her pen down. It was the first moment of peace she had experienced since the incident had started. When Pete Higgs returned, she planned to review the circumstances and police response to date. She was determined to get Lee out of this mess and didn't want to miss a trick. She looked at her watch; where is Pete? He should be back by now. She hadn't eaten all day and was feeling pangs of hunger and light-headedness. Andrea felt guilty for thinking about food whilst Lee was in such a dangerous predicament.

She called Pete's mobile, but he didn't answer. Her mind wandered back to Lee, reluctantly. She accepted that she had feelings for Lee, the chemistry between them had been flirtatious. This situation and her fear for his safety had confirmed how she felt about him. In turn, the realisation made her feel defensive and vulnerable. Was he just the same as the other fellas?

Her dad had been a drinker and gambler. He had led her mother a dog's life, wasting all their money and contributing nothing. Andrea's memory drifted back to the night he abandoned them. She was only eight years of age at the time but still remembered it well. Her poor mother was crying and pleading with him to stay, probably from a misplaced sense of loyalty to him. He slammed the door shut behind him and eloped with his younger model. They heard nothing of him for many years until Andrea received a phone call, not long after joining the cops. Andrea had had sufficient time to build up some resilience by then. She limited her relationship with him to the odd phone call every now and then. By which time, she had drifted into an even worse relationship with her ex-boyfriend. But this wasn't the time to be contemplating her failed relationship. Andrea put the brakes on her racing mind and returned her focus to the present moment.

Caroline was monitoring Gaz's conversation; he was progressing well with Jason. He was good at his job, a safe pair of hands. This conversation had been going on for a good fifteen minutes.

"What are you thinking Jason, are you going to do the right thing and let Lee walk out of the front door?"

"Wow, steady on there. I said he was safe for now. I didn't say I was releasing him."

"It's the right decision, Jason. And it takes guts to make the right decision."

"I need some time to think."

"Okay, Jason, we can easily help you to sort this. Once you let Lee out of the house, I'll make sure you're safe to leave too."

"You've forgotten one thing, I'm not prepared to go back inside. You can't help me with that, can you, Gaz?" Jason pressed the red circle.

Twenty Eight

DS Pete Higgs was feeling under pressure. He knew it was now or never. The silence in the room had afforded him time and space to think. His mind was free of clutter for the first time in weeks. He decided that he had no other choice; he was confident of achieving a result. He had to act, and he had to act now. The apprehension and fear were growing inside him, fuelling his determination. His focus returned to the two detectives, huddled over their gadgets, running frequency checks.

"I don't think you need me here. I'm going to get something to eat. Do you want any food bringing back fellas?"

"No thanks, mate, we'll be done here in an hour or so," DC Walsh said curtly, not bothering to look up. Pete left the lounge and walked past the entrance to the kitchen. The firearms team were sitting around the dining table, busy on their smartphones.

"I'm just stepping outside to check the receiver," Pete said, purposefully misleading the group.

"Are they going to be much longer?" The sergeant asked.

"I don't know," Pete grimaced with a shrug of his shoulders. He opened the door slowly, trying not to make any noise and stepped outside into the darkness. An intense feeling of doubt prompted him to consider returning to the incident van. He was very tempted, it was the easy option, but he had made his mind up. He walked around to the back of the apartments, keeping close to the wall. When he reached the rear aspect of the building, he could see the patio doors of Lee's flat. A tiny slither of light escaped through the edge of the curtains, drawing a straight line across the concrete paving stones. He crouched down under the kitchen window, carefully in the pitch black, his hand trailing against the abrasive texture of the bricks.

Andrea was sipping a coffee when Frank took a seat at the table. She thought he looked tired and more stressed than he usually did. He stank of cigarette smoke and looked as if he hadn't shaved. She thought she could smell a whiff of whiskey and wondered if he was a man under pressure. She was looking to exploit any cracks in his armour.

"Is Pete out there?" Andrea asked.

"No, I'm not sure where he went. He mentioned something about picking some food up," Frank lied.

That's weird; it would be the first time that he'd gone for food without asking if I wanted anything, Andrea thought, especially as I'm stuck here.

The takeaway run was a well-established ritual during an extended shift. Andrea looked at her watch; she had been on duty for twelve hours. She tried Pete's mobile again. No reply. She looked over towards Frank.

"He's not answering his phone. What's he really up to, Frank?" Andrea sensed something was amiss.

"As I said, I think he's gone for something to eat," Frank said dismissively, not looking up from the table.

"How do you sleep at night representing low life like Hamilton?" Andrea asked as if she was goading Frank for a fight. She was venting her frustration and anger at Frank, who happened to be sitting in the crosshair of her sights.

"Quite easily, Andrea, everyone has the right to legal representation. Whether 'low life' or not.

Therefore someone needs to be there to provide it, to ensure fairness. History tells us miscarriages of justice do happen. Perhaps just as well we are here to represent them," Frank answered in an unconfrontational manner, probably having heard it all before. Andrea left it there; she'd taken a dig, and Frank hadn't risen to the bait.

"I'll go and check if Caroline needs you for anything else," Andrea said. She was getting irritated by his presence, exacerbated by her tiredness.

"Do you need Frank Burton for anything else, Caroline?"

"No, we're fine. It would be useful if Frank can remain available on his mobile phone. We might need him present if Hamilton decides to give himself up."

"Right, I'll let him know. I'll also update the Chief Superintendent on the negotiations. What are your thoughts, Gaz?"

"It's going well, and he's calmed down since we first spoke with him. He's become more rational and is engaging more. There's nothing to suggest that Lee is being significantly mistreated, but we know Hamilton has a history of violence and is capable of inflicting serious harm. Our strategy is progressing well," Gaz reported.

"I agree, and hopefully, we will be able to hear the conversation from inside soon. If the firearms teams have to move quickly, they will have a better idea of what they're walking into. Great work, Gaz, thank you."

Andrea's phone started to ring, "Ah, this must be Pete at last. He'd better be heading this way with the kebabs," Andrea said, she left the negotiating room and took a seat in the incident room.

"Andrea, it's Ollie. What the hell is Pete Higgs up to?" His voice sounded like he was agitated.

"I don't know, Ollie, what's happening? Andrea felt a surge of adrenalin and was dreading whatever it was she was about to hear.

"He's stood at the rear patio doors looking into the target address. Did you not know?"

"Oh shit, what the bloody hell is he doing? I thought he'd gone to collect a takeaway. I've not seen him for the last hour. I'll call his mobile. Keep me updated." Andrea ended the call and selected Pete from her contacts. The voicemail blurb kicked in, "Pete, what the hell are doing? Get your arse back here now." Andrea felt numb in a state of disbelief. She couldn't bring herself to believe what Pete was doing. Not only was it out of character, but it was also reckless and dangerous. He could mess the whole operation up. What the hell was he thinking?

Andrea turned around, realising that Frank Burton had heard her conversation.

"You can go now, Frank, thanks for your help. Would you be able to return if we need you?" It was Andrea's turn to fake sincerity.

"Yes, I'll keep my phone on. What's Pete doing?" Frank said quizzingly.

Andrea laughed, "Police business Frank, see you later." Frank stood up lethargically and left the incident room. Andrea took a seat at the table, rubbing her temples slowly. She considered giving Parkinson an update but thought better of it. He would quite rightly fly off the handle in response to Pete's maverick course of action. She couldn't cope with an angry boss right now. Andrea made another futile attempt to ring Pete again, the call again going straight to voicemail.

Pete felt his mobile phone vibrating in his trouser pocket. He suspected it was Andrea, and that she would want his balls on a plate. He tried to focus on the present, ignoring the inevitable wrath that he would be facing at the end of all this. He had to move quickly to keep the firearms officers at bay.

The curtains were closed. He carefully pushed up the lever on the patio door lock. It clicked into the open position a little too noisily. He felt relieved that the door wasn't locked. He slowly started to slide the door open, just giving him enough space to squeeze in behind the curtain. An ominous silence met him.

He knew he couldn't afford to startle Hamilton, so he called out, "Jason, it's DS Pete Higgs. I need to speak to you."

Jason looked towards the curtains closed across the patio doors, and instinctively sprang up from the sofa. "Don't you fucking move," he snarled at Lee whilst focusing on the patio doors.

"I ain't going anywhere," Lee replied

"Jason, can I come in?" Pete repeated a little louder. Jason stalked up to the patio doors with the pistol thrust out ahead of him in his outstretched hands.

"Jason, I need…" Before Pete could finish his sentence, Jason grabbed the curtain and yanked it back. Pete's eyes struggled to adapt to the instant light as he stepped forward.

"I'm on my…" Again, he didn't manage to finish his sentence. He felt a sharp pain in the side of his head and saw stars as Jason pistol-whipped him. Pete stumbled to the floor, ending up on all fours.

"Lie face down, you piece of shit," Jason shouted as he turned the key, locking the door, cursing himself for not having checked it. He pushed the curtain back and spun around. Lee was still motionless.

"Fucking hell, there's no need for that," Pete groaned, feeling disorientated. He lay face down on the floor, trying to recompose himself. His left ear was burning with pain and buzzing, his hearing was impaired, giving him further discomfort.

"I said no one was to enter the building. What part of that don't you understand?" Jason said, towering over Pete.

"I need to speak with you. The bosses don't know I'm here. They'll go ape-shit when they find out." Pete looked up from the floor, wincing in anticipation of more pain. He realised he'd never known proper fear until now. He saw Lee on the floor in the lounge.

"Stand up," Jason instructed. Pete stood up slowly; he felt sick and nauseous, "That's a proper right hook you have there; you don't know your own strength," Pete said, trying to lessen the tension, "I need to speak in private, Jason," Pete continued, nodding towards Lee conspiratorially.

He was more perturbed and shocked at the scene before him than he thought he would be. There was a sinister feel about the apparent calmness in the room. Towards the far side of the room, to the left of the front window, Pete could see Lee lying motionless on the floor. Hamilton was standing halfway between himself and Lee, pointing the pistol at Pete's head. Hamilton looked anxious and rattled, nothing like his usual self, as on previous occasions. He looked tired and irritated. Pete felt scared, and with good reason too.

Pete gestured in the direction of the kitchen, then placed his hands in the air in a non-threatening gesture. Hamilton nodded towards the kitchen in approval. Pete slowly walked, making sure he gave Hamilton no excuses to shoot him.

"Go and stand by the sink," Hamilton instructed. Pete walked to the far end of the kitchen, now wishing he was still sitting in the lounge next door, with the safety of the firearms team. He turned around at the far end to face Hamilton and leant back against the worktop.

"I shouldn't be here. Frank wanted me to offer you a way out of this," Pete lied. The shock and fear of Hamilton pointing a pistol at him were fading. He felt his confidence returning, and he was trying to use Hamilton's apparent anxiousness as a positive.

"Oh yeah, and how are you going to do that?" Hamilton replied. Pete felt reassured that Hamilton at least seemed willing to listen, rather than dismissing him immediately.

Hamilton's phone started ringing. He looked to his right towards Lee, then back towards Pete, shaking his head.

"Hello Gaz, I'm a bit busy right now. The local bobby has just called unannounced. I need to put the kettle on and get the custard creams out. Can I call you back?"

"What's happening, Jason?" Gaz asked.

"You tell me, Gaz, you're the one pulling the strings around here."

"I just meant, was everything okay in there? Are you both okay?"

"Stop playing fucking games. You said you wouldn't send any cops to the flat. And now DS Higgs has just popped in. What the fucks going on, Gaz?"

"Jason, I've not been in the loop on that. It's the first I've heard. Let me speak to the boss and get back to you."

"Don't play fucking games with me, Gaz. I'll blow them both away if you push me."

"Jason, this wasn't planned; I'm as surprised as you are. Don't hurt either of them, and I'll speak to the boss and call you back. In fact, can I just speak to DS Higgs?"

Jason ended the call without answering the question.

Pete imagined the rage Andrea was in right now. She was probably in the room listening to Gaz speak and was now holding forth, telling everyone who cared to listen what a liability and disgrace Pete Higgs was.

"Jason, you need to listen to me. We haven't got much time. You don't want to kill Lee. You've made your point loud and clear. You've won. Lee's lay on the floor with a bag on his head. He knows he's at your mercy…" Pete was tripping up over his words, trying to sell his case convincingly.

"Cut to the chase then. What's your plan?" Jason interrupted. Pete felt a wave of relief run through his body. Hamilton was still interested in getting out, and there was hope of resolving this yet.

"It's simple; we don't have many options. But we need to act quickly, we need to be audacious, whilst they're trying to work out what the fuck I'm doing here. We switch clothes, and you text the DI on my phone that I'm leaving the apartment. You then make your getaway. Initially, they will think it's me leaving. It buys you a minute or so to clear the immediate area. It's down to you then. There's plenty of rat runs for you to disappear into." Pete braced himself for Hamilton to start laughing or tell him to piss off. But it didn't happen, and Hamilton looked thoughtful.

"I'll tie you two together. Can't have you alerting your colleagues as soon as I'm away," Jason thought out loud.

"That's fine, but we need to move now, or we lose the element of surprise and confusion I've created." Pete was trying hard to push the momentum faster. If he didn't convince Jason to go now, he was here for the long haul trying to save Lee by the seat of his pants. He was also confident that Hamilton wouldn't get too far before being picked up by his colleagues.

"Is Frank in on this?"

"Yes, it's my last debt to him. My cover story will be that I came in, you tied me up, nicked my clothes and escaped. We all get what we want. We all move on. Frank and Wayne are behind this plan."

"Give me your clothes then." Pete couldn't believe his ears; Hamilton was going for it. He must be desperate to getaway.

Gaz turned his swivel chair around to face DI Andrea Statham, "What the hell is Pete doing?"

"Well, it looks like Hamilton's got two hostages now. What a clusterfuck. You need to get back onto him. Our best approach is to go down the line that Pete has acted of his own volition. You must maintain some level of trust and integrity," Andrea suggested.

Caroline nodded, "I agree; it is what is it. We just need to deal with what's now in front of us."

"I'll go next door and telephone Parkinson. He will be flapping his way up to the ceiling in panic when he hears this. I can't hold him off forever."

Gaz picked up the phone and dialled Lee's number, shaking his head.

Twenty Nine

Pete's arms were going numb, and he was struggling to ignore the throbbing pain. They were pulled back tight behind him and tied tightly to the dining chair by plastic ties. The edges were cutting into his wrists, causing excruciating pain. His legs were bound to the legs of the chair. He looked over towards Lee; Jason had shackled him to the radiator piping with plastic ties. Pete couldn't help himself but envy Lee. Lying on the floor looked like heaven compared with his bolt upright position. Neither of them would be going anywhere soon. Jason had made sure of that. Pete looked over towards Jason, who'd made a reasonable effort at fitting into Pete's suit. Jason grabbed a beanie hat from the coat stand and put it on, immediately concealing his blonde hair. Pete was surprised at the complete change in his appearance; Jason now looked like a convincing DS Higgs imposter, he would look even better outside in the dark.

Pete couldn't hide a smug feeling of contentment, hoping that the listening devices would pick up their conversations. In which case, there would be a reception committee of armed cops waiting for Jason outside.

Pete had been careful to whisper in the kitchen and hoped the tech guys hadn't recorded his initial conspiratorial conversation. All the same, he wasn't too concerned if it had been picked up, he would explain it away as a mere ruse to gain Jason's compliance.

Jason walked over to Lee and crouched down alongside him, pressing the pistol's muzzle into the back of Lee's head.

"Time to die, you fucker," Hamilton uttered menacingly, "you didn't honestly think I was going to walk out of here without killing you, did you?" Pete froze and felt dizzy; a chill ran through the length of his body. How had he been so naïve? He had seriously underestimated Jason Hamilton; he had to stop this, but how?

"Christ, Jason, don't shoot him; they'll hear the shot and storm the flat in minutes. We'll all die!" Pete shouted in desperate stone-cold fear, and the fear was exacerbated when he realised he would be executed next. "Bloody hell, Jason, don't do it. You need to be on your toes now before it's too late. Jason, you've won. Put the pistol away." Pete was in a desperate panic, and he felt helpless and woefully inadequate.

Hamilton withdrew the pistol away from Lee's head then swung it back with some force, striking the side of his head with the butt. Lee cried out and recoiled in pain. His body almost left the floor from the force of the blow. Blood started to pour down the side of his face.

"That's all you're getting for now. But remember, I will be back for you, and I will kill you." Jason stood up and made his way to the utility room door. Pausing, he sent the text that Pete had written to Andrea on Pete's mobile phone as he stepped outside, 'Did my best, couldn't get Lee to safety. He's tied up but unharmed. I'm coming out.'

Andrea was briefing Chief Superintendent Parkinson with a situation report on her mobile phone. The latest development of Pete Higgs entering the target address sounded even more bizarre as she relayed the circumstances to him. Parkinson went quiet; the pause was uncomfortable. Andrea was saved by the pinging text alert on her phone; she looked at the screen, it was from Pete Higgs.

"There's been a positive development boss, I'll call you back," she said and ended the call before Parkinson could reply.

Andrea read the text; this was getting crazier by the second. Had Pete managed to get in without being seen? What the hell was happening?

"All call signs, I've received a text saying that DS Higgs is leaving the target address, any sightings, over?"

"Foxtrot Charlie One, Sighting confirmed, a male has left via the side door, looks like the male that entered the patio doors. I can't be one hundred per cent sure. He's just gone down the side path. He should be at the front in a few seconds. I've lost sight, over."

"All call signs, confirm any further sightings over?" Andrea responded on the radio. She stepped into the negotiation room. Caroline was holding her radio to her ear following developments. She held a puzzled expression but gave a thumbs-up to Andrea.

"He's ignored my last three calls, Ma'am; something isn't right here," Gaz said, immediately trying to make contact again.

"Control, task air support to deploy to the target address asap," Andrea instructed over the radio. She redialled Pete's phone; there was no reply.

"Any sightings? Over," Andrea sounded desperate over the radio.

"This isn't right; he should have appeared outside by now," she said, picking up her phone.

"Ollie, it's Andrea. Have you got enough teams to commence a search of the exterior? Something isn't right here."

"Leave it with me." Ollie recognised the need for urgency and allocated an armed response team to move in.

Jason was operating on a tidal wave of adrenaline. He left the house calmly, but as soon as he was under cover of the garden vegetation, he began to move with stealth. He squeezed alongside the sub-station and the concrete fence, keeping low, making full use of the cover. His face and hands were getting scratched and were stinging from squeezing between the fencing and shrubbery. The fear of being caught and the adrenaline rush fuelled his escape. Lee's route plan had been genuine. It was going well or was he about to walk straight into the sights of an armed officer's machine gun? He reached the end of the hedge and paused momentarily. Looking around, assessing the threat. It looked clear.

He was just about to set off when he noticed an armed officer lay on a flat garage roof, facing the direction from where he had run.

He crouched back down into the cover, considering shooting the officer, but he was just out of range, and the gunshot would give his location away. Jason calculated that he was only just within the cop's peripheral vision. The clock was ticking, and the pressure was building. But he had to keep going. He felt around in the dirt and found a stone. He looked behind him and selected a house window, close enough to hit. He threw the stone and listened as the glass smashed, shattering the silence. A dog began to bark, and then another.

He set off, swiftly walking alongside a detached house, activating the sensor security light. He cursed and started to run out of the spotlight, hoping the cop remained focused on his distraction of smashing glass.

Within seconds he was out of view; he had reached the road and could see the cemetery. Jason felt vulnerable and exposed, but he needed to stay calm. He couldn't afford to look suspicious and draw the attention of residents. He walked towards the wall of the cemetery.

"Foxtrot Charlie Four, I have heard the sound of smashing glass. I cannot confirm the location. It sounded close to the target address on the Southern aspect. Stand-by."

"All patrols observations for any males on foot. We cannot confirm that the male leaving the address is DS Pete Higgs. Report any sightings," Andrea requested.

"Foxtrot Delta two, we have searched the target address garden. No trace. We are moving towards the garden backing onto the target address."

The firearms commander directed other armed teams on a systematic search of the gardens over the radio.

"Hamilton's still not answering the phone," Gaz said aloud to the room. Andrea rang Pete; the phone went straight through to voicemail again.

"I'm going to ask the boss for authority to send the firearms team into the apartment. This isn't looking good…" Andrea was interrupted by her mobile ring tone.

"Ma'am, it's DC Walsh. We've got the listening device up and running. We can hear two male voices in the target address: DS Higgs and DS McCann. They keep repeating that Hamilton has left the address…"

"Thank you, I'll call you back," interrupted Andrea.

"All call signs, it is believed that the male who left the target address is the suspect Jason Hamilton. He is in possession of a firearm. Report any sightings and approach with extreme caution," Andrea said over her radio, just as her mobile started to ring.

"Andrea, I'm listening to the radio. How the hell has he got past the firearms containment?" Parkinson sounded flustered.

"We don't have a confirmed location for him yet, boss. We need to get the firearms team into the address. Will you authorise it?"

"Well… I could do with more information…" Parkinson sounded hesitant.

"It's looking very likely that Hamilton has left the address. We need to ensure the safety of Lee McCann and Pete Higgs. He may be injured and require medical assistance. We need to go in now," Andrea interrupted in a demanding tone.

"Yes, I agree; firearms entry is authorised. I will drive over and join you at the scene."

"Thanks, boss." Andrea got straight onto Ollie, the firearms commander and gave him the green light for an armed entry into the address.

Jason calmly walked along the pavement. He didn't think he'd been seen by anyone but couldn't be sure. The hairs on the back of his neck were standing up as he saw the exterior wall of the cemetery. He anticipated hearing the sound of police sirens and seeing flashing blue lights at any moment. "Almost there. Come on, keep it together," Jason said aloud.

Jason felt a wave of panic on seeing the headlights of a car approaching. His heartbeat started to race, and his body tensed with trepidation; he felt deflated. Was it a cop car? He was just about to leg it towards the cemetery when he realised it was a taxi. He stood in the road and waved it down. As the car stopped, he opened the front passenger door. The driver was a middle-aged man with a large beer belly touching the steering wheel. He looked irritated at being flagged down.

"I'm on a call. You will have to ring the office pal. I'm not insured otherwise."

"No problem, Sir, I'm a police officer. I just wanted to ask if you had seen anything suspicious whilst driving up here."

"No, I've just been pulled over by the cops back there. I've got passengers waiting. I'm already late. I need to go."

"No problem, Sir, thanks for your time." Hamilton shut the door. He watched the red tail lights disappear into the distance as the taxi was driven away, the driver unaware that Hamilton had dropped

DS Pete Higgs's mobile phone behind the front passenger seat.

Hamilton walked beyond the row of houses and entered the darkness of the hedge-lined road. Having had a final look around, he was content that no one was watching. Jason vaulted the cemetery's stone wall and dropped into the surrounding woodland. He could see the shadows of the gravestones in the distance. He set off running, building his speed into a sprint. For the first time since dragging DS McCann into the flat, he was now feeling confident of escaping. His arms and legs were pumping like an athlete sprinting.

His lungs felt like they were burning. The twigs were cracking underfoot as he entered the maze of paths between the graves. The taste of freedom urged him to go faster.

A sudden fear resonated within him. He heard the sound of the police helicopter in the distance, getting louder. He needed to reach Wayne's car quickly. The heat-seeking cameras on the aircraft would pin-point him. He sped up his pace for the final thousand metres or so to the cemetery entrance.

Thirty

Andrea stepped into the technical operations van, sliding the door shut behind her. DC Walsh and DC Nolan shuffled along to make more space on the vehicle's fitted bench, and they listened intently to the ongoing live broadcast from the address. In addition to the three occupants, the van was host to an array of electronic, hard-cased equipment and multiple LCD screens occupying much of the remaining space.

"If you can hear me, this is DS Pete Higgs. I am in the target address with DS Lee McCann. Hamilton has left the address; he is armed with a pistol. I repeat, Hamilton has left the address…"

Andrea's phone started to ring. It was caller withheld, probably a landline from the police station.

"DI Statham."

"Ma'am, it's DC Nadia Khan from the force intelligence unit. We have triangulated the phone number you gave us, and we have a hit. A vehicle heading south along Oldham Way."

"Excellent news Nadia, will you contact communications and get them to allocate an armed response vehicle?"

"Already onto it, Ma'am, the force duty officer, has authorised it. They're on route. She has also diverted air support to assist."

"Thanks, Nadia. Keep me updated, please," Andrea felt relieved; it wasn't a certainty, but they might be onto Hamilton; he may be travelling in a stolen car. She placed her phone into her pocket and could hear Pete Higgs repeating his situation report. Andrea was relieved to listen to his voice and the news that they were both okay. But she was still furious with him. He had some explaining to do. Her thoughts were interrupted by a series of loud bangs and smashing glass together with the repeated cries of "Armed police do not move." The siege was over, but the assailant was still at large.

Even though DS Pete Higgs knew it was the armed police entering the flat, the loud noises made him instinctively want to find cover and hide. First, the windows were smashed, then the front door was bust off its hinges by an entry team with a wham ram, and then pyrotechnic flash-bangs were thrown into the room, leaving him feeling disorientated, his ears were ringing.

He opened his eyes, feeling dazed, to see armed officers methodically searching the flat, dressed all in black, carrying MP3 machine guns at the ready. Repeated shouts of "Room Clear," reverberated around the flat. The actions of the armed officers became less hectic, and the noise started to die down.

"Target address confirmed clear, no trace of the suspect Hamilton. DS Higgs and DS McCann present they both look okay," the team leader updated headquarters on his radio.

Scenes of crime officers had entered the apartment once it was safe to do so. Both hostages were freed from their restraints, which were forensically recovered to preserve any DNA traces left by Jason Hamilton. The armed response medic checked them both over and recommended that the cut on Lee's head required hospital treatment.

Pete Higgs got to his feet and dusted himself down. He was overwhelmed with relief. The intense feeling of guilt had drained from him. It was replaced by the apprehension of what he was about to face next.

"I wasn't expecting to see you tip-up here," Lee said.

"I just felt like I had to do the right thing, Lee. Unconventional, I know, but he wasn't messing about, and I couldn't sit by watching."

"I'm not complaining, mate. Whatever you said in the kitchen worked," Lee said, looking at the blood on his hands from having examined his head.

"DI Statham wants to see you both in the major incident vehicle. We will escort you out of the address. We can't be sure that Hamilton isn't still in the vicinity," the firearms team leader advised. Pete's feeling of relief and euphoria quickly sank at the thought of facing Andrea. Even though he was sure that his actions had probably saved Lee's life, he was convinced he was still in deep trouble. He had a great relationship with Andrea, but this time he knew he had crossed the line, and departed from police protocol. Worst of all he had probably lost the respect, from his boss and colleagues.

Jason picked up his speed when he reached the smooth tarmac path; his leg muscles were starting to burn. He was running at full pelt and breathing heavily. He suddenly had a rush of anxiety. What if Wayne hadn't shown up? No problem, nick a car, he thought to himself. He reached the entrance to the cemetery and saw a car parked just inside the gate, under the canopy of the trees. He glanced inside and felt instant relief when he saw Wayne in the driver's seat. Jason opened the front passenger door and collapsed into the seat.

"Fucking hell mucker, I'm glad to see you. Let's get out of here," Jason said breathlessly and burst into a fit of loud, nervous laughter. Wayne gave him a wry look and cautiously drove out of the cemetery.

"We've got to get past the cops yet, it's a bit early for celebrations," Wayne said shaking his head. He got off the main road at the first opportunity and took the side streets through the housing estate. Both of them remained on a high state of vigilance for police patrols.

"I cannot believe I did it. I thought I wasn't getting away," Hamilton laughed.

"Did you kill the cop?" Wayne asked, bemused.

"No, he got lucky and saw me. We ended up scrapping on the driveway, and I dragged him into the house. Then the cops showed up. I either killed him and got banged up again or got on my toes."

"You took a big needless risk there. You should be in Amsterdam by now. The Dutch boys aren't happy. They think you've messed them about."

"Fuck them. We put enough business their way. It's only a short delay, for Christ's sake. You should have seen the shock on the coppers face, it was priceless."

"I just hope it was worth it, Jason. We're now at risk of getting lifted by the cops, and Dirk and his boys are pissed off with you. You should have stuck to the plan."

"Wind your neck in Wayne, and remember who pays your wages." Hamilton glared at Wayne, an uncomfortable silence followed.

Jason sat back in his seat and closed his eyes. They were out of the immediate vicinity and putting some miles between themselves and the police.

DI Andrea Statham thanked DC Nolan and DC Walsh for their work as she carefully stepped out of the technical operations van. DC Walsh looked bewildered and eager to get away; it had been one of those days. Andrea felt the temperature had dropped, or maybe it was the tiredness kicking in. She strolled to the major incident truck. Looking towards the target address, she could see lots of uniform activity under the glow of the yellow street lighting. She had achieved her priority; Lee was safe, as was Pete. But she was keen to find out what had gone on in the address. Had Pete saved Lee? What would have happened if he hadn't gone in? DS Higgs had plenty of questions to answer. But Hamilton was still at large and she still had work to do. Her phone started to ring.

"Hi Andrea, it's Sophie, the force duty officer."

"Hi Sophie, please tell me Hamilton is in custody," Andrea said more in hope, than expectation.

"It's never that easy, is it? The vehicle was a taxi. The driver is making a statement at the moment. He denies any knowledge of the mobile phone, which the patrol officer retrieved from the car's back seat. He says he was waved down by a male, matching Hamilton's description on Middleton Road near the cemetery. Hamilton must have slipped the phone into the car to send us on a wild goose chase."

"At least that gives us a confirmed sighting of his last known whereabouts. I can get some CCTV enquiries allocated to help us get us back on his trail. Thanks, Sophie." Andrea couldn't help but feel a tinge of disappointment.

She stepped up into the Incident Room and closed the door behind her. Caroline, Gaz, and Becca had packed their gear away and hovered in the incident room holding their coats.

"Unless you need us for anything else, we'll get going," Caroline suggested.

"That's fine. Thanks for your work guys, great job as usual," Andrea said.

"We're still on-call, so we'll get some rest. We can meet up for a debrief tomorrow if you like?" Gaz said.

"Sounds good; see you later."

"I'm available on the mobile if you need me," Caroline said as she left the room. The quiet prompted Andrea to put the kettle on and take stock of the circumstances. She took a seat at the table and was just enjoying her first sip of coffee when Chief Superintendent Parkinson stepped into the room.

"Great news Andrea, good effort. DS McCann is safe and well."

"Yes, it's a big relief boss, I've just got to locate Hamilton now."

"How the hell did we not pick him up? He's walked through an armed containment, for god's sake." Andrea cringed inside; the boss had a point. She felt embarrassed and could feel her cheeks colouring up.

"Schoolboy error boss, it looks like the subterfuge of DS Higgs leaving the address worked for him. It all happened in a matter of seconds. I'll know for definite shortly. I'm about to debrief Lee McCann and Pete Higgs. I've got some fast-track CCTV enquiries ongoing to locate Hamilton. He's not clean away just yet." The latter positivity did nothing to diminish the fact he'd escaped.

"Do you need me on the debrief?" Parkinson asked.

"Probably best if I do it on my own boss. They're more likely to clam up with senior command present."

"Yes, I agree. Right, I'll go and speak with the firearms officers; perhaps Ollie can shed some light on it." Parkinson left the room, leaving Andrea to her thoughts. She took a tentative sip of her coffee to see if it was warm enough to drink, it was lukewarm, but she needed the caffeine and emptied the cup anyway. Ollie, the firearms commander, entered the incident room with Lee McCann and Pete Higgs.

"Am I glad to see you two! Are you both okay?" Andrea asked.

"I've had better days. I thought I was a dead man. Thank god Pete came to the rescue," Lee mumbled. Andrea thought he looked terrible with dried blood on his swollen face and a haunted look in his eyes. She felt anguished, looking at the state of him. She couldn't hide the contempt in her eyes when she looked over to Pete as he started to speak.

"I don't think the bosses will see it like that, Lee. I did my best; sometimes we have to go off-piste and take more risks," Pete replied with his pre-emptive mitigation. Andrea refrained from giving her opinion.

"Get a brew, guys and wait in the negotiation room. We can do the debrief in there. We won't get disturbed." Whilst Lee and Pete made a brew, Ollie hung back with Andrea.

"Parkinson has just left here to go and speak with you," Andrea said.

"I'll catch up with him after we've spoken," Ollie said, sounding deflated. He declined the offer of coffee and continued, "sorry about Hamilton, I've held a hot debrief with the officers covering that aspect of the building. It was a perfect storm for the

253

lucky bastard. The radio transmission informing that DS Higgs was leaving the flat coincided with Hamilton leaving. He was wearing DS Higgs's clothing. For a split second, it looked legitimate. We deployed a team towards him from the front aspect of the building, but he was gone. Our searches on the ground and air support were negative. There was one blind spot, and he found it."

Andrea could see that Ollie was gutted; it would take his team a long time to live this one down. It would certainly be the gossip in the canteens for a while.

"He's moved through those gardens at some speed. Air support is still searching for a heat source, but I guess he's nicked a car by now," Andrea said, unable to offer Ollie any consolation.

"I guess so, the dog handler followed a trail to the cemetery, but the dog lost the scent there." Ollie looked down, shaking his head.

"Shit happens Ollie, at least those two are safe and well. We can nick Hamilton another day. Okay, I'd better get on with the debrief."

"Lucky you, I've got to go and face Parkinson," Ollie said, looking like a man already condemned.

Wayne turned onto the slip road for the motorway services. The parking area was deserted but for a few cars. The darkness provided a cloak of anonymity as Wayne parked close to the landscaped seating area.

"Are you waiting here or coming in?" He asked Jason.

"I won't risk it. Just get me a couple of beers if they have any and something to eat, mate. And stop looking at me like that, for fucks sake, get over it."

Jason said, looking out of the passenger window into the darkness.

Wayne walked towards the restaurant and shopping area. Once out of the sight of Jason, he made a call.

"Hi Dirk, are your boys still in the water?" he asked hopefully.

"Yes, at some risk, thanks to Jason, they're not happy. What the hell is he playing at?"

"Look, mate, I've apologised already. He's becoming a liability, but I've got things under control. He's not leaving my sight until I hand him over to you. Are the tides okay for you to collect him? I can get him to the RV point in about an hour."

"There's no rush; five o'clock would be the optimum time," Dirk replied wearily.

"That sounds good. I've got a plan to make sure Jason behaves himself. I'll call you back in a couple of hours to see if you agree. I think you'll like it."

Wayne entered the building, pulling his baseball cap lower and avoiding the security cameras where he could. He paid cash for the sandwiches and drinks, then headed back to the car.

"Give me your phone. I need to call Burton," Jason demanded.

"It's too risky, mate; the cops will be monitoring everything. Anyway, more to the point, I think I can get you out of the country from Whitby in the early hours."

"That's a good move. I'm probably on Britain's most wanted list right now; a bit of distance from this place would be a good thing," Jason said, sounding pleased with himself at the thought of his newfound notoriety.

"You'd be mad to come back for a good while. You need to go completely off the radar."

Jason could sense that Wayne was still pissed off with him. But he decided not to make an issue of it. Jason was well aware of his current vulnerability and knew he needed Wayne on his side, at least for the time being. Once he was safe in Amsterdam, he would begin to reassert his authority and take the business to the next level. Jason took another swig of his beer then opened his sandwich. The smell of egg mayonnaise filled the car. Wayne opened his window, letting in the cool fresh air.

Jason couldn't help himself; he couldn't tolerate Wayne's attitude any longer.

"Have you got a fucking problem, Wayne? You're pissing me right off."

"Look, Jason, I've not only kept the business running whilst you've been locked up, but I've increased profits. I'm making us more money. I sorted out the Amsterdam move for you, and then you disappear and take a cop hostage, risking fucking everything. Of course, I'm pissed off with you!"

"We're back on plan. We're sitting here drinking beer, not sitting in a police cell. You need to remember what I've done for you over the years. Not sit there fucking sulking." Jason took another drink of his beer. Wayne didn't reply. The silence was deafening.

Thirty Two

DI Andrea Statham pulled out a chair and joined DS Pete Higgs and DS Lee McCann at the table. She smiled sympathetically at Lee. Pete looked uncomfortable, fidgeting with a pen. Andrea sensed that Lee was still in shock, albeit he was putting on a brave face.

"First things first, fellas, I'm so relieved to have you both out of there safe and well. Do either of you need anything, medical or counselling wise right now?" They both shook their heads. She anticipated that being the answer but was obliged to ask.

"The uniform Inspector covered all the wellbeing stuff when we came out. Hamilton knocked me about a bit, but aside from that, I'm fine," Lee said.

"Go next door, have a minute and grab a coffee, Lee. I'll debrief Pete first." As Lee closed the door quietly behind him, Andrea turned her attention to Pete.

"Well?" Andrea almost spat the word out and glared at Pete.

"Whatever I say isn't going to be a good enough explanation. I probably know Hamilton better than any of us. I was in no doubt that he would shoot Lee. I had to do something. He was a cornered animal; it was only going to end badly. You would have had no other option than to reject my plan if I'd run it by you. And besides, I didn't want to drag you into the shit with me. I was confident I could pull it off. I know it looks reckless, but it wasn't."

"Reckless? It looks bloody crazy from where I'm sitting, Pete. What the hell did you say to him?" The thought of Pete assisting Hamilton on behalf of Frank Burton was gnawing away at her.

"I offered him an alternative to spending the rest of his life in prison. I knew you would be able to hear our conversations over the listening device, so you would have the heads up and have been prepared to grab him when he came out."

"He was dressed in your clothes, for Christ's sake."

"I know, but I had to make the plan plausible. Hamilton's not stupid; he wouldn't have come on board otherwise. I knew that you had the listening device operating, and therefore the knowledge of what we were planning."

"We didn't… the device wasn't set up in time to capture that conversation," Andrea lamented.

"Look, Andrea, I'll take what's coming to me on the chin. I know it was a maverick unauthorised course of action. But guess what? It worked! Lee is sitting out there enjoying a coffee. Rather than having been collected by the undertakers in a body bag," Pete said, sitting back in his chair with a self-righteous look on his face.

"But the flip side of the coin is, Hamilton is on the run again. Did he give anything away at all?" Andrea asked hopefully.

"No, but he can't have had much time to plan an escape. He's flying by the seat of his pants and, therefore, he's more susceptible to making mistakes. Have you got anything from the CCTV trawl yet?" Pete asked, trying to move the conversation onto catching Hamilton.

Andrea shook her head and lounged back in her chair. Somehow Pete had made her feel less angry. He had always been good at digging himself out of a hole. But she still had a nagging doubt about his relationship with Frank Burton. She leaned forward and folded her arms onto the table.

"I'm not stupid, Pete; I've known you for years. What the hell have you got mixed up in here, with Burton and his cronies? You need to do the decent thing and be straight with me. I may be able to help you get out of it." Andrea held eye contact for longer than she would typically have done, looking for any non-verbal leakage from Pete. There wasn't any. He raised his eyebrows and leaned forward from his chair, hands on the table.

"I've told you before, I may have stretched the relationship boundary more than I should have, but that's all. Frank Burton thought he was using me, but I was getting more out of him. Just old-fashioned coppering. Applauded not so long ago, but now frowned upon." His apparent smugness grated on Andrea.

"I hope you're telling me everything for your own sake. This is your last chance to be honest with me, Pete. After this, I won't be as understanding if I find out you've taken the piss out of me."

"You've always trusted me, Ma'am; there's no reason not to now. I'll help you to get Hamilton locked up. Lee's safe. That's our number one priority."

Andrea placed her pen on the pad of paper; Pete was right, for now. "Ask Lee to come in, will you?" Andrea asked, feeling irritated by Pete's ability to make his actions sound like the most reasonable and obvious thing to do.

"No worries, I'll get hold of Frank Burton and get what information I can out of him."

Andrea wanted to believe Pete, but her gut feeling was telling her otherwise. She couldn't put her finger on it, but something wasn't right. Anyway, she'd allowed him to come clean, and he hadn't taken the opportunity. If there was more to it, then he was on his own.

Lee ambled back into the office with two coffees. He placed one down on the table for Andrea. She thought he looked pretty calm and composed, considering what he had just been through. But shouldn't that be expected? He was a trained undercover officer.

The flirtatious side of their relationship had faded; the boundary was now much clearer, a professional one. Andrea wondered if this was just a natural reaction to the circumstances. Or was she running away from getting emotionally close to someone once again? Time would tell. For now, she was just happy that he was safe.

Lee slowly recounted the events from when he first saw Hamilton outside his flat. Andrea was taking notes and highlighting areas of interest, which she would want to explore further.

"What was your gut feeling, Lee? Did you think he was going to shoot you?"

"It was just lucky that I saw him; if I'd have entered the flat, he would have got in and killed me without a doubt. I felt like it was more important for him to escape. How did the uniform patrol respond so quickly? They probably saved my life."

"We received some intelligence and got worried when you didn't answer your phone."

"That's interesting. I wonder where the intelligence came from, Frank Burton maybe? Pete's intervention was timely too. He gave Hamilton an alternative to killing me. But like I said, Hamilton threatened that it wasn't over, and he would be back for me. Pete deserves a break; I honestly think he saved my life in there. I know he acted outside of protocol, but I've got to say, it must have taken some guts. He placed himself in danger. Hamilton could have shot the pair of us."

"How was Pete with Hamilton? I know it's a difficult question, but what was their rapport like?"

"Professional, he had the rapport from interviewing him for the contract kill offence and other stuff. There was tension between them. Pete had planned that you would be listening to the conversations. It's sod's law that the listening device wasn't activated in time, and the firearms teams didn't manage to detain him...My head is banging. Have you got any pain killers in your bag?" Lee digressed, tired of Andrea's questioning.

Andrea slid a foil of paracetamol tablets across the table. She watched Lee remove the tablets from the foil and wash them down with coffee. If it wasn't for Pete's actions, there was a good chance he wouldn't be sat across from her, safe. She decided to let Pete continue working on the case, for now, having accepted that the mitigation of saving Lee's life would probably get him off the hook. Maybe he could use Burton to their advantage to help locate Hamilton. But the nagging doubt was still there, had he gone into the flat to save Lee or to help Hamilton escape.

Pete was relieved to have left the debrief with Andrea. He'd felt uncomfortable under the spotlight. He thought she had gone easy on him, either that or she still hadn't uncovered anything significant about his clandestine activities. It could have been a lot worse although he felt pretty confident that he had talked his way out of a disciplinary hearing. The fact he had saved Lee, together with his exemplary service record, stood in his favour. At worst, he might have to accept a formal reprimand.

But he still had work to do. He turned the ignition key and drove away from the scene, relieved by how well things had gone for him. In a perverse sense, he felt sorry for Andrea; because so far, he had managed to pull the wool over her eyes, but how long would his luck last for?

As Pete walked into the office. Frank was sitting at his desk smoking.

"Open the window, Frank; how many packets have you been through?" Pete asked, wafting his hand across his face. Cigarette smoke hung heavy in the room. "It's like being back in the CID office in the seventies."

Frank stood up from the desk and pushed up the old wooden sash window, which creaked until it jammed, refusing to rise more than a couple of inches.

"There's some coffee on the side; help yourself, mine's black, please," Frank said coughing.

Pete carried the coffees over to Frank's desk and took a seat on the red leather Chesterfield wingback chair. He was starting to feel relaxed. The room lighting was dim, just the green desk lamp illuminating a small area of the old-fashioned office, leaving the remainder in the shadows. It created a dramatic ambience, exacerbated by the current circumstances. Pete felt at ease; and didn't feel any threat from Burton. He had grown begrudging respect for the old rogue. It hadn't extended to trust, though, and he certainly didn't underestimate his potential threat.

"I'd say I've paid my dues beyond doubt, Frank. I risked my life and put my job in jeopardy to get Jason out of that mess," Pete said purposefully whilst being economical with the truth. He gave Frank a somewhat tainted account of his intentions and actions at the flat. Frank lit another cigarette and took a long drag.

"I certainly can't argue with that Pete, maybe we move forward with a more cordial and mutual understanding?"

"Fine by me, but you're stuck in a deep rut with Hamilton, and by my reckoning, he's lost the plot. He's a loose cannon," Pete let his words hang. Frank took another long drag of his cigarette and looked forlornly into the darkness.

"I can't argue with that either."

"Where's he gone, Frank? It's probably the best outcome for all of us to locate him. Once he's back inside, the cops will move on and leave us alone."

"I don't have a clue where he is. Let's see how things pan out over the next few days." Pete got the impression that Frank had something up his sleeve, which he wasn't about to disclose.

"I need to get back. Let me know if you hear anything," Pete said, walking to the door.

Thirty Three

It was well past midnight when the police vehicles vacated the scene, and the police incident cordon tape had been removed, allowing residents to get on with their lives unrestricted. A stillness had returned under the glow of the residential street lights. The scenes of crime team remained inside the flat, completing their forensic examinations, the only remnant of the siege.

Andrea had returned to her office, to co-ordinate the manhunt for Jason Hamilton. Her mobile phone ringtone made her jump; she was miles away, trying to make sense of Hamilton's actions and what his next move would be.

"Hi Ma'am, it's DS Booth at the CCTV unit. Good news. We've recovered a decent amount of footage from the area of the cemetery. The taxi driver's evidence has helped us pinpoint the time frame, which has made life a lot easier. We think we have narrowed down a get-away vehicle to one of four possible cars. The analyst is still working on it, but I'm confident we're on the right track. Three of the cars have been located locally. Only one is still unaccounted for."

"Fantastic, great work. I'll get a couple of detectives from our office to come over and assist you with the legwork. We can set up an ANPR camera trawl; hopefully, our target vehicle may still be on the road and get clocked by the roadside cameras before they park up for the night." Andrea felt tired, but the update lifted her spirits. There was a realistic possibility of locating Hamilton through this new line of enquiry.

Andrea opened the HOLMES investigation database on her laptop. She read through the notes she had made earlier, following her review of enquiries and intelligence surrounding Frank Burton. Not surprisingly, he had covered his tracks well. Communications with Jason Hamilton could be accounted for legitimately, lawyer to the client. The confidential privilege given to their communications provided them with further protection. Andrea knew she would need more substantial evidence to be given authority to delve further into that area, which she didn't have. The intelligence suggested he used burner phones, which in itself wasn't a crime. The behaviour, however, made her more suspicious of him. The economic crime unit had focused on his finances, at her behest, yet again another door closed. At this stage, they concluded that his finances were consistent with his employment. Where is his stash of dirty money? She wondered.

She looked at Burton's contact with other phones of interest to the investigation, established by the analysts. There were several contacts with Pete Higgs's personal mobile and Andrea suspected he'd been sloppy on those occasions. No doubt, Pete too would have used burner phones for any corrupt activity. However Pete could easily account for these calls with the explanation he had previously given in relation to meeting Frank at the Crown Court. She concluded that she didn't have much evidence on Pete at the moment. His irrational behaviour at the siege wasn't right. She had known Pete for longer than she cared to remember. It was out of character, to say the least. Why did he really go into the flat? What were his real intentions for going into the apartment? That was Andrea's hunch, but she was miles away from proving it… for now.

Keeping him close would be a good move, she decided. He was still an accomplished detective and more eager to impress than ever. She reached into her bag for her mobile. There was a text from Sarah Lovick, inviting her out for lunch the next day. Chance will be a fine thing, she mused, knowing she would be working long days until Jason Hamilton was apprehended. She declined, due to work commitments and then selected Pete from her contacts.

"Pete, where are you?"

"I've just left Frank Burton's office. I've lent on him to give us the heads up on where Hamilton may be heading. I'm pretty hopeful he will come up with something. He seems to be losing patience with his client."

"Good work, come over to my office. I'll put the kettle on, and we can review the lines of enquiry and where we go next." Andrea felt a strange feeling of ambivalence towards Pete after the call. Their history meant a lot to her, and they worked well together. But if he had crossed the line and gone down the route of corruption, then that's all it would be, history.

Her mind shifted to Lee McCann, god, he had been lucky today, for which she was grateful. She felt a need to chat with him but reluctantly accepted he was probably asleep, and she didn't want to disturb him.

Wayne pulled the car over into a layby on the A64, not far from Whitby.

"I need a leg stretch and some fresh air. I'm knackered." He looked over towards Jason, who was sleeping in the reclined front passenger seat.

The coolness of evening air was a welcome respite from the car, and listening to Jason snore. The road was quiet as would be expected in the early hours of the morning. He checked his phone for the time and then selected Dirk from his contacts list.

"Morning Dirk, we're almost at Whitby. Is the plan still a goer?"

"Morning Wayne, yes, all is good at this end. I've just spoken with our guys on the boat. Apparently, your associate has lost some considerable weight through seasickness. When he heard of the delay, he contemplated throwing himself overboard." They both laughed.

"Yeah, I'm sorry for messing you about, pal. I've got Jason on a tight leash. I promise you we will be there on time. I won't let him leave my sight until I've handed him over to your boys. Are you still okay with the arrangement?"

"Of course, Wayne, you have paid for a service, and I will deliver."

"Good, it's the best outcome for both of us. It has been a minor hiccup; normal service will be resumed soon, mate."

Wayne opened the door and was greeted with the sound of Jason snoring, and the car didn't smell great either.

Wayne shook his head and opened the driver's window. He looked over to Jason. A feeling of resentment overcame him. This once close friend and business associate had become a burden. He had changed for the worse and was now pissing everyone off. But he knew the burden would be lifted very soon, once he was on the boat.

Pete entered the office. He was wearing jeans and a dark blue hoody.

"New look Pete?"

"It's all I had in my locker; Hamilton had my suit away. Look, I know I've pissed you off monumentally. Give me a break, and I'll make it up to you." Pete said, sounding sincere.

"Let's run through the events of today and see if there's anything we've missed, shall we? Then we can get home for a few hours' sleep," Andrea said, making no reference to Pete's request and getting straight down to business. She wasn't in the mood for placating Pete or reconciliation at the moment.

"Okay, I'll make some notes on the whiteboard." Pete stood up and took a pen from the shelf.

"Right, it would appear that Jason Hamilton was waiting outside Lee's address. He planned to follow him into the flat and shoot him. So, how did he know Lee's address?"

"They probably had Lee followed?"

"Or somebody told them?" Andrea's eyes didn't leave Pete's. She was watching his reaction carefully.

"What the hell, Andrea, that's a cheap shot. Do you believe for a minute that I'd do that?" It was a while before Pete was able to regain his composure. Andrea had got the reaction she was looking for; Pete had let his guard slip. Innocent Pete wouldn't have reacted that way. Was this guilty Pete?

"Bit of an overreaction, Pete? I wasn't inferring that you told them. Is there something you want to get off your chest?"

"Look, I'm shattered, my heads all over the place. It's been a tough day. Let's just concentrate on getting Jason Hamilton banged up."

Andrea's mobile started to ring.

"Ma'am, It's Nadia at the Force Intelligence Unit. The car registration number has activated an ANPR camera on the A64 towards Scarborough."

"Wow, that's looking good. Who would be driving from Chadderton to Scarborough at this time of the morning? I think we might be onto our man here. Great work, Nadia. I'm not sure who covers that area, Humberside or North Yorkshire Police. Will you get onto them and request observations and armed response to any sightings of the car?"

"Yes, Ma'am, the force duty officer is briefing her counterpart in North Yorkshire as we speak."

"Excellent, speak soon, Nadia." Andrea placed her mobile on the desk and booted up Google Maps.

"One hundred and ten miles to Scarborough, the roads will be empty. I bet we could do that in just over an hour. We need to get up there and make sure the search is effective. I've got a good feeling about this, Pete. Grab a car; we need to be there when they lift him." Andrea couldn't hide her enthusiasm. It would be a great result if Hamilton was back in custody before the 9 am 'you should haves' booked on duty in the morning, after having had a good sleep.

She welcomed constructive feedback from colleagues, but got irritated by the hindsight experts, holding forth from their air-conditioned offices.

Thirty Four

The motorway was almost deserted, only a scattering of red lights in the distance.

"If only motorways were like this all of the time," Andrea said, feeling obliged to create some small talk.

"Especially this one, you're lucky if you don't get caught in standing traffic these days," Pete replied. The tension between the two of them had subsided for now. Andrea sensed that Pete was on a charm offensive, trying to make amends.

"I've tasked the intelligence unit with researching any links Hamilton has with Yorkshire or this neck of the woods generally. There's nothing that springs to mind from the investigation so far."

"The only obvious one I can think of is Amsterdam. But if he's heading for there, the Port of Hull would have been the obvious destination."

"But he's switched on, and he probably knows we will have an all-ports alert in place and so I don't think he'd take that risk. He'll keep his head down and take the less obvious route."

"I just hope that the local cops are up to the task. There are a good few places to sail from along that stretch of coast, not only the main towns. Let's hope they've got it covered."

"Even with good local knowledge, it's a difficult task; due to the lack of cops these days, they've probably got a skeleton staff on duty at this time of the morning. I envisaged that being the case, so I've pulled together all the support I can get my hands on. Dave Ferguson was chuffed when I woke him up at three o'clock; he's turned an extra surveillance team out for us. The duty officer has allocated us an armed response team too. I've also tasked one of the duty night detective sergeants to make her way with three constables. Can you think of anything else we might need?"

"I was considering phoning Kirsty Hamilton and Frank Burton regarding any links Jason may have in Yorkshire, but they'd probably tip him off that we were on to him." Pete replied, "it's not worth the risk, especially as they'd probably say nothing."

"Yeah, if he has got a bolt-hole up there, they should know. Put that on the backburner for now. It's always an option for later."

"We're not far away now. We should be there in about an hour." Pete announced.

Andrea sat back in her seat and considered her options. She was satisfied that she had all bases covered. Her phone started to ring.

"Hi Andrea, just a quick update for you from Yorkshire police. They've completed an initial sweep of the waterfront at Scarborough; no luck there, I'm afraid. They are checking out the other locations as we speak. Nothing further on the vehicle location either. Do you have an estimated time of arrival that I can pass on to them?" The Force Duty Officer asked.

"Hopefully, in about forty minutes or so." Andrea ended the call and selected google maps; she studied the area northwards on the A64. The coast was the most likely destination; it had to be, she concluded, but where?

"We need another sighting of their car. The obvious destination is Scarborough, but it could also be Whitby. And that's assuming he's heading for the coast. There are too many coves and bays to check out in the time we've got." She felt a wave of travel

271

sickness and immediately placed her phone into her bag.

"I can't read whilst I'm in the car, I get travel sick. She looked ahead at the almost empty motorway lanes stretching ahead of them into the darkness. Frustrating though it was, for now, she was relying on the local police force to be vigilant during their searches and ANPR cameras.

"Not far now. We need to switch cars; my fingerprints will be all over this one. Let's lift one from around here," Wayne said, looking around for a suitable replacement.

"Where are we? We can't be far off now, surely?" Jason had awoken from his slumber and was rubbing his eyes.

"Pickering, not far now. We'll burn the car on the Scarborough road to keep them guessing which way we've gone." Wayne slowed down, checking out a potential car parked on a driveway but saw a better option nearby, "There's a motorbike over there, by the flats, that's even better. You drive the car, and I'll meet you further up the road." Wayne was quickly able to hot-wire the electrics on the bike and pull away with low throttle, avoiding drawing attention to himself. He pulled over a short distance away by the entrance to a builders' merchant, where Jason was waiting, standing next to their car. "Good move Einstein, no helmets, we're going to stand out like a sore thumb," Jason said, still groggy and irritable after waking up.

"Right, let's get this sorted," Wayne grabbed the petrol container from the boot and dowsed the interior. Jason ignited it from the other side of the car; the flames shot into the air with a whoosh and started to spread across the vehicle in no time. Wayne felt a wave of intense heat across his face and stepped back to safety. He picked up a brick and smashed the red plastic brake light on the motorbike. He jumped back onto the bike; the engine was still running. Wayne signalled for Jason to jump on the back.

"Let's get out of here," Wayne shouted over his shoulder as they accelerated away, putting distance between them and the burning vehicle.

He stretched his leg over the seat and grabbed Wayne around his waist. Wayne ignored his negativity whilst feeling uncomfortable by Jason's close embrace. The bike clunked into gear with a jolt and accelerated away.

Wayne's timing had gone to plan. He would be at the meeting point in just over ten minutes. The back roads provided great cover from the police. He felt Jason's grip on his waist tighten as he opened the throttle up and accelerated to eighty miles per hour. He laughed out loud at Jason's obvious discomfort and pulled the throttle back a little more. He couldn't afford to keep the Dutch boys waiting.

"Slow down! How can you see where you're going with no lights," Jason shouted in fear. Wayne reacted by accelerating more, pulling back on the throttle. The dark tops of the hedgerow contrasting against the moon-lit sky provided a line of the road to follow. He wobbled the handlebars and felt Jason's grip tighten as the bike veered around on the road. He was enjoying the ride, especially as Jason was freaking out on the back.

"This is great; I've not had a blast on a bike for years," Wayne shouted. Leaning into a sweeping right bend, a rush of blood indicated he should have slowed down more; in anticipation. The bike was straying dangerously close towards the edge of the road. He fixed his eyesight to the right, willing himself to pull it around. The back wheel slid on the loose gravel as he accelerated out of the bend. Shit, that was too close for comfort, he whispered with relief.

"Fucking Hell, Wayne," yelled Jason, hanging on for dear life.

"Hi Andrea, it's the duty officer. Local patrols at a village called Pickering have attended a car on fire. They're waiting for the fire brigade to attend; it's looking like the car from Chadderton. I guess this all but confirms it's Hamilton."

"Pickering? Where's that? Is there an obvious destination from there?"

"It looks like the obvious direction of travel was Scarborough, but Whitby is just as feasible. They're both about thirty minutes away."

"Damn, we don't know what car they're travelling in now."

"The local cops are checking CCTV opportunities, but that's going to be difficult at this time of night."

"Okay, thanks for the update," Andrea said, tapping her mobile phone on her thigh. Her anxiety was growing. She felt like the odds were stacking up against her.

"That doesn't sound good. I saw signs for Pickering a bit back." Pete murmured.

"You can say that again. Hamilton's totally off the radar now. We're dependent upon the local cops seeing him. We don't know what car he is driving anymore."

"He must be heading to Amsterdam, so we can still be fairly confident it's Scarborough, Whitby or nearby?"

"Pull over, Pete. It's shit or bust time. Let's take the risk with Burton, see if you can get us something positive out of your dodgy dealings." Andrea looked towards Pete as he brought the car to a halt. He shook his head slowly and wrinkled his eyes momentarily, picking his phone up.

"Hang on, Pete, I'm in bed. I'll call you back." Frank sounded groggy.

"He's going to ring me back," Pete said, "He needs to stop smoking. I could hardly tell what he was saying."

"I don't think Kirsty would help us," Andrea thought aloud, "She's more likely to tip him off."

"I doubt it very much, but what have we got to lose." Pete's phone started to ring.

"Frank, sorry to get you out of bed. We've located the car Jason Hamilton is using. We've got an ANPR camera activation on the M62 heading East, Yorkshire way. Any ideas where he could be heading?" Pete went for damage limitation with the vague M62 location.

"The only place he visits in the Northeast, to my recollection, is Newcastle." Frank lied. "Where was the vehicle clocked? Are you sure it's him?"

"I've not got an exact location yet; the information is just coming through to us."

"Sorry I can't be of more help, Pete. I'll see what I can find out for you in the meantime." Frank left his mobile on the desk in his study and walked back up the stairs, shaking his head, "I think you're too late to foil Wayne's plan, old boy," he said aloud as he got back into bed, giving the matter no further thought.

"Were you talking to me?" his wife whispered.

"No, dear, go back to sleep. The plod wanted the duty solicitor and rang the wrong number." Frank pulled the duvet around himself and thought no more of Pete's request.

"He said Newcastle was the only place Jason frequents up here. I'm taking that with a pinch of salt," Pete said.

"Let's hedge our bets, we'll head to Whitby, and I'll ask the night cover detectives to cover the Scarborough waterfront. We can ask the local cops to check out the lesser-known bays and coves." Andrea felt drained. She had been on a high after receiving the news about the ANPR activation. But now they didn't even know what type of car they were searching for, depending on a chance encounter. She feared Hamilton was slipping away into the night, completing a successful escape.

"We're only twenty minutes away from Whitby. It's not over yet." Pete didn't sound convincing. But he was clearly trying to be upbeat. He put his foot down, wheel spinning from the lay-by.

Andrea grabbed the sides of her seat instinctively. Usually, she would tell Pete to slow down, but not this time. Hamilton must be close-by, she contemplated, looking around for a likely getaway car. A road sign illuminated by the headlights of the vehicle displayed 'Whitby 5 miles'.

Thirty Five

Wayne was racing against the clock; the route from Pickering had taken longer than expected. On reaching Whitby, he became more cautious, approaching junctions guardedly in a state of hypervigilance. He couldn't afford to be seen by the cops at this late stage; that would be a disaster he couldn't even contemplate. He turned onto the last stretch of road. The small fisherman's cottages whizzed by in his peripheral vision. His eyes squinted to avoid the dryness caused by the wind in his face. Wayne felt vulnerable because his position could be seen from miles around, but it was the only route he knew, and he didn't have the luxury of spare time, to risk getting lost. He brought his focus back to riding the bike. His mind had wandered, contemplating what he would do if they were too late for the pick-up.

He was accelerating to the final stretch, the old town cobbled street that led to the meeting point. The cobbles sent an uncomfortable vibration through him, and he felt Jason's grip tighten, which irritated him. He approached the final row of cottages on his right and slowed down to a crawl to minimise the engine noise. He rode slowly at the sloped path leading down to the jetty, remaining vigilant, looking for the boat. As he rode onto the jetty at an engine tick-over speed, he looked over the water towards the other side of the harbour. Not a soul was to be seen. It was looking good.

At the end of the jetty. Jason jumped off the motorbike with gusto unexpectedly, causing the bike to wobble and almost fall over; Wayne fought hard not to lose his balance and drop the bike, cursing Jason.

"We're lucky to have got here. You nearly lost it on that bend," Jason moaned. Wayne let it go over his head. He knew any gratitude for helping him to escape was unlikely to be forthcoming. Jason's arrogance verified Wayne's reasoning for wanting him out of the way.

"We're here; that's all that matters," Wayne retorted dismissively.

"I'm no expert, but it looks like high tide. Can you see them?" Jason asked, looking relieved to have escaped from the white knuckle-ride.

"Walk past the lighthouse and drop down to the lower level. Wait there for them. I'll ditch the bike," Wayne said looking around; he felt a feeling of relief that he'd almost got the job done. He flicked the bike off its stand with his foot and wheeled it to the edge of the jetty not far from the lighthouse. It didn't take much effort and it plummeted into the water. The bike disappeared instantly, swallowed up by the sea with a resounding plunging splash of white foam, and spray, the dark inky water concealing its existence.

Meanwhile, Jason dashed towards the end of the jetty like a man on a mission. Having ditched the bike, Wayne looked towards the end of the jetty; he was just in time to see a rib motorboat leaving with three figures in dark clothing crouched on board. The boat was disappearing into the swell of the sea. The outboard motor being no more than a faint hum against the competing noise of the sea.

There was no time to waste. Wayne needed to get back to the safety of Bridlington. He walked briskly along the jetty and scrambled up over the rocks heading up the hill towards the church, off the beaten track.

Pete parked the car up on the road next to the public toilets. He saw vehicle headlights in his rear view mirror and climbed out of the car.

"It's a patrol car," He shouted over to Andrea as she got out. Both of them walked briskly to the water's edge, scanning the moored boats in the harbour area for any signs of life. The crews of two fishing trawlers were on deck were preparing to leave the harbour. Pete started to run towards the first one, "We might just be in time," he shouted over his shoulder to Andrea, who was trying to keep up with him.

As Pete approached the uniform officers, he directed them to check out the second boat. They turned about taking his lead on the need for urgency and sprinted towards the second boat.

All four regrouped at the harbour side a short time later, following negative searches of the trawlers.

"We've been checking the location for you in-between answering calls. It doesn't look like your suspect has been here, but I can't be a hundred per cent sure. The problem is, there are so many places to sail from along this coast. It's like looking for a needle in a haystack. The helicopter carried out a thorough sweep of the coastline but had to refuel. I'll request another flight shortly."

"Thank you for your assistance. I've got officers searching in Scarborough. We will crack on here. Can you revisit the lesser-known coves again?" It's probably our last throw of the dice; we're running out of time. The uniform officers ran back to their patrol car.

"I think we were bloody close Pete, but I'm guessing we've missed him. The local cops were our best chance. I think they had good intentions, but they've not got the resources."

"It's not over yet. Let's work our way around the harbour. They could be holed up in a boat waiting for us to leave," Pete said.

Andrea was still unsure about Pete. Is he in on this? Is he just playing along with me? Even keeping tabs on me? She looked away from Pete, over to the other side of the port; the sky was starting to get light. The skeleton-like shadow of the old Abbey on the hill looked spooky, like a haunted mansion, casting doom on their mission.

Their search proved fruitless, and they reluctantly walked back towards their car.

"Let's go and get a coffee before I debrief the duty officer," Andrea said. They both walked back along the harbour until they reached a fisherman's café. Pete stood looking towards the water, watching for any activity on the boats in the harbour.

The cardboard cup was burning Andrea's hand; she placed it on the wooden table, having checked in with the other patrols and briefed the duty officer at headquarters.

"Hamilton's luck has to change soon. He's used more than the nine lives of a cat. His luck can't last forever. The sound of the police helicopter broke the silence; they both craned their necks towards the sky.

"That's probably our best chance now. Hopefully, they have a heat-seeking camera on board," Andrea said, standing up to join Pete at the water's edge.

Meanwhile the rib was bouncing heavily on the waves, violently jolting the occupants from the wooden benches. Freezing spray from the sea was smacking Jason in the face. He was beyond cold, holding onto the rope for dear life. But nothing could dampen his spirits now. The water was ink black, the lights of Whitby were almost out of sight, he was scanning for a fishing boat but couldn't see one. His two rescuers were dressed in black clothing, wearing balaclavas. One was busy fighting to keep the rudder on track, while the other followed a compass bearing and indicated the direction with hand signals. Jason had never been so cold in his life.

"How much longer?" he shouted into the wind. They either ignored him or didn't hear him. He wedged his forearm under the rope to secure himself better.

Jason started thinking back to Chadderton, primarily to take his mind away from the current journey from hell. It was making the motorbike ride feel like first-class travel. He regretted not killing McCann there and then, but that was easy to think now, with hindsight, having escaped the clutches of the police and whilst sat in the apparent safety of the boat. He resolved that his chance would come again and settled for having humiliated him for now. He was brought back to the moment by a flash of light from the horizon. "It's the fishing boat," he shouted on relief. The engine of the rib de-accelerated, confirming his observation. Almost there, he thought longing for the warmth and safety of the trawler.

Thirty Six

As the rib slowed down and came alongside the
trawler, Jason felt his spirits lift, another step towards
freedom achieved; with the prospect of a few beers
with Dirk in store, he suddenly felt warmer.

He sat back and watched as a black-clad crew
member from the fishing boat threw a rope down to
the rib. His uncommunicative companions
immediately grabbed the ropes and pulled the boats
together.

Jason jumped up and stepped towards the rope
ladder leading up to the deck of the fishing boat. The
taller of the two guys shoved Jason hard in the chest,
causing him to stumble backwards and fall onto his
arse.

"Move when I fucking tell you to," the aggressor
shouted.

"Do you know who I am? You wanker," Jason
retorted, stunned. He glared at the guy but decided to
stay seated and revisit the matter once aboard. One
after the other, the two crewmen climbed up the rope
ladder and boarded the vessel. The shorter of the two
guys turned back to Jason.

"Okay, climb the ladder now." Jason nonchalantly
stood up and climbed the ladder. He consciously
tried to make the climb look effortless as a show of
strength. The crewman held out an arm and helped
him onto the deck.

"Ignore my colleague; he's a stickler for health and
safety procedure," The guy laughed loudly at his own
joke and walked away towards the cabin. Jason
looked around but couldn't see the tall guy, who he
wanted to remonstrate. Jason followed the shorter

guy into the wheelhouse cabin. He was standing chatting to four other men. Jason felt conscious of their lack of hospitality. He felt like they had forgotten about him, or worse, they were ignoring him.

"Where's Dirk?" Jason asked impatiently, raising his voice to be heard above their cackle.

"Dirk is not here," The taller guy said, stepping out of a room at the rear.

"Who's in charge here?" Jason asked with challenging authority.

"I am," the tall guy replied assuredly.

"What's with the tough guy attitude?" Jason challenged.

"Shut up, that's not important right now," the tall guy replied.

Jason was not used to being spoken to like this. Especially as he had been expecting a warm greeting from Dirk over a beer, he sensed something wasn't right. Jason was feeling confused by their behaviour and contemplated whether to act on the offensive or just roll with it for now.

"Okay, what happens next?" Jason asked, toning down his attitude.

"Are you armed?" The tall guy asked.

"Yes," Jason said. At the exact moment, the sliding door behind him closed with the motion of the sea, creating a loud bang. Startled, Jason looked behind him. The Four crew members burst out laughing at his reaction. Jason was fuming. Who the hell do these muppets think they are? He raged in his mind. He needed to remove himself from his tormenter before he acted on the urge to put the tall guy on his arse with a right hook.

Jason stepped forward towards the sliding door. One of the crew stepped into his path, blocking the door. "Staff only. Give me the weapon. You'll get it back when we dock."

"Fuck you. I'll be keeping hold of that." The words came out of Jason's mouth like second nature. He felt the need to stand his ground and stop taking shit from these nobodies. He felt on edge. His reaction made the tall guy appear agitated.

"Okay, it's like that, is it? Have it your way. But it will be a long journey for you, my friend."

"Fuck you," Jason said as he turned around and opened the other door, returning to the deck. He needed a minute to make sense of this situation. He reasoned that it was their boat, there were four of them, and for now, they held most of the cards. He just needed to control the anger and frustration that was rapidly growing inside him.

Jason heard the door slide open behind him. He turned around, this time there were five crewmen, his senses felt weird, he recognised the one standing at the back. Ryan!

"Ryan, what the fuck are you doing here?" Jason was shocked. He wondered whether this was some strange dream induced by hypothermia.

"Jason, it's been a while. How was your time in Strangeways?" Ryan asked confidently.

"It's your fucking fault I was sent down in the first place, but it was a piece of cake, thanks, all the same." Jason directed his misplaced anger towards Ryan. Always the easy target. Jason found Ryan's newly found confidence strangely menacing.

"Priceless, you take out a contract, to get me killed, hire a cop to do it… and it's my fault," Ryan said laughing ostentatiously. If Jason wasn't sure before, he was now for certain. It wasn't looking good. He was in a spot of bother, putting it mildly. He also knew the odds were stacked against him; five against one in the middle of the North Sea.

"Okay, Ryan, you've said your piece. What the fuck are you doing here anyway?"

"I'm afraid things have caught up with you a little, Mr Hamilton. There's an interested party that doesn't want you to go to Amsterdam," The tall guy interrupted.

"Which leaves us in a quandary," Ryan said. Jason was unnerved by Ryan's new confident disposition.

"Look, fellas, who the fuck is pulling the strings here? Does Dirk know what's going on?" As Jason finished speaking, he began to suspect that Dirk had double-crossed him. "Is Dirk setting me up, for fucks sake?

Whatever he's paying you, I'll triple it if you get me safely ashore. Ryan, we need to put all that contract kill shit behind us and move on. I have already instructed Wayne to get you back on board with us," Jason lied in desperation.

"Can't do that, Jason," Ryan replied.

"Ryan, you've not told me yet. What are you doing here? I heard you'd left all this shit behind you." Jason found himself playing for time but wasn't sure how he would benefit from it.

"I've been asked to come here and report back, confirm if you like, that the job has been done."

"For fucks sake, I've told Wayne and Frank…I don't have a problem with you anymore," Jason lied again.

"Carl was the grass, and he paid the price," Ryan said. Jason was rattled. He was reaching flight or fight time.

"Okay, who is it that wants me dead?"

"You'll never know, Jason. What goes around comes around. It's nothing personal; you of all people will understand that, of course," Ryan said, unable to hide his satisfaction at watching Jason, as he slowly accepted his predicament.

Jason's right hand had been slowly moving towards his waistband. Suddenly he grabbed the stock of his pistol and thrust the pistol upwards, pointing towards Ryan. Instinctively Ryan dropped to the floor and rolled away from Jason. Jason was too late; the crew member furthest to his right had seen his move coming, and his pistol was already half raised. The crew member fired a double-tap into Jason's forehead. Jason lay on his back lifeless, inches away from Ryan. Ryan was too close for comfort and rolled away from Jason's grotesque death stare.

The crew acted swiftly, securing iron weights and heavy chains to Jason's body. Four of the crew members just about managed to pick him up, struggling with the weight, and bundled him overboard.

The tall guy dropped the remaining weights into the rib, then shot several bullets through the toughened composite structure. He watched as the sea slowly swallowed the rib. Finally, he cut the ropes, and the rib totally disappeared under the water.

The captain took the wheel and set off for Rotterdam. The remainder of the crew retired to the messroom and resumed their card school.

Ryan returned to the deck; he typed 'job done' and pressed send. He could hear laughing and shouting from the mess, competing with the accelerating engines as they headed further out to sea. He launched his mobile into the blackness of the night and headed back into the cabin.

Thirty Seven

Wayne opened his eyes, the ringtone having woken him from a deep sleep. He had been in a deep sleep on the sofa, and his neck felt stiff and sore as a result. He sat up and rubbed his eyes. The mobile stopped ringing. After a moment, he recovered his bearings and looked out of the window of the holiday cabin; squinting in response to the bright sunshine. He picked up his phone, which still displayed the last text he had read; job done. He saw the missed call was from Dirk. He walked to the kitchen and took a bottle of orange juice from the fridge. He sat down at the wooden table on the decking outside and took some deep breaths of the sea air. The orange juice soothed his throat; the Irish whisky from the night before left his mouth dry as if he'd been eating peat. Wayne couldn't help but smile; he'd always loved being at the seaside since he was a kid. He had happy memories, an early rise on the morning of departure, a walk to the newsagents to buy the summer specials of his favourite comics and then…

His mobile phone started to ring again inside the cabin. He walked back inside and answered the phone.

"Wayne, how are you? I was getting worried when you didn't answer."

"You woke me up; otherwise, I would still be asleep. I was well out of it. A few too many whiskies last night." Wayne returned to the decking and sat down gingerly, leaning forward, placing his elbows on the table.

"The king is dead; long live the king. We completed your request."

"I never doubted you, Dirk. Did it go to plan?"

"Yes, the fish will be feasting. He cut a rather pathetic figure in the end. Pleading with Ryan to do a deal to save his life, ironic, really."

"Excellent, I'll get my man to transfer you the payment. It sounds like a job well done. That was much easier than getting him sorted out in Columbia."

"Yes, but at least we would have benefited from some sunshine if we had gone for that option," Dirk laughed.

"I'll be in touch soon to make the arrangements for a visit. Pleasure doing business as always. Is Ryan still with you?"

"He dined with us this morning, and then he left. He took great pleasure in taking part once he recovered from the seasickness. He had a spring in his step this morning."

"He's re-joining me back in the firm. He's a good asset. Thanks again, mate, I'll be in touch." Wayne slid the mobile onto the table and sat back, closing his eyes, enjoying the warm sun.

A short time later, Wayne took a stroll down to the beach. He stood still, looking out to sea. He had no regrets. It was the start of a new era; he felt in control for the first time in a long time. He intended to bring stability back to the firm. His relationship with Jason had deteriorated, and something needed to give. Jason's reckless behaviour made his decision easy. He brought himself back to the present, enough rumination.

Not that he didn't trust Dirk, but... he needed to call Ryan, just to make sure Jason wasn't sitting nursing a beer in some lap dancing bar in Amsterdam.

"Wayne, you should have been on that boat mate, it was cathartic," Ryan sounded relieved.

"I take it he's at the bottom of the North Sea?"

"He is mate, I've got to be honest; it's fantastic knowing he's no longer coming after me. He got his comeuppance, a taste of his own medicine."

"Where are you now?"

"I'm at the airport. I've got some business to sort over here, and then I might have a trip to Manchester at some stage."

"Well, I'm looking for a new partner if you're interested?"

"I'm done with it, mate. I'm lucky I'm still alive. I need to quit whilst I'm ahead."

"Don't be hasty, mate; it's an open offer. I've told Dirk you are back with us, he respects you. Anyway, run me through what happened on the boat." Wayne listened intently whilst he walked back to the cabin; he took no pleasure from listening to the detail; it just satisfied a morbid curiosity. Wayne asked Ryan to get in touch on his return and ended the call.

He had another call he needed to make.

"Good morning Wayne, I was getting worried. How did it go?"

"The deed has been done, Frank. It's not a pleasant business, but sometimes these things need to happen for the greater good. It's you and me now. Onwards and upwards."

"Well, I feel relieved. I don't want to see anyone suffer, but it was the right decision."

"Don't be feeling any guilt, Frank. We made the right decision. He knew the score. I'm in no doubt he would have lost it with me next. The paranoia had pickled his brain. Going back to kill the cop was the last straw for me. I couldn't give a damn about McCann, but what did Jason think he was going to achieve?"

"Exactly, he'd have made himself public enemy number one. They take it personally when one of their own is attacked."

"It's a dirty business, Frank."

"We need to meet up and run through things."

"All in good time, Frank. I'm going to have a few days up here. I'll text you when I'm back."

Frank got up from his desk and refilled his coffee cup. The wave of relief that washed over him was intense. It surprised him. For a while now, he had quietly feared he would be going to prison if Jason had been allowed to continue down the path to self-destruction. Perhaps he hadn't realised how toxic their relationship had become. He was better off with Jason dead. Nothing personal, of course.

As if appeasing his guilt at the death, he decided he should let Kirsty know. He stood at the window and lit a cigarette. His first deep inhalation felt good. It was a strange feeling that Jason was gone, one of disbelief but liberating at the same time. He sat down at the desk and picked up his mobile.

"Frank, I'm glad you've called, DI Statham has been on my back again. She threatened to take the salons off me, under the proceeds of crime act. The cheeky bitch."

Frank quite liked it; when Kirsty got feisty, it suited her. He stubbed out his cigarette in the already full ashtray.

"Don't worry about that for now, Kirsty. I've got some terrible news. Jason is dead." A silence followed.

"What? How did it happen? You told me he had escaped. What's happened?"

"It looks like the Dutch boys double-crossed him. He had planned to be taken by boat to Holland. Once aboard, he was shot." Frank kept his account as close to the truth as possible. There was nothing to be gained by implicating himself and Wayne. Silence followed again.

"I feel numb. I don't know what to say, Frank."

"Say nothing. Just give it some time to sink in. It will take a while to get your head around it and grieve for him."

"It was always going to happen, wasn't it, Frank?"

"Let's just say he did business in high-risk circles."

"Thanks for letting me know, Frank."

"If you need me for any support or whatever, I'm still here for you. Nothing changes. If the police come knocking, just refer them to me. Oh, don't worry about DI Statham's threats. Jason was cautious with the finances; the police won't find anything amiss in his accounts. We paid the best people to make sure of that. You have some space, and I'll check on you in a few days."

"Thanks, Frank."

Andrea arrived at the office early. She was recovering from the effects of sleep deprivation brought on over the last few days. Andrea studied the intelligence reports once again. She was looking for a clue between the lines that probably wasn't even there. The intelligence was from two different sources, both with a reliable rating.

A rival OCG has assassinated Jason Hamilton. They have gone to extreme lengths to dispose of the body. The source is confident it will never be found. She placed the documents back in her drawer and took a drink of coffee.

It was nearly eight o'clock, almost time for her meeting with Pete Higgs. She switched on the wall-mounted flat-screen television and selected the news channel.

Pete appeared at the door spot on at eight o'clock. "Where's the team?" he asked, having walked through the empty office.

"They're on rest days. I'm on senior CID Force cover today, a favour for Dave Ferguson. Close the door, Pete." They both took a seat at the meeting table. There was tension in the room.

"Have you read the intelligence reports?" Andrea asked.

"Yes, I read them this morning. The intelligence seems to be accurate. I had an off-the-record chat with Frank Burton, which of course, he will deny ever happened. Hamilton was double-crossed by some gangsters who were supposed to be helping him to escape. I guess that we weren't far behind him but got the wrong location. Word has it, he sailed from Scarborough but never reached his destination."

"A cosy off the record chat with Burton, eh? You've sailed close to the wind there, Pete. Far too close for my liking."

"I know, Ma'am, but Lee is still alive. I like to think I played a big part in that."

"Maybe, but Hamilton got away as a result."

"And now he's dead." Pete smugly pointed out.

"Which has made it easier for the Chief Superintendent to decide you will receive a formal verbal warning. You're bloody lucky, Pete. It could have so easily gone tits up for you."

"Look, Ma'am, I know you're angry with me but, it all turned out good in the end. Maybe I sailed a bit close to the wind and got a bit close to Burton, but there was no harm done at the end of the day."

Andrea bit her lip; she had left no stone unturned whilst looking at Pete's relationship with Burton. But, she had no evidence to prove any wrongdoing. Her hunch told her that there was more to it, but a hunch wasn't good enough.

"I'll take your word for it, Pete. But you mustn't forget, Burton would drop you like a stone to save his skin, be careful."

There was a knock at the door; Lee McCann walked in, "This looks serious. Have I missed something?"

"No, we were catching up, that's all. Pete was just leaving." Pete took the hint and stood up to leave.

"Good to see you both. I'm taking some leave, a family break in Cornwall. I'll catch up with you in a few weeks." Pete closed the door behind him.

"How are you feeling, Lee?"

"I'm fine, Ma'am, ready for our next job."

About the Author.

CJ Wood is a retired career detective. He served in the Royal Military Police and UK Police Service in a career spanning over 30 years.

For his last 15 years he undertook the role of Detective Inspector investigating Serious Crime and Major Incidents.

CJ is an avid reader and passionate about writing, when not engaged with a book he can be often be found hiking the mountains of the Lake District.

Website; www.cjwoodauthor.co.uk

Facebook CJ Wood-Crime Fiction Author

Twitter @CjAuthor

Disclaimer.

This is a work of fiction. Names, characters, businesses and incidents are the products of the authors imagination. Any resemblance to actual persons, living or dead, of actual places and events is purely coincidental.

Printed in Great Britain
by Amazon

63407608R00177